ALWAYS

Single Dads, book 4

RJ SCOTT

Love Lane Books

Copyright

Dedication

Always for my family.

Always

RJ SCOTT

Chapter One

Cam

"HE WAS lucky to get away with seven years," Jim, my exhausted counsel, and only real friend took a seat opposite me in the small room off the main corridor of the courthouse. I hadn't been able to afford a lawyer of my own, and when Jim had turned up at my door, telling me he was my court-appointed liaison, I was horrified. I needed better representation, but how would I pay for any of it?

Turned out he was the best thing to happen to me. He'd done everything to keep me from being dragged into the case by the DA who insisted I must know things I wasn't revealing. Hell, I wish I *had* known something that would help put my husband behind bars because his actions had put Finn—*my son*—in danger.

How could I know anything when I'd coasted through the last few years in a daze of uncertainty, lies, and pain?

Finn hiccupped a sob into my neck. I held my son so

tight that I hoped he felt safe. He didn't need to hear anything else about what his other dad had done, or how hard Jim had to fight behind the scenes to exclude paper thin lies created by my husband's team.

The defense had painted Graeme as a solid family man who'd simply found himself caught up in things he had no control over. They'd been lying. If there was one thing the court case *had* shown everyone it was that Graeme had had all the control all of the time. Over money, and people.

Over me.

Graeme had been born into a rich family, given more money than he knew what to do with and went on to hold a respected position with a group of investment managers who'd courted him as if he were a king. He was a smooth talker, able to con even the most normal of people. Even me.

Pathetic. Idiotic. Blind. Me.

Falling for Graeme had just been step one in a tragic story. I'd fucked up, and I should never have fallen under Graeme's spell or allowed him to control me as he had.

I'm a strong, principled man who knows right from wrong. I'm a good dad.

Repeat as needed.

"There's nothing lucky about what happened to us," I whispered back, aware that Finn, huddled into my side, could hear everything I said, and some of it I never wanted him to know. Thankfully, Finn hadn't been in court for the long closing statements, sitting instead in this small room with a kindly court officer who'd played computer games with him and fetched him lunch. I'd been on my own to listen to the defense as they lied to explain away what

Graeme had done as trying to please his money-obsessed husband. It was apparently my fault. He loved me too much. He wanted to please me. Me? I'd never wanted a single dime of his money.

I wanted a family, a husband who didn't fuck about on me, a dad for Finn who cared enough to be at home. I didn't want money, or maids, or a chef who lived half the week in our house, or private schools and exotic holidays, although that was how I was painted. They argued that the pressure on Graeme was intense, and the defense team cited me wanting Italian marble tiles in a bathroom as the straw that broke the camel's back. I never said anything about a bathroom, let alone tiles.

The lies were many, and through all of it I could see the way people stared at me, one of them, an angry white-haired man, never took his eyes off me. Simon Frederickson had everything going for him—a newly retired pension fund manager he was expecting a retirement full of good things. But, he'd bet everything on Graeme which was the start of his downfall. He'd been a key witness for the prosecution and had given gut-wrenching testimony about how he'd lost everything, his money, security, family, his entire life—and it had all been Graeme's fault. Simon had become my touchstone in this whole thing. From watching him I could see the lies that would be believed, and the way the jury was slowly buying into the defense's rhetoric.

It was somehow all my fault, and the way that the witnesses stared at me, Simon included, showed me what they thought.

I could see the point where every single one of them

thought I was getting away with hiding money, living the life, and that I needed to pay as well. My only blessing was that there was not a single shred of evidence to say I was involved.

There wouldn't be, because I wasn't part of what Graeme had done, unless my naïveté counted. I just wish I could push the guilt away, because they were right in one way—I *should* have known. Finn shifted in my hold, but it wasn't to move away, it was to bury himself even closer and I smoothed my hand on his back.

"What next?" I asked Jim, staring right into his eyes, able to see the very moment where optimism and relief died, replaced with defeat.

"The house is gone," he said.

"We knew it would be."

The house was where I'd thought we'd be happy, where I thought I could give Finn the life he deserved, where I'd fallen in love. But now, all I could recall was Graeme in the kitchen holding a knife, a lifeless body next to him, as he held a pity party for one where he blamed everything except himself for cold-blooded murder.

How does a man kill another person and not end up behind bars with a life sentence?

The prosecution had wanted him put away for anything they could find. They'd settled for a plea bargain, in exchange for passwords to a multi-million dollar bitcoin account, and now Graeme was locked away for seven years for the white-collar crime of embezzlement. Seemed to me as if other people's money had helped him again, and I could feel the weight of everyone staring at me in court.

"There's no money in any accounts, it's all gone."

I nodded. Every cent that was legitimately mine was in my backpack—all five thousand dollars that I'd stashed away over the last six months from helping out on small renovations in my spare time. It wasn't enough to start over, let alone even rent a place, but it would get us a bus ticket away from here.

He held out his hand, and I managed to shake his without dislodging Finn. "It's been a pleasure working on your behalf." He crouched in front of us, his round glasses reflecting my image. "Finn?"

Finn stirred in my arms and finally peeked out of my coat, his dark hair mussed and his eyes red from crying. "Yes, sir?" he asked, his voice cracking.

"You're the bravest boy I've ever had the pleasure to meet. You look after your daddy if you can, but also, let your daddy look after you. Pinkie swear?" He held out a pinkie, and Finn didn't hesitate to offer his as they shook, and then Finn buried himself again. With a smile that softened his normally stern face, Jim patted Finn's knee before nodding to me. "You know how to reach me if you need any advice."

"Thank you for all you did, Jim. I don't know how I can ever thank you."

"You're welcome—I'm not bad for court-appointed counsel, right?" His eyes twinkled, and I winced, recalling our first conversation where I'd told him outright that we needed a *real* lawyer who could look out for me and Finn. He'd been better than any high priced lawyer I could've imagined.

"Not bad at all," I turned the joke back on myself, and

we exchanged smiles. He was filing divorce paperwork as a favor, and I knew I'd never be able to pay him back in this lifetime.

"This is for you," he held out a large envelope, and I took it without hesitation, used to being passed this and that, and long past questioning anything. "It arrived by courier to our office, but it's addressed to you. Is it something I need to deal with?"

I needed to open it and see, so sitting on the hard bench with my nine-year-old son crying in my arms, I managed to open the envelope, and pulled out a handwritten note. I skimmed to the name at the bottom—Nick. My chest hollowed with pain. Why was Nick writing me notes when I'd told him to stay out of my life? What did Nick have to do with me right now? As far as I was concerned I'd burned any bridges between me and my best friend a long time ago.

"Cam? Are you okay? You look pale. Do I need to get help?"

I shook my head. "It's from an old friend."

"You're sure?"

"I'm sure."

Only when he was gone did I pull the note out again to read it.

Dear Cam,

PLEASE READ.

I found a place for you to stay. I promise Finn will be safe from the media circus there. All the details are in the other envelope.

Don't be stubborn about this. Don't run. You don't even have to see me. Just come home.

Nick.

INSIDE THE OTHER smaller envelope were details of someone called Adam Williams, and an address in La Jolla, San Diego, not far from where I'd grown up in Carlsbad in the same neighborhood as Nick.

Nick had started as my childhood nemesis, then become my very best friend, and even my boyfriend for one night, until a kiss had determined that we were better off as brothers than boyfriends. He'd been the one to support me when I'd adopted Finn—I'd asked him to be Finn's godfather—that was how much he'd been part of my life. I'd been unnecessarily cruel to Nick when he'd called me just after Graeme had been arrested. He'd asked if I wanted help. I'd still thought my husband was some kind of innocent victim, and with hindsight I'd acted in an emotional form of self-defense. The last thing I needed was Nick to say I-told-you-so because he'd never liked Graeme at all.

I'd asked him to leave me alone, irrationally distrustful and harsh. He'd backed off... so why was he contacting me now? Shocked, worried, uncertain about what I was reading, I sat for the longest time, hugging my son, and spiraling back to that last conversation with Nick when I'd told him that he couldn't understand what I was going through and to leave me and Finn alone.

How could I face him? Was it even possible that San Diego was the right place to stay for a while? Was it time to go home? Finn and I had been living out of suitcases in a cheap motel, sharing a room for so long it had become our normal, we spent most of our time dodging journalists and people hurt by what Graeme had done. At times I feared for our lives.

So, what is keeping me in New York?

"Dad?"

"Yeah?"

"What do we do now?"

I didn't have a clue. New York was nothing to us. No friends. Nowhere to live. No money. And, worst of all, the media frenzy around us that wouldn't abate for a long while. And in the middle of it all, Finn.

"I think we need to head home."

He stiffened in my hold, and pulled back. "I don't want to go there. Can't we go back to the motel?"

We wouldn't be going back to that motel now, everything we'd left there was going to stay, not that it was much. I'd already put a plan in place for us to slip away, but never with a destination fixed in my mind. I pressed a kiss to his head. "We already talked about this, you don't have to worry, we're not staying in New York and we have plans, right?"

"A horse place in Montana with a river."

"And a new job for me."

"And I can get a dog."

I side-hugged him. "Yep, a dog of your own. But we can't do that straight away, we need to…" *hide, avoid the press, lick our wounds.* "… just take some time. Back to my old home, California, then it will be you and me against the world, Finn."

He processed the information with a frown, his eyes red from crying and his hair in tufts where he'd hidden in my hold. Then he wrapped his arms around my neck, tight as he'd done since last June, over a year ago. Everything in his world had been destroyed, he wasn't going back to the private school. He didn't have friends here. It was the two of us, starting over.

"You and me against the world, Finn," I repeated, and felt his tears hot on my skin.

I'm not sure either of our hearts would heal from this.

But we had to try.

Security guided me to the exit, but determined journalists had gathered outside, a whole mess of them waiting, and I hovered inside, hiding Finn behind me. I could see the road to the train station, and if we could just get there then we could make it anywhere.

I crouched in front of Finn, zipped up his coat, pulled up his hood, and clicked the snaps so that the lower half of his face was hidden and the furry hood shielded his eyes. I did the same with my coat, and then I gripped his hand and pointed out of the front window.

"You remember what we're doing now."

"Running away," he said with renewed confidence.

"It's the last thing we have to do. Just as we planned, okay, we're heading for McDonald's. Can you see it?"

Finn nodded, and swiped at the tears on his face with his free hand.

"Don't let go of me," I said. "If you get scared I'll carry you."

He was nine, small for his age, I could easily carry him, but he pushed his shoulders back and shook his head.

"No carrying."

"That's my boy," I praised, even as my chest tightened.

Then, we opened the door.

"Cam! Where's the money?"

"Cameron   Hastings!   Did   you   agree   with   the sentencing?"

"Can you give us an interview, Mr. Hastings?"

"Cam! Over here! Over here! Did you lie for your husband?"

"Is your son okay?"

"Cam! Cam! How is it possible that you don't know where the missing money is?"

It broke my fucking heart that I didn't know about the money, or where it'd gone, and that I couldn't give back what Graeme had stolen. It killed me that people had lost everything, and that somehow I was part of the awful loss they'd experienced. If I'd seen what was happening then maybe I could have done something—stopped him. A blanket of despair settled on my shoulders, and for a second I indulged the hopelessness, before shoving it away. I was going to give Finn a new start, and it didn't matter about the rest of it—Finn had seen too much, and he needed a safe place where he could learn to be a kid again.

"You fucking asshole!" Simon Frederickson was there, eyes sparking with temper, his lips twisted in a snarl, reaching for me and Finn, and yelling in my face. This wasn't the first time he'd come at me, but this time I had Finn at my side and I moved to protect him.

"Sir!" Security moved in.

Everything inside me snapped, and I reached out to

grip Simon's arm. "I'm sorry, I don't know. You have to believe me."

"I have nothing!" he screamed in my face, and next to me Finn buried himself in my side.

"I wish I could help you."

"I will make you pay, you fucking lying piece of shit."

"Sir!" Security bundled him off me, my hold on him ripped away, and then with utter determination I shoved through the crowd. Other security attempted to keep the media away but god knows who else was in this crowd who hated us. I couldn't breathe until we made it through the barrier which trapped the journalists long enough for us to get to the crossing, over the road, and into McDonald's. The media followed us, I glanced back to see Simon face down on the sidewalk, the cops there, and I wanted to go back and plead with them to take care of him. He had a family—a wife undergoing cancer treatment, two kids with families of their own, and he had no money. He'd been destroyed more than I was.

Please don't hurt him. I almost went back.

"Dad?" Finn tugged my sleeve, and that dragged me back from compassion to fear in an instant. I had to keep Finn safe. We took the side door, went through a book store, left via the rear exit, hid in a Starbucks for a few minutes, doubled back on ourselves, and finally I felt we might be free from being followed. Cautiously, I headed for the station, Finn holding my hand, blending in with the tourists, and went straight in with a group to find the lockers, opened the one we'd rented the month before and pulled out our bags. Once inside the bathroom I messed up my styled hair, pulling it down to frame my face, then shoved a scarlet NY beanie on, took off my coat and dumped it on the floor, and then set about helping Finn to reverse his two-sided jacket, adding a matching NY beanie. I changed out of my suit into jeans and a jersey, and then, with Finn watching, I hacked away at the beard I'd let grow long, taking it back to smooth skin as much as I could. All I had in the bags was a couple more change of clothes, all the cash I had left in the world, our passports, and as many of Finn's baby photos as I could fit.

I don't know what was in Finn's bag—I'd let him pack it himself, to take reminders of our old life that would see him through enough until we could go home one day and get more.

Home? It's not our home anymore.

"You remember what to say if anyone talks to us?" I wrapped the suit and coat in a bundle and pushed it into a plastic bag. I'd drop it with one of the homeless guys outside, surely I could do one more good thing before we vanished.

Finn blinked up at me, his eyes full of tears, but his shoulders were back and determination was written in every line of him. My little man was so brave, even after everything I'd allowed to happen. "I remember. I have to say we're going to visit family, and I can't talk to anyone about anything else. Oh, and my name is Finn Bellamy, not Finn Hastings anymore." He worried at the zipper on his coat and I knew he had something else he wanted to say. "Dad?"

"Yeah?"

"Will people ever stop hating you?"

I thought of all the people searching for someone to

blame and turning their gazes on Finn and me. They were right to accuse *me* of being naïve, they could harass *me* and call me every name under the sun, but they weren't touching Finn. I just knew they weren't going to stop for a long time.

"They will do one day, I'm sure," I lied, and then patted his head. "Ready for an adventure?"

"I don't know, Dad, I'm scared."

My heart cracked and I cradled his face, staring into his dark eyes and wondering what was the best thing to say. I couldn't exactly say I would never let anything happen to him because I had so let him down, and I couldn't promise him that everything was going to be okay, because I didn't know that. So I went with what Finn's counselor had said—that honesty was the only way to go.

"I'm scared as well."

His eyes widened, and he grabbed at me. "You are?"

"How about we both pretend we're not scared, and get on a bus or a train and head away from here."

He tugged me close for a hug, almost unbalancing me.

"Okay, Dad."

I hugged him, then bopped his nose and smiled, waiting until he gave me a returning smile, and only after he did was I ready to leave the confines of the bathroom to find a seat on a train or a bus heading anywhere. For better or worse, we had a destination now—San Diego.

One day Finn and I might return to a life in New York, after all it was a big city, but there was something so warm when I thought of heading west to the place I'd been born. All I had in New York was a shit-ton of miserable memories, and a marriage that had gone to hell, catching Finn in its destructive force. I was happy to leave.

We headed out and tried to lose ourselves again, and it was only when we were on the train that I could even think of relaxing a little.

"Hi, is this seat free?" I looked up and all I saw was white hair. My mind made the connection to Simon Frederickson and fear gripped me. My heart raced, but it was just a random guy looking for a seat, that was all. I was losing my shit—seeing phantoms.

"Yeah, sure."

The man smiled, then sat down and immediately put in ear buds before closing his eyes. Thank goodness he didn't want to sit and chat because that was the last thing I needed right now.

I just needed time to think. Finn and I could hide out together for a few months, just while I planned a fresh start and got my head straight. Simon wouldn't know where we were, nor would others like him whom Graeme had wronged. Neither would the media, or the senders of the hate mail that arrived every day, not for a while at least. I hoped we could be anonymous, to give ourselves time.

"Let's get this adventure started."

Chapter Two

Adam

"Red! Hey!"

I'd tried my hardest to avoid seeing anyone but I couldn't exactly ignore Eric's yell across the engine house.

"Hey, Tree." I calculated the chances of me being able to make a run for it with my aching knee, and it came out at zero. It was vital that I didn't appear to be in pain in front of Eric, because the asshole would start fussing over me. The last thing I needed was fuss. I limped toward the fire truck that was being polished with loving care and attention by the big man, and tilted my head as if I was judging the work, then glanced over at Eric preening and waiting for praise. The fire truck was his baby and he spent all his downtime making it look good. Not that there was a lot of downtime right now, coming off the back of the latest fire which was finally under control. I could see the exhaustion on Eric's face, and the faint bruising from the breathing equipment. The Lewis fire had swept from peak to peak and left nothing much in its wake, including destroying three small farms and nudging the boundaries of two towns. Even in January there were fires now—it was hell out there.

And, I should have been out there helping them.

"You staring at me or the truck?" Eric crossed his arms over his chest and fake-pouted.

"In your dreams would I stare at you," I deadpanned. "Why? Do you want me to stare at you?" I ran a suggestive hand down my chest, "I'm gonna tell Brady you're flirting with me."

He went as scarlet as the truck and blustered, "I didn't, all I said… he wouldn't… asshole."

"That's my name, don't wear it out." I brushed my shoulders and despite the pain, I swaggered closer, inhaling the scent of oil, and polish, and pressed my fingers against the reassuring solidness of the huge scarlet truck. I'd been so proud to be part of this team, because from the very first day I could remember I'd always wanted to be a firefighter.

From engines built with Legos, to a firehouse made from cardboard boxes and paint, I quickly moved on to model-making, and reading every book on the subject. Living in Cali, I watched every change in the weather, knew every path of the fires in the hills and the tragedies around us. All of it merged into one big dream for a very small kid. Firefighter. Not a paramedic, or a cop, or military—always firefighter. The day I'd finished my degree in fire science I'd applied for the service, made it through boot camp, passed all the exams, and received a probie position with Engine sixty-three, one of the youngest they'd hired.

Taking forever to come off probie status hadn't worried me one little bit, I could've spent all day cleaning the bathroom, mopping floors, and taken more than my fair share of cooking duties, although I'd burned more than my colleagues could tolerate, so they'd edged me away from that. I'd genuinely tried, but for someone who knew all about combustion points, I wasn't so good at watching food as it burned to a crisp in the oven.

I would spend hours standing with the guys, my second family, talking shit as we worked on the truck, prepared for every eventuality, trained, ran drills, and I was the youngest, proudest, bravest, most educated, and keenest firefighter that I could be. I'd also been impetuous, unruly, and filled with the desperate need to be the one who saved everyone.

Now I wasn't part of the team, because a year ago I'd fucked everything up. So now, when I had to come to the engine house for these regular check-ins I crept around like a cat in a room full of rocking chairs trying to avoid everyone so I didn't have to see their pitying glances, or worse, have to tell them if I felt okay.

"How you doing?" Eric asked, and dropped cloths into an empty bucket. The chrome gleamed and he'd taken special care of the engine logo, a panther in full pounce, claws extended.

"Good," I lied. Pain cramped in my neck, and I was blurry-eyed from the remnants of last night's migraine. There was very little that was *good* about today. "What about you?"

"Maddie got an A in math, Lucas made an awesome photo frame in shop, and Brady's students at the college got funding for an online web comic."

I gave him an utterly genuine smile. Eric meeting Brady and the kids, settling down, making a family, was what it was all about. Family. Love. Career. I had a big extended mess of loving family; loving parents, two brothers, a sister, nieces and nephews, but what I didn't have was a partner. I hadn't had one before the accident because I'd had a career to focus on and filled the sex-jar with one-night stands. I didn't have a partner *after* the accident because I was mixed up in pain, and therapy, grieving the loss of self-esteem and the obliteration of my career. If I couldn't respect and love myself, how could anyone else?

Particularly when they'd have to sit with me through seizures, migraines, and pain from twisted muscle and bone that was so intense I would sometimes just sit and sob.

"Are you here for a reason? Is it for a kids' thing?" Eric pulled me out of my introspection as he closed the lids on various pots of polish. I'd done some volunteer work with children affected by fire, physically and mentally, becoming an informal big brother to a couple of them. The last one I'd worked with, a girl who'd been the only one rescued from a house fire, had moved in with an aunt and uncle in Ohio, and unless I made the scheme an official thing I wasn't about to get departmental support. I couldn't decide if I wanted to make it a real thing. Hell, I couldn't decide what T-shirt to wear in the mornings let alone something that might shape my life, but I at least had some ideas of where I could help. Battalion Chief Lewis had told me what I'd already known—there wasn't a lot of support for something that wasn't in the remit of the firefighting service.

He loved the idea, appreciated the concept of outreach, acknowledged I wasn't looking for funding as such, but offering up much in the way of Fire Department support was something he couldn't do. I still had free use of the rec room, and as much support from the guys as I needed, but actual signed documentation to make it all official was a different matter altogether. Unspoken was the fact that it wouldn't be long before I was heading for a discharge from this role, because I wasn't getting better in any appreciable way.

I lived with my injuries, and that was about as good as it was ever going to get.

Without endorsement, I wasn't getting access to the right kind of support for the kids which I'd envisioned as a multi-departmental team, from social care to PT. Finding homes, working with family, I had it all in my head, but it was all too much to do on my own. I liked working with kids, and outreach was a good fit for me.

On my good days, at least.

Not that I'd tell anyone that, and no one would see my anxieties because I was the world's best at fronting it out.

I think.

I wasn't surprised by the news that my ideas might never get off the ground, even if the words fell like dull thuds. I'd hoped that this might've been easy, even if the reality was bound to be something different. I already had a folder full of information on how to look for private backing—I had plans to talk to schools, to maybe start a company specializing in post-trauma support. So many plans, and all I could hope was that my pain levels would let me make them all real, because I was one of the best people to help. Not that my heart was really in it, but then my heart wasn't in anything right now.

"Earth to Red? You okay?"

Eric sounded worried and I wished he'd stop asking me that. "Yeah, I talked to him about the big brother scheme."

"Cool. Let me know if you need anything from me or the guys."

"I will."

"Brady said that you're renting rooms at the house."

"Yeah, to a guy and his son. If that's okay?"

Why was I asking him that? It was my house now.

"It's not our house anymore," Eric was patient, but I could see that he thought I was being weird. I'd bought the house from Eric, Leo and Sean, and yeah, it was *my* house now.

"I know," I huffed a laugh as if I wasn't being an idiot. "Talk later, yeah?"

My vision blurred, and I knew I needed to get to a quiet place and close my eyes, pull out some yoga, chill, rest my neck, so I sketched a wave, and was almost at the door when Eric stopped me.

"Are you coming to Ringwood on the seventeenth? Leo reminded me it's on his schedule."

Leo's schedule was famous, and even I relied on his text reminders for when I'd been able to fit time for working at the foster home into my schedule. *My non-existent schedule now.* "Of course."

"Great." Eric bit his lip, wouldn't quite meet my eye. "Uhm, Brady's coming to do some yard projects if you want to do something different from construction work."

I knew what Eric was doing—he'd probably prepped Brady to have some easy job ready for me. Maybe counting seeds in a packet while sitting at a table in the shade, all so I wouldn't have to do any heavy lifting. I wasn't that badly fucked up that I couldn't hammer a few nails in wood.

Who am I kidding?

The heavy impact of a ton of concrete on my shoulder as a bridge support disintegrated around me had injured my brachial plexus. The buildup of scar tissue had led to neurapraxia, which resulted in muscle fatigue and pain. But, the vicious cycle would start whether I did physical work or not, and I'd been doing better recently—apart from the migraines, that was.

"Nah, I'm good with the construction." I struck a bodybuilder pose and didn't wince once, making Eric smile.

God, how many times was I going to lie today? I'd gone through the stages of grief, and come out the other side, and I'd learned all kinds of coping strategies, but the one where I pretended everything was okay was the hardest of all. I waved again, and the door shut behind me. The Santa Anas swirled around me and ruffled my hair, and for a moment I thought I could scent the smoke from the hills, but that was my imagination, a visceral connection to memories that I had to stow away. I called a cab and made it home to my new place, heading for the kitchen, taking meds, and two water bottles, and then climbing into bed. I pulled the quilt over my head, closed my eyes, and wished for sleep.

And I did all of that without crying.

I call that a win.

I woke up feeling clearer and more focused, with no sign of the promised migraine which I had apparently caught in time. By the angle of the light through a space in the drapes it had to be early evening, and the crackers I'd eaten so I could take the meds were long since digested, and I was hungry. After a shower, and dressing in loose sweats and a worn T-shirt, I headed downstairs, using my cane and gripping the bannister just in case, to find three messages and two missed calls on my phone.

I answered the important one first.

"Hi, Mom."

"Adam, I had this awful feeling and needed to know you were okay." That was my mom, not waiting to ask me the real questions. At least with Mom we got the worries up front and personal, and not couched in conversation about other mundane things.

"I'm fine, Mom, I wish you'd stop worrying."

"You buy a house, you move out, you're on your own, what if you have another seizure?"

"Mom, you don't have to worry, I haven't had a seizure in months, the meds are working, and I'm not having headaches." Okay, so I was lying. Mom asked the hard questions, and my siblings and I had learned how to lie without giving ourselves away. "Also the house is perfect, and the pool is just what I need with the rehab, plus I have a doctor living right next door."

"I'll still worry.

"I know, Mom, but did you hear that Erin thinks Harper is allergic to wheat?"

"No."

"Yeah, apparently."

The final weapon to get Mom off the hunt was to sic her on a sibling—part of the tried and tested Williams siblings battle plan.

"Okay, sweetheart, stay well, and I'll see you on Sunday. It's your dad's turn to cook, so make sure you're early."

"Will do, Mom, love you."

As soon as we ended the call I counted down from twenty and sure enough a text arrived from my sister who called me an asshole for siccing Mom on her, and even feeling wobbly and pathetic, I couldn't help laughing. I loved my family, but I was a long way past the softly worded questions about my health, and I wanted to get back to normal. A year was long enough for me to have to be a victim, and they had to get their heads around how I was facing the world and getting my feet back under me.

I changed for swimming, pulled on a T-shirt and then slathered any exposed skin with sunscreen. I was the typical redhead, freckles, pale skin, and I burned in an instant, and a scare with a college friend and melanoma was enough for me to respect my pale skin. I'd ordered a sun shade for the pool which was arriving next week, then I wouldn't be *as* exposed to the sun, but for now I went swimming late in the day, when the sun was low and evening was pulling in. There were steps into the pool, and when I sank under the water, in an instant there was less strain on my legs with the buoyancy helping to support me. The stretches were the hardest part, repetitive motion designed to pull and rearrange each muscle, a long list of movements that I could recall in my sleep. Then there was the slow swimming from end to end, front crawl, moving the warm muscles into a natural rhythm that gave me space to think.

That first step out of the pool, when gravity pulled me down and made me feel heavier, was always a bitch, but by the time I reached the house, a towel around my neck, I was looser than I had been all day, and there was no sign of a headache.

I made food, or rather my microwave reheated food, and as I sat to eat my cell vibrated with an incoming call. I answered it without looking at the screen, expecting my sister to ream me out for the early go-fetch I'd performed to get out of the way of the worried-mom bus.

"Adam? It's Nick."

This was the third call I'd had from Nick, one of the guys from a support group that Ash attended—Single Dads something or other.

Ash lived next door with Sean, the doctor I'd been reminding Mom about, and their daughter Mia. Sean, and then Eric and Leo had found love in this house—all I wanted was to find peace. Although I'd have been lying if I didn't think maybe the place had a little bit of magic in it.

Leaving my parents' garage conversion had been necessary for my mental health, but moving to this house had been a huge step and only done because I wanted to recreate the buddy relationships I'd seen with Leo, Eric, and Sean. I didn't want anyone to witness my daily humiliations inflicted by a body that refused to work the right way, but the idea of a less empty house had seemed good at the time. It was a big house, with three bedrooms, and I had been kind of lonely. Add in that I'd fundamentally lost my old career, I was still floundering over a new career, and I'd agreed to the proposition immediately.

"Hi."

Nick cleared his throat, "I'm just checking in about your agreement to host my friend and his son."

"It's all good," I confirmed when he paused.

"Don't ask Cam for the rent, I'll send you the money for them," he said, "so if you could text me your details, I can get it sent over. I'll cover a year."

"Wait, I thought they were only staying six months?"

He sighed with great drama, and he didn't speak for a while and I wondered if maybe the call had dropped, then he cleared his throat.

"I don't know. And they might not even come here, but I'll pay you anyway."

"You don't need to—"

"I want a safe place for them to relax." He cursed under his breath and then changed the subject. "Asher was explaining that you volunteer on the Ringwood project? I didn't realize we had that connection."

I was caught on the word *safe*, but when he forged ahead with mentioning Ringwood and effectively got me to restart my thinking in a different direction. "I am, when I can."

"Thank you for your time, it's a project close to my heart." He paused a moment and I wasn't sure what to say. "Anyway, I'm thinking that Cam, could take on paid work on the Ringwood project? He's a carpenter—was a carpenter—so if that's okay, he's got experience."

"Paid? We don't have—"

"Ringwood contacted me to say that the construction company working there has pulled out."

Huh? This was the first I knew, and it messed up everything. The work at the foster home was being driven by the small company, and utilized a team of volunteers to back them up, but if the professionals had pulled out then it would have to be up to the volunteers, and none of us were construction experts.

"Okay—"

"So you sounded worried, can you still help?"

Seemed this Cam guy was important to Nick, and if I was reading between the lines then he needed work and a place to stay. Was he an ex-boyfriend or something? Or was that me jumping to conclusions? I was intrigued why he wasn't moving into Nick's place, and that was going to be my next question.

"Sure, but—"

"Okay, done," Nick interrupted. "I gave Cam your address, he might arrive tomorrow, or the day after," he sighed again, "or not at all."

Oh, that created many other questions. This Cam guy *might* arrive? He might not? He needed to be safe? And now he was going to work at Ringwood on the extension?

Paid. Probably by Nick who was already fundraising for the bulk of the work. Plus what had happened to the construction crew we were using? There was something weird about them just up and leaving.

"What about—"

"Good, good," Nick added. "All sorted, I'll have my finance team send you enough for rent and incidentals, if you can text me the bank details on this number. Then I have one more favor from you."

"Okay?"

"Please, it would mean a great deal if you could let me know as soon as Cam gets there. Just don't let him know you told me, okay? Thank you, and talk later."

Confused, and wondering what I'd just listened to, I sat and stared at my phone for a long time.

What in hell was all that?

Chapter Three

Cam

THE BUS DROPPED us off outside a park and as soon as our feet hit the ground I stumbled on the sidewalk, managing to catch myself before I face-planted. I'd been so wired during this last leg of our journey that I hadn't slept at all, wavering between fear and worry, with nothing much in between. Escaping was maybe too dramatic a term to explain our rush from New York cross country to San Diego, but I certainly felt free knowing there was a distance between *them* and us. I took a moment to check the area, getting my bearings, the cool wash of a breeze welcome against my heated skin. January wasn't the hottest time of the year out here, but the bus had been cramped and noisy, and familiar panic had gripped me and wouldn't let go.

"How much longer to go, Dad?" Finn had managed to sleep curled up on the seat next to me, his head on my lap, but he'd woken and was crabby and narrow-eyed, and I didn't blame him. This was day four of our crazy, convoluted journey, and after a series of bus changes and going from one train station to the next to cover our tracks, we'd finally made it to the West Coast, and in the vicinity of the house that I'd been heading for. I checked the printed map and gestured down the road.

"Just here," I murmured, although I'd been telling Finn that it wasn't far to go for the past couple of days, not only to reassure him, but to help me out as well. We'd made best use of motels, slept on trains and buses, and eaten crappy food, but as far as I knew, there wasn't anyone back east who knew where we were, and as long as they didn't look too hard at my life before I'd met Graeme then we'd be okay for at least a while. It would be easy to find out I was originally from California but I don't think this mattered.

It wasn't as if I had family in San Diego, my mom had died young, and my dad not long after my eighteenth birthday, no siblings, just a few friends who'd long since moved, and Nick of course who I wasn't going to be visiting anytime soon. How long our anonymity would last I didn't know, but at least I'd probably get some time to think, and I was hoping for at least a few weeks.

"I'm hungry." Finn slipped off his backpack, pulling out the remains of a Snickers bar he'd started on our final bus from the train station. I couldn't avoid seeing one fluffy ear of Fred-Bear, a comfort that had been a part of Finn's life from the day I'd taken him home from the hospital. My chest tightened. All he had left in his world was an iPod, a few clothes, and one ratty teddy bear that had seen better days, and it was all my fault.

He pushed the chocolate bar back inside. "It's squashed," he muttered and then sighed with the drama of it all. How strange was it that I felt warmth at hearing his complaint? He'd been through so much the past year or more, and he'd been so good at attempting to take care of me that he'd lost some of his spirit. "Sorry, Dad," he added after a pause, and there it was again—a normal healthy nine-year-old reaction to a shit experience and he was apologizing for himself.

That had to stop—he had to have time to explore being a kid again, and I was completely focused on providing that for him.

"We'll get something to eat after we get to the new place," I said with the best helping of conviction I had in me. I had to believe that this Adam guy didn't know my backstory, and if he did that he wouldn't judge us for Graeme's actions, that he *would* take us in and give us somewhere for Finn to sleep tonight, and he *would* have something for Finn to eat. Those were the only things I wanted for now and I didn't care if he recognized me, got pissed at me, and made me stay outside, he surely couldn't turn Finn away. If worst came to worst we'd tell Adam we weren't staying, and then head... somewhere else.

I checked the street signs, got my bearings, and started down the road, across the corner of the park, heading towards Birds View Court. We walked past a café full of moms and toddlers, then reached an exit gate from the park, and all too soon we were outside our new place. I stopped dead as fear gripped me so hard it outweighed my courage.

What had possessed me to think that there was a better life for us here in San Diego?

What am I doing?

Back in New York we'd had nothing but smoke and mirrors, lies and betrayal, but was heading west to my childhood city going to be any better? Here I would have to face finding a school for Finn, and dealing with seeing Nick, and my defensive barriers were low and my emotional reserves spent.

"What's wrong, Dad?"

It wasn't fair to stand here as though my feet were encased in concrete, because in a few minutes we'd be checking out the house we'd be living in for a while. Hopefully undisturbed. The chance here, of work, plus a place to stay, even if was only for six months, was what Finn and I needed, away from the creditors and the reporters that had hounded our every move. Away from the detritus of the rest of our lives.

"I'm good, excited," I lied. He took my hand and little did he know how much braver that made me feel even as he glanced up at me with apprehension. For all his bravado he didn't want to do this either. "Ready?"

"Are you sure this is the right road?" Finn asked doubtfully.

"This is it, our new home for the next six months."

"It's kind of small," Finn whispered, as if he was afraid someone might hear him. Anything would be small compared to what we'd come from, but the simple houses in this quiet cul-de-sac with neat yards and privacy looked a lot like what I wanted home to be for us both. The front door of the house was unassuming, painted red, surrounded by bushes, and with a wide porch that jutted out at the front. It was one of two houses that mirrored each other, and I liked the symmetry of it all.

Drawing in a breath, I knocked.

The door opened after a short time, and as it did Finn shrunk into my side.

"Hi."

I couldn't see who spoke, the bright midday sun flooding the front yard with light, and the owner of the voice in shadow.

"Hi, I'm Cam Ha—Bellamy, and this is my son, Finn."

"Come on in, do you have bags or anything?" The man limped into the light to check around us, and where I'd expected an older, burly, white-haired retiree, I was faced with a young man with dark red hair, and bright green eyes. He seemed to be around the same age as me, with freckles, sharp cheekbones, and full lips that were quirked in a welcoming smile. He was sexy-cute and hot and smiling so broadly that he made me want to smile back, and for a second I wasn't a dad, or a husband escaping a life he hated, or a man needing help. For a brief moment I felt a tug of attraction, and that threw me because that kind of thing did *not* happen to me, nor would I let it happen. I tamped down the general appreciation and took a closer look at the man I was trusting didn't recognize us. He leaned on a cane, and I was confused by my expectations versus reality. How could this guy be a *retired* firefighter, and why was he leaning on a cane, and... oh shit... was that why he was a former firefighter now? Maybe this wasn't the Adam I was supposed to be meeting, and I guessed I better check.

"Nick told me that… I'm looking for Adam?" I asked with caution.

"You've found him." He took my hand, his grip was firm, and I was lost in his green eyes, my ability to form a sentence having fled. The entire change from what I'd expected and the reality facing me was throwing me off balance. "Hey, Finn, I can get some snacks ready, and I have lemonade. Do you like lemonade?"

Finn scuffed his feet next to me, and it dawned on me that I was standing outside our new home in a daze. Maybe part of me had hoped for the huge firefighter of my imagination. Maybe I craved a hero who could watch out of us.

I don't know what is happening.

"How about you?" Adam asked.

"Sorry?"

"Do you want to come in for lemonade? Or come in at all?" Adam made the joke, and I knew that in polite company it was proper to react, but I'd lost the plot. Adam's wide smile faded, and wariness filtered into his eyes. His expression changed as if all the hope had been knocked out of him, because I was staring at the cane, and then his eyes, and I was saying nothing at all. What must he think?

"Please. We'd love some." I smiled then, but I couldn't grin the same way as I used to, not fueled by sheer happiness or pleasure, and I don't think it worked because Adam backed away into the dark interior and allowed us in.

He looked uneasy.

And yet again I'd fucked up.

We closed the front door then followed him into a hallway and left to a big kitchen with a kitchen island in the center. Adam busied himself pulling chips out of a cupboard and fetching chilled lemonade in a large jug.

"Nick wasn't sure what day you'd get here, so I made some lemonade each day just in case. It's just out of a packet—nothing fancy." He was one hundred percent polite and careful, and there was no sign of the smile.

"We've been traveling a while so we're exhausted, sorry if I'm not seeming… right."

He poured three drinks and side-eyed me. "Where did you travel from?"

I shrugged off my backpack and helped Finn with his and then the two of us sat on the stools at the counter, then ignored the question. "Buses, trains, I feel as if I left half of myself in a hundred different places."

Adam hooked his cane on the door handle and took a seat opposite us, and the smile that had vanished returned.

"Help yourself to food, I can make you a PB&J if you want one, Finn?"

Finn mumbled something to himself, and I knocked elbows with him. "Do you want a sandwich, Finn?"

"Yes, please," he said and then dipped his head again. I recalled a time when he hadn't been shy—when he'd been boisterous and happy and in love with life. I was determined that we'd find our old selves, but for now it was important for him to eat, and sleep, and feel safe and secure.

"I can do it if you like." I offered immediately.

"I've got it," Adam sounded determined, and he was right, he could. Leaning against the counter, he created a plate of PB&J sandwiches. Finn nibbled on the first one, then it disappeared so fast I couldn't help smiling at my son's enthusiasm.

"Thank you," Finn said when he'd finished the first quarter.

"It's all good. So, Nick said you need the rooms for six months."

"How do you know Nick?" I shouldn't assume there was a connection between Adam and Nick that went further than Nick searching for a place to live. He'd assured me in that note that Finn and I would be safe so I assumed he must have known Adam somehow.

"I was going to ask you the same thing."

God, that was a long story. Starting with being best friends, and then disintegrating into accusations and arguments and then with me ghosting him.

"He's a friend from way back," I hedged.

"No, he's my Uncle Nick. He's not a friend," Finn said, and I froze. Nick *was* Finn's godfather, and when we'd been close, Finn had called him uncle, but I didn't realize Finn still remembered him at all, let alone the familiar term.

"Finn's godfather," I amended, or explained. I didn't know what the hell I was doing.

Adam moved on the stool and I caught him wincing, then just as quick he covered it up with another smile. "Nick is a friend of Asher's, he lives next door and his husband, Ash's husband, Sean, is the best friend of a firefighter I worked with, Eric. In fact, Eric, Sean, and Leo who is a cop, owned the house before me." He shook his head. "You don't need to know all that, sorry, but yeah, I was looking for someone to rent a room, and Ash said he'd mention it on the SDT forum and voila, you were recommended by Nick."

I didn't follow a lot of that, but the mention of the SDT forum, Single Dads Together, was yet another icy knife in my chest. Nick and I had set that up, way back, when his husband Danny had passed, and before I'd let Graeme into my life.

"Well, we're happy to be here." Happy was a vast understatement. This was somewhere to stop and take stock, and it might have only been temporary but I felt a flush of peace.

Tonight we would sleep in a real bed, and there wouldn't be the specter of journalists baying for blood right outside our front door. How long our anonymity would last I couldn't imagine, but for now we were somewhere calm, and I felt the overwhelming urge to hug Adam hard for agreeing to have us in his home. I hadn't realized how much I'd needed a friendly face, or understood how starved I must have been for affection when all I wanted to do was grab Adam and hold on tight.

Tomorrow, the hard work started, the first day of trying to rebuild my life one day at a time then fix everything for Finn.

Chapter Four

Adam

I WATCHED Cam very closely because he was a very hard person to read. He connected with his son, his expression softened whenever he glanced at Finn. Talking about Nick had hurt hard, and the stony expression when I rambled on about how I ended up having housemates made me wind the story up until it was a blurted mess of explanation.

Why in God's name I explained who owned the house before me, or that Eric was a firefighter, or Leo was a cop, I don't know. He was lucky I didn't point to the discoloration on the refrigerator door where their schedule had once hung. I'd seen it when all three of them had lived here, a neat explanation of who was where saving lives at what time. A reminder that there was no point in my putting any kind of schedule up, given I wasn't on shifts, or keeping any kind of office hours.

Stow the self pity.

Cam flustered me, and I wasn't sure it was in a good way.

I'd seen his expression change from a spark of connection to shock when he saw me leaning on the cane. I hadn't wanted to use it today, but a particularly brutal PT session had left me shaky and off-balance, and if a stick to hold me up was what I needed to get me through the day then that was it. No sense in crying over a man checking me out and then avoiding me as soon as they saw the cane, or my scars, or the way I sometimes couldn't even walk in a straight line.

Rejection was one more facet of the post-trauma experience, and one more thing that I'd had to get used to. He'd shaken my hand, seemed friendly, but he'd checked me out, raked his gaze from my head to my toes, only not in a good way where he lingered on my groin. No, this was a very different observation where I'd been judged and found wanting. Add in the pain snapping in my shoulder when we shook hands, and his quick release of said hand, and I was left in a bad place. Hence the rambling. I subscribed to the adage that the more I talked, the less people wanted to ask intrusive questions.

I'd expected Cam to be an older guy, mostly because he had a nine-year-old son, and I'd assumed that he'd be well into his thirties, or even forties if he'd gone through adoption and started late. It turned out I was wrong, and the brief flash of holy-shit-he's-hot subsided quickly when he stared. Then I couldn't quite meet his gaze in case he started asking questions.

Why are you using a cane?
Did you have an accident?

Are you okay?

I wasn't ready to answer any of those right now.

Of course, none of that boded well for the happy living together experience I'd hoped for. I didn't need the money, but the company might've been nice, and a kid in the house would give me something to focus on. Kids were cool, they asked questions about my injuries yes, but their questions were born out of innocence and not out of ignorance or a need to work out if I was worthy of attention.

Okay. Let's get off this thought train before it derails.

"Thank you for letting us stay," Cam said, and picked his bag up. "Do you want to show us our rooms? Or just tell me where we need to go?"

"I'll show you." I needed to get up the stairs, and it was on my list of things to do today. Along with washing a mug or two without leaning on the sink, emptying the dishwasher without sitting on a chair, swimming without nearly drowning, and three sets of climbing the stairs. Small steps for some but giant mountains for me, each mountain with the ogre of pain guarding the peak. I'd already achieved washing up my breakfast bowl, but the dryer was still full, and I'd managed the stairs once, which was when I'd come down that morning and only counted as half.

"Do you have other stuff coming? More bags?"

I saw him flinch. "This is it for now." He wouldn't meet my gaze. "We'll need to go shopping for some things later."

"Okay, cool, I can show you the stores around here. Follow me." I wasn't going to poke and pry when it was

obvious he had secrets he wanted to keep. I knew all about
secrets, and he was entitled not to explain a damn thing.
Ending up at my house with no bags, in fact no life at all
apart from a backpack each, was weird, but it would have
to be a puzzle I left for a later time. What were they
running from? Why did they need somewhere to stay?
None of that seemed important when I saw how exhausted
they both looked.

Using a combination of limited muscle strength, my
cane, the judicious use of the rail and ignoring whatever
pain stabbed me with fire, I made it to the top of the stairs
in record time. Well, record time for me. Cam bumped into
me a couple of times from a combination of
overestimating how quickly I was moving and probably
exhaustion, and then made a big show of apologizing
before waiting for me to get to the top first. Yes, I felt like
a fucking idiot.

"This is the biggest of the two rooms," I gestured into
Eric's old room at the front of the house. It came with a
king-size bed and an attached bathroom.

"You have this one, Finn," Cam murmured.

Finn slipped past him and into the space before
stopping by the bed and shrugging off his backpack. I
didn't know what I was waiting for. Maybe a comment
from Finn about the bed, or the storage, or god knows
what. I had assumed that Cam would take that one,
because the other one was kind of small and didn't have an
attached bathroom.

"And this is the other room," I pushed open the door to
the final bedroom, which came with a large bed, but not
much else, although the view over the valley was stunning.

"It's not a lot," I began, but stopped when Cam waved a hand.

"It's great, I don't need a lot of room like Finn, just a bed is all." He moved to the window and stared at the view. "Stunning."

"I have the same view," I leaned on the cane and crossed to the same window. "We have a pool beyond the scrubby bushes there, it's warm, big enough to do an approximation of laps and I have a canopy to fix up because I easily burn." I gestured at myself.

He blinked at me as if I was speaking a different language. "Is there someone else living here?" he asked.

I was lost and staring right into velvet brown eyes. "Sorry?"

"You said 'we have a pool.'"

"Oh, my bad, I meant *I* have a pool. Well, *we*, now that you and Finn are here I guess."

He was watching me again, but this time he was staring right at me, and when his gaze dropped it was only as far as my lips before his focus returned to my eyes. I wish I could say he played for my team, and that he was checking me out because of attraction, because he was sexy-gorgeous in his rough and ready sleep-deprived way, but there was no evidence of that.

"Feel free to use the pool whenever, same with the grill because I don't use that a lot. Ash and Sean live next door, with Mia. I meant to ask, do you know Ash?"

He stared at me, then frowned. "I don't think so."

"I thought maybe you were on the forum, the single dads thing, you know, through Nick?"

"Oh. No, I'm not on there at all." He turned to stare

back out at the view. "I've lived away for a while now, kind of lost touch with Nick."

"Okay, well, as I said, they're next door, and sometimes I babysit Mia, she's a toddler, but the cutest thing, only just to warn you she is going through a major crayon stage and if you leave anything out then it gets scribbled on."

"Mia. Crayons. Okay."

"We can sit and talk later about food, but for now there is plenty of breakfast things, and bread, cold meats, that kind of thing for lunch. Help yourself to anything you want from the kitchen and there's a ton of portions in the freezer from one of my mom's manic cooking days. Chili I think, and maybe lasagna. There's nothing with nuts or gluten, because my niece is allergic to everything, allegedly, and I say allegedly because I'm sure it's my sister being overprotective, but who knows, because I don't have kids so I don't know what it's like to worry about them."

He stared at me and there was the faint hint of a smile at my yammering on with no purpose.

I coughed to clear my throat. "Anyway, there's a key on the hook with a red fob which is for the house, so help yourself, and there's extra bedding in the closet, and for the toiletries I just went out and got one of everything and left it in the attached bathroom, so you'll need to put them away."

He went for his wallet. "How much do I owe you?"

"Nick already gave me your money," I reminded him and the color leached from his face. I'd just assumed Nick was passing on funds, but yeah, I'd misread that.

"Fuck," Cam muttered, and closed his eyes for a moment, so much emotion passing over his face that I was confused. Was he angry? Shattered? Happy? I couldn't tell, and the reaction went on for way too long.

"Do you want to ask me any questions about anything?"

"I need to check on Finn because he's not sure what… I just need to…" He gestured at the door, and I moved aside to let him pass. He disappeared into what was now Finn's room.

Well, I sure made a good impression. Such a good one that he didn't want to stand around and talk.

I stopped at the open door, found dad and son both staring out of the window at the front yard, their heads close together, and Cam talking.

"I'll be downstairs," I interrupted gently, "but whenever you're ready, if you want, you can find me and I'll show you the pool."

"Thank you," Cam murmured, and that was my cue to go downstairs. At least this way I didn't have an audience, because I was more awkward going down than I had been climbing up what with the whole fear of tumbling headfirst down the steps. Still, when I reached the bottom I felt a great sense of achievement. Considering I used to be able to run up and down ladders carrying pounds of equipment, this was small

That was then. This is now.

I sent a quick text to Nick to tell him that his friend and son were here, and he replied instantly with a thank you, as if he'd been waiting for the message.

I stopped in the kitchen, feeling as if I should wait for

Cam and Finn to join me, to be a host or something, which was stupid because they were paying rent, but that didn't matter. I wanted to care for their needs before they got caught up in any strange ideas about looking after me.

Flicking on the television, I sat back on the sofa, went through some short stretches as the news ticker showed statistics for the Low Pass fire under footage taken from cars of flames jumping the highway. I stopped stretching when the camera zoomed in on first responders, knowing that Eric and the team might've been out there somewhere.

A familiar blackness began to creep inside me, a regret, pain, memories of a future that had been destroyed, and I turned off the television.

"Hi, Mr. Williams, you said about the pool?"

Finn startled me, and I jerked upright so fast that I knew I'd pay for it later. I didn't know how long Cam and Finn had been standing there watching me, because when I went to the dark place it was very hard to connect with the real world. But his words had pulled me out of it, yanked me away from the memories, and for that I felt grateful.

"Call me Adam, please, and yes, the pool." I used the arm of the sofa and my cane to stand, then opened the doors that led onto the patio and then down through the yard, past the scrubby bushes that were tall and tangled, and to the end of the garden with more views over the valley. "Ta dah," I announced with a fake fanfare, hoping to raise a smile from Finn because I hadn't seen him do a lot of smiling yet.

"Can I sit with my feet in there?"

I was at least rewarded by seeing interest in his expression and for now that would have to do.

"Sure you can. If that's okay with your dad?" I glanced at Cam who nodded.

"Go for it, but sit in the shade. I need to get sunscreen as well." The last thing wasn't for Finn, I think he was adding to his mental list of things to buy.

Finn sat cross-legged by the side of the pool pulling off his shoes and socks at speed then rolling up his jeans before sitting in the only shaded part, on the edge with his feet in the water and his head tipped back.

"How old is Finn?" I was just making conversation, but when Cam didn't answer immediately I glanced over at him and he was worrying at his lip.

"He's nine. Nearly ten."

"My brother's son is nine, it's a good age. Into everything and not afraid to look stupid doing it." I repeated what Luke had said to me last weekend, when he'd been explaining how Seth had climbed the tree in the backyard and then gotten stuck. All I could think was thank god he hadn't had to call 911, because sure as shit that would come back to me through the grapevine. Everyone knew my family, but that was what came of having a dad who'd been a senior cop, and a mom who made it her business to be involved in everything.

Cam nodded, but that was all I was getting out of him. I pulled a chair from the sun and into the shade.

"Let's sit for a while," I encouraged, then waited for Cam to follow, which he did after a short while of making it seem as if he'd rather have been anywhere than with me. I knew for a fact that if Leo had been there then his cop senses would've been tingling, but it wasn't my place to think that Cam, or his son, were in trouble, or even consider the possible cause of any trouble. Nick had asked for them to stay, said they needed safety, and that I could do, so it was all golden as far as I was concerned.

"Nick said I could trust you," Cam blurted as he sat down, the words spilling out of him as if he'd been thinking about how to start the conversation for the longest time.

"He's right. You can."

"How can he even say things like that, when I don't know you at all?" He sounded tired.

I offered my hand with a reassuring smile. "Adam Williams, former firefighter, youngest son of a strong mom with a need to meddle, three siblings, my dad is a retired cop. Gay, pretty much an all-around good guy." I was teasing, but Cameron's expression relaxed a little and he shook my hand.

"Cameron Bellamy, call me Cam," he hesitated and gripped my hand, his eyes shadowed with incredible pain. "Currently going through a divorce from a husband that…" he stopped and I squeezed his hand to let him know I'd heard and understood the first part of his statement.

"Hello, Cameron Bellamy," I murmured, and the connection of our joined hands went from natural to slightly too long—as if neither of us wanted to let go. I was pulled in by his intense gaze, attracted to the collection of features that made up his handsome face, albeit shaded with exhaustion. What I wouldn't have given to be able to kiss away the tiredness, snuggle into him and…

The fuck? Where had that come from? I was losing my

shit here when a handsome guy with a soft smile made my non-existent attraction gene spark to life. I hadn't had sex since… hell, my libido after the accident had tanked at the same time as my career, and it had only been in recent weeks that I'd been interested in anything south of the pain in my back. But Cameron was pretty much the kind of guy I would've gone for—tall, gorgeous, sexy, and with the most perfect smile. In fact, if he was here in my house, and he felt like a connection then maybe we could—

"Hello, Adam Williams," he interrupted my fevered imaginings, which was a good thing. I had to keep my head in the game. Just because Cameron was sexy-hot and my idea of a wet dream didn't mean I was anywhere near the kind of person he might be interested in. I forced my thoughts back to where they belonged.

"So, Nick told me—"

"Did Nick tell you I used to be Cameron Hastings?" He steamrolled right over what I was about to say, then let go of my hand.

I felt bereft because his grip was firm, and I'd had an excuse to stare into his eyes. I could see he was waiting for me to react, but the name Cameron Hastings didn't ring any bells, even though the weight of the words appeared to be enough to push Cam into the ground.

"No, what do you mean *used to be*?" I tried not to sound as though I was demanding an answer, settling for a milder curious tone, just to encourage him to keep talking. I think if I'd done my usual thing where I had verbal diarrhea then he'd take Finn and run in the opposite direction.

"New York…" He stopped and bit his lip, then ran the tip of his tongue over the bitten spot.

Is it just me or is it that the sexiest thing I've ever seen?

He wasn't talking, if anything I got the sense he was done and that he was considering leaving.

"City on the East Coast, I know of it." I teased, but I didn't get a smile in return.

"Jeez, I don't want to…" The internal battle was written in every line of his frown. "My soon to be ex-husband is Graeme Hastings." He waited again, but I had no idea who that was either and I shrugged to indicate that fact and to encourage him to carry on. "My whole world was caught up in him and what he did, and I assumed everyone would know."

"Meh, New York is another world, and way too cold." I was teasing to get him to smile but I doubted anything would've shifted the frown that was etched onto his face.

"He embezzled, swindled, and basically lied to line his own pockets after losing our money, and that of many other investors, in deals slap-bang in the middle of a gray area. He singlehandedly gambled with hundreds of thousands from pension funds, and he's in prison starting a seven-year sentence." He hesitated for a beat, for me to acknowledge that yeah I knew this asshole, but I couldn't give him anything.

"I genuinely don't know the story." I winced that I'd used the word story. That implied it was an easy thing with a happy ending, when it wasn't.

He deflated and then made this dismissive gesture. "I

suggest you Google it then you'll have a *real* picture of who I am."

There was that stoic but frowny expression again, the one that said he expected me to do what he said, and then throw him onto the street. Maybe he'd seen a lot of adverse reactions to who he was, but it wasn't typical for me to judge people without knowing the facts, and there was only one thing I needed to know.

"You're the husband of a bad guy, doesn't mean you're a bad guy too. I don't judge people on what Google says."

He shook his head and sighed all at the same time with sluggish resignation in the exhalation. "I have to warn you that you might end up with people at your door because of who I am."

"What kind of people?"

"Journalists. Wanting to ask questions." Shadows filled his eyes as he stared at me again, expecting me to freak out. "Nick never actually explained any of this before he talked you into opening your house to us?"

I could've lied, but Cam and his son needed me, or at least my house, and being a hero was kind of a nice feeling. "No, he didn't."

He stood so dramatically that his chair toppled. "I knew it, that's just like him, assuming everyone will do what he says. I'm sorry. We'll just leave, thank you for the snacks—"

"Hang on," I scrambled to stand about as carefully as I could, at a speed which wasn't that fast, and only just managed to grab the sleeve of Cam's T-shirt to stop him walking off. "That doesn't mean I'd have said no. Believe me, I've seen my fair share of paparazzi for one reason or another. You're a dad, with a son, and you need a place to stay, and I'm certainly not here to judge anyone."

He endeavored to shrug me off, but I had a perfectly good right hand and had found my center of balance, and unless he pushed me to the ground there was no moving me. In the end he stopped tugging and I released my hold on his shirt.

"You don't know me."

"Did you have anything to do with whatever your ex did?" Simple question, and I catalogued all of Cameron's tells. The widening of his eyes, the way he held himself, and the anger that made him clench his fists.

"I might have been able to stop him…" He let out a sigh and scrubbed at his face, and I knew there was a whole backstory there. "But no," he finished.

"Dad?" I hadn't realized but Finn had left the water and was by his dad's side, his expression screwed into something super-fierce.

"I'm good, Finn, promise. I was just explaining to Mr. Williams about your… about…"

"Dad—"

Cam put a hand on Finn's shoulder. "It's okay, Finn, he's not—"

"I can fight you," Finn announced and took an angry step toward me.

"Finn, he's not Graeme."

Finn crossed his arms over his chest and then stared at me with a mutinous expression. I did the one thing I could think that might work, and sat again, knowing that I had to back down otherwise the two of them would leave. I got the sense that Finn would do anything for his dad, and if that meant leaving then that was the way it would be.

"I barely know either of you, so why are you telling me all of this?"

"What are you telling him?" Finn rounded on his dad. "I thought we were being a secret?"

Cam looked defeated. "He has to know, Finn, because otherwise, if anyone wants to find us…"

The two of them were locked in their own world, an unspoken conversation passing between them, and only after Cam pulled Finn in for a hug did Finn appear to relax.

"I'll be right there," Finn pointed at the pool, sitting where he had before, but he didn't dangle his feet in the water this time. I could feel the weight of his stare on me.

"He's so protective he's forgotten how to be a kid," Cam mumbled, but I'm not sure he meant to say it out loud, as he changed direction. "What were you asking me?" Cam sat back down as if his strings had been cut and the flimsy garden chair creaked.

"Why do I need to know the reason you're here?" I reworded the question.

"Just to reassure you I guess, because this place is the space we need to just breathe, away from cameras, and people who want us to hurt." He straightened in his chair. "I can handle whatever people throw at me, or write about me, but Finn is still a kid. I'm not stupid, I know the media will find out where I am somehow, but we'll move on before that happens. I swear."

"Not that it changes you staying here, but what should I expect?"

"Journalists maybe, possibly one of the people affected by what he did. I don't know, but whatever it is I will fix it, and move on."

"Well, in the spirit of honesty, I should tell you that I have migraines, I take all kinds of meds for pain, I'm seeing a counselor, and I haven't entirely come to terms with my entire life being dragged out from under me."

He faced me, and I saw compassion in his dark eyes, and maybe even some understanding. I guess his world had changed the same as mine, just in a very different way.

"Is there anything I need to know to do?"

Well, that was the responsible thing for a housemate to ask, and I appreciated it, but there was only one thing I needed.

"Judge me for the bits you can't see," I said in all seriousness, and then quirked a smile. He could take that anyway he wanted, but most of all I wanted him to not see a broken man, but someone who was in his corner. Someone worthwhile.

He nodded and I hoped he meant it. I needed to be a hero, I had this stubborn streak and wanted to help. He'd looked so fierce and determined, telling me that he could handle what he was going through when he was struggling with some big things. I was struck with a desire to protect this man and his son, which was at odds with the pain I felt and my inability to move faster than a freaking snail.

Well, that's new.

Chapter Five

Cam

"Judge me for the bits you can't see."

That summed up how I felt about what I'd told him.

Don't see me as Graeme's husband. Don't judge me as a failure. See inside my heart. Adrenaline from telling Adam enough to warn him, made me shaky, and even though he'd settled back in the chair and the conversation had ended I could see more questions in his eyes. I really did want him to Google me, then I wouldn't have to go through everything in detail, but he seemed the type of person who wanted to know things from the source. I should've been happy about that—Nick had said I could trust Adam, but there was always that doubt that people wanted to make money off my story.

"Dad?"

I snapped myself out of the contemplative mode I'd drifted into, and smiled at Finn.

"Yep?"

"Are you really okay?" That was Finn's default question, and he wasn't looking at me as much as he was staring daggers at poor Adam.

"I'm good. We're good. Are you okay?"

The confrontational stance melted away as he stared at my expression, which I'd schooled into a reassuring smile, and my sweet nine-year-old kid came back slowly. "Yeah, but…"

"But?"

"I can't swim without trunks, and there wasn't room in my bag to hide them." He shrugged a thin shoulder. "It's okay though, I don't really have to swim."

I ignored the slightly manipulative words and settled on feeling guilt again—pretty much my default setting. We couldn't bring much of anything, and trunks weren't a necessity, not when he needed to bring Fred-Bear as his comfort. We both needed so many things, and with Nick covering the cost of rent, something I needed to accept for the time being, we had some spare cash to at least get the essentials. We'd need a ton of things to make a new life, but it had to be only just enough that we could pick everything up and run at a moment's notice. Swimming trunks were a necessity for as long as we stayed here at the house with the pool.

"We need to go shopping." I turned to Adam. "You said there was a store near here?"

"Yeah, I'll call a cab and come with you, if that's okay. I need to get food. Are you okay with grocery store clothes?"

"Yeah, that's good." Christ, I'd have taken anything I could get, and I'd long gotten over the need for designer clothes to maintain an appearance. I'd have been happy with cheap jeans and a clean T-shirt right then.

"Okay then," he opened an app on his phone and ordered a cab. "Fifteen minutes out, okay?"

"Great. Finn, shoes on, we're going to buy what we need."

The ride to the store was quiet in the back with Finn and me staring out of the window, learning our new neighborhood as best we could, and second, looking at things that would mark our stay here. The park, the café, the school that I wouldn't be sending Finn to. We passed a group of kids in a front yard close by, and I couldn't help but see the way Finn hunched in on himself. He'd told me he'd had to leave all his friends behind, but every single one had dropped him a long time ago.

When we pulled up outside the store, we grabbed a cart and went in to find that they sold one of about everything we needed. Trunks were at the top of Finn's list, and he got me some too, then we added shorts, underwear, T-shirts, shoes, enough to get a basic wardrobe together, plus a ton of sunscreen, sunglasses, and the pile seemed to be getting bigger with every pass we did of the aisles and shelves. Things that Finn approved went into the cart, although when he thought I would wear the purple and pink hibiscus shirt I don't know. Still, it made him smile and I would go to the ends of the earth and back just to make him smile.

Adam had stayed with us for a while, and then he'd wandered off for food, and we headed for the stationery aisle to get everything we needed to start homeschooling. Not that I had any idea of what we needed, but I did recall the first day of a new term and the excitement of new notebooks and pens. Maybe if Finn chose what he wanted then I could encourage some enthusiasm in myself for being responsible for his education.

As we were investigating options Adam returned, items in bags and leaning heavily on a cart. I took a second glance at his face, because something wasn't right. He'd been in pain back at the house, but that was with his body, this was different. He was gaunt, pinched, one hand resting on his temple and pressing there, and his already pale skin had a gray hue, his green eyes dull with agony. Something had changed since he'd left us, and none of it was good.

"I'm sorry, I have to head back," Adam said. "I'm not feeling good."

"We're nearly done, I just need to get some books and then, we'll pay and come with you."

He nodded, and winced. "I'll call a cab… meet you… outside."

Adam leaned heavily on the cart and limped past the checkouts, then out through the main door, and Finn and I did the stationery aisle in record time, yanking one of everything into the cart. I should have spent more time getting notebooks for each subject, but we could come back in a few days once we had a feel for what we needed for homeschooling. Still, it was a good ten minutes before we joined him, and by the time we got out there he was so pale I thought about calling 911. I didn't get a chance to ask him what was wrong because the cab arrived, and he was very quiet in the car, supporting his head in his hands, and I didn't know him well enough to tell him that he looked like shit.

When we got back, I grabbed all the bags from the

trunk and still made it to the front door before Adam. He attempted to get the key in the lock, but was missing by a country mile, so I took the key and opened it, then headed inside, by which time he was leaning on me for as long as it took to get to the kitchen table and for him to drop like a rock into the nearest chair.

"Shit. Do I need to call 911?"

"No. Meds. Sleep."

"What can I get you?"

His face was pinched in pain. "I was stupid... just my... top shelf, the sumatriptan." He gestured to the stove, and I went to the nearest cupboard there and found a basket with prescriptions. Later I'd think about asking him to put them somewhere else, given that Finn was in the house, but right now all I could think was that he appeared close to passing out. I didn't know what this drug was for, but I poured water from the filter jug in the refrigerator into a glass, and then put the meds and the drink in front of him. He picked up the tablets but couldn't open the childproof lid, so I gently took it from him and with the lid off, passed it back.

He swallowed two, but the action itself made him wince, and then he closed his eyes, rocked back in the chair.

"I need to get upstairs," he ground the words out and gagged, and for a moment I thought he was going to be sick. I put the lid back on the pills and wondered what the hell to do next.

"Is he okay, Dad?" Finn asked.

"Just a headache, Finn. Can you start putting the food away?"

"Sure, Dad, I don't know where everything goes, though."

"Just put the cold stuff in the refrigerator, and the frozen in the freezer. Leave the rest on the table."

"Okay."

"Bed," Adam interrupted, and tried to stand. "Left it too long…"

I couldn't let him struggle. I helped him to stand, and step by cautious step we made it out of the kitchen and to the bottom of the stairs. The climb was nothing for me, but I could see how it would be a mountain for him, and without being too clumsy I assisted him with each step, taking his weight, hearing his labored breath, and when we were at the top of the stairs, I thought I saw tears in his eyes. He took over from there, used the wall to support himself, managed to get to his room, and got as far as the bed before crumpling to the mattress. If this was a migraine he'd need darkness, and I pulled the drapes, then considered the fact he was still wearing sneakers. I took them off, assisted him in moving to a more comfortable position, and then stepped out of the room and closed the door.

"Dad?" Finn was right there waiting for me.

I gave him a reassuring side-hug. "It's okay kiddo, he's fine. I'll go put the rest of the groceries away, then come back and we'll go through our new clothes."

Groceries stowed, we then put everything away in Finn's room, but I dumped my purchases onto the bed, because I didn't have the heart to try to organize anything right then. I hovered outside Adam's door wondering if 911 was an option, or was he okay in there? Having only known him for two hours, I didn't know him well enough to make a judgement call, but I felt responsible. He'd opened his home to me and Finn, and for that I would be forever grateful. He'd fed us, given us rooms, not said one word in judgment about what I'd told him.

There was even that thought that he *might be* one of the good guys, as Nick had promised.

I knocked, didn't hear anything so opened the door a little, to check he was still breathing, much as I did every time I went in to check on Finn. From the daylight in the hall the covers moving with each breath was easy to see, but he'd buried himself under a quilt and I wasn't going to peel it back if he needed darkness. I closed the door and turned to find myself face-to-face with Finn.

"I'm hungry, Dad," and he rubbed his belly to underscore the sentiment. I ruffled his hair before he could duck, something I took great pleasure in, and then we chased each other down the stairs and into the kitchen.

Adam had mentioned pre-cooked meals in the freezer, and I pulled out a container marked *Lasagna* and then put it back into the freezer, loath to take his food, and checked the refrigerator instead, finding the chorizo he'd bought today, tomatoes, then hunting around for pasta. Cooking was my happy place, recipes, ingredients, love for the food, and the pleasure I got when Finn ate everything in front of him.

Within thirty minutes Finn was devouring a plate of hot pasta and I had a helping myself, along with another bowl ready for Adam if he woke up hungry. Exhaustion began to blur the edges of my thoughts even though it was early evening, but I had a long list of things I needed to do.

First was to find out more about this job that Nick suggested without talking to Nick directly, which was an impossible thing, oh and agree to a schedule for repaying what he'd given Adam for the rent. Christ knows how much it would be—six months' rent and utilities—it had to be a big sum, and it hurt my chest when I checked my bag and saw the remainder of my cash in there. Five thousand dollars less the money we'd spent today. I didn't have a hope in hell of paying Nick back anytime soon and I needed to get an account set up.

Too much to think about.

Then, I had to spend time searching through the supplies we'd bought. Homeschooling Finn was the single option left for now, even if it meant he wouldn't make new friends. I wasn't planning on staying in San Diego for any longer than the six months I'd imagined at first, and already had the idea of heading north to somewhere super remote, like in the center of Montana where Finn could just be a kid who didn't have to worry about what I'd gotten myself wrapped up in. Then he could go to school, and I would have to hope that I hadn't fucked up his education too much.

Homeschooling was an option, but was I going to be any good at that? I didn't have a college degree, but it wasn't because I couldn't have gone—I had other things to do, and a carpentry apprenticeship with my dad had been every hope and dream I had come true.

I miss you, Dad.

He'd never have allowed me to make the mistakes I'd made—although Nick had tried to stop me, and look how *that* had ended up.

"Your face is all funny," Finn observed, and scooped the last of his pasta onto a fork then scraped his plate clean of every speck of sauce.

"Your face is weird," I snarked back.

"Not as weird as yours." Finn forgot the serious observation he'd made and instead we went into a cycle of saying shit about each other. Normal dad/son stuff. A decision on how to approach the homeschooling could be made tomorrow, when I wasn't so tired, when my head wasn't full of everything else.

We cleaned up, and Finn went into the living room, taking his new cheap tablet with him—the only frivolous thing we'd bought at the store. We'd charged it then set up a new email, set the address as here, discussed how and when he could visit sites, and that he wasn't to connect with anyone back in New York. He'd listened to me in all seriousness, pinkie swore that he'd keep me safe. He broke my heart with that simple promise and I hugged him until he squeaked in protest. Then we downloaded some games within a budget—enough to keep him occupied as I found some paper and a pen and began making lists of subjects, curriculums, outcomes, and whatever else I assumed Finn should know. I was utterly out of my depth, but this was important.

Let's get this done.

I was on my eighth try at a list when everything began to make sense.

Shame I can't just teach him shop every day, because that is one thing I can *do.*

This current list, number eight, had two columns, one marked with a hopeful, *what I know*, and the other one

with a more honest, *everything I don't know.* So far it was
the don't-know list that was winning, and it started with
any kind of basic algebra and ended with fraction
equivalence, and that was as far as I'd got. I'd borrowed
the tablet quickly, long enough to look up curriculums for
a fifth-grader and I knew what he was meant to follow but
why did a nine-year-old need to know algebra for fuck's
sake?

And what even *was* fraction equivalence?

I was so screwed.

Chapter Six

Adam

I WAS SO FREAKING embarrassed about what had happened. Not only had I misjudged my abilities, but I'd pushed past the first warning signs in the grocery story as if I wasn't completely broken. I'd managed to sleep, the meds did their thing, but I'd had the night from hell with pain, and I was so over everything this morning.

And to add to the embarrassment, my new and sexy housemate with the dark eyes, strong hold, and thoughtful smile had put me to bed. And not in a good way.

He didn't mention it at breakfast, apart from asking me if I was okay, and when I said I was fine he believed me, or at least he didn't call me a liar outright. It was only after Finn went up for a shower and I successfully managed to cross loading the dishwasher from my list that he relaxed enough to talk to me.

"Do you often get migraines?" he asked as he blew and sipped a hot coffee.

"They're not even… I don't…" Where did I start? I guess I should tell him part of why I was hobbling around the house like an old man in case I did something stupid and he found me rocking in a corner. "I was injured on the job and manage nerve problems with meds, yoga, and relaxation, but when they get messed up, or my muscles get tight, then I get the headaches. So thank you for your help yesterday."

"It's no problem."

"I could have made it upstairs myself, though." I had to say that in case he thought I was completely incapable.

"I know," he lied, and I was pleased for the lie. "I'm sorry for your injury."

That kind of sympathy was something I'd gotten used to. At first I would push back, ask them what exactly they were sorry for, and it was my family that got the brunt of that kind of shit, but now it was an easier to just smile. I'd long since given up adding anything about it being okay, because it wasn't okay.

It was far *fucking* away from okay.

"I know a bit of massage, if I can ever help."

My head went straight *there*. Direct to imagining him massaging me, and now was not the time to think any kind of erotic thoughts, at least not before coffee.

"I'm okay."

He gave me a measuring glance, then there was silence —a slightly awkward silence which wasn't surprising since Cam had been in the house for less than a day and already seen me at my weakest. I helped myself to coffee and a dry bagel that was about all I could manage, and headed straight for the patio with a nod of goodbye as I passed Cam. There was this big part of me that wanted to stay and talk about everything and nothing, but this awkward stage was made so much the worse for what had happened last night.

I walked the edge of the yard, past the bushes, around the pool, following the gravel path as it twisted in and out of cultivated beds, then ended back at the patio before repeating it.

"Hey, Uncle Red!" A squeaky voice came from next door, and all I could see was Mia's head, but I knew that wasn't Mia's voice, nor was she tall enough to be looking over the fence. I also knew that Ash wasn't the one holding Mia, because Ash was sensible and Sean was an idiot.

Ergo, it was Sean.

"Morning, Mia, morning, Sean."

Sean popped up from where he'd been bending, scooping Mia up and over his shoulders so she sat on his neck, her hands in his hair and a wide grin on her face as he held her legs.

"Unca Red!" she yelled, and my heart melted. Mia was adorable, and loved her Uncle Red, even if she patted my shoulder a lot and muttered about ouchies which convinced me that Ash and Sean discussed me when I wasn't there. Yes, I get she saw me with a cane, but the fact she patted me? I wished people didn't talk about me behind my back, but then again I knew that Ash and Sean would discuss the consequences of injuries with compassion.

Still, it hurt.

"Mia wants to come over and swim," Sean announced, but I could see Mia and Sean were both ready to swim. Mia in her tiny flowery costume and Sean naked from the waist up. I imagined he'd be wearing trunks, I *hoped* he was, otherwise his husband would kill him.

"You never have to ask."

"Yeah, we do, it's not our place anymore." Sean went from cute dad to all kinds of serious in an instant, and then back to dad just as fast. "Ash wants to come too, so he can meet the new guy, he was pouting when he said that by the way," he added.

"Of course he was." Ash wasn't the nosy neighbor— nope that would be Sean. "The canopy arrived, so we need to get it up and over the pool."

"We'll be round in five," he said, and then jogged down the garden with Mia squealing with delight. I headed back indoors, abruptly feeling lighter because I would have a buffer between me and my housemates, and that could only be a good thing. As long as Sean didn't go into doctor mode and ask me questions about how I felt, because if he did then Cam might tell him about the migraine, and right now I didn't want Sean discussing the whys and wherefores of why I shouldn't be pushing things. I met Sean at the front door, and he had a cooler and a toolkit. Ash was holding Mia who scrambled down and flung herself at my legs and held on tight.

She pressed a kiss to each of my knees. "Kissing the booboos," she announced, and then beamed up at me.

I leaned against the wall, then scooped her up, because

she weighed nothing, and pressed a raspberry kiss into her hair. "Hello, Miss Mia." I hugged her and she wrapped her arms around my neck, then kissed the booboos better there as well.

"Swimming," she announced imperiously.

I wasn't going to be able to carry her to the pool. Hell, I was only upright because I had the wall propping me up, but Ash took her from me, tickling her belly and holding her aloft. He didn't make a thing of taking her, but when he walked off Sean and I were left in the hallway.

"How are you?" He slipped into doctor-tone when they were out of earshot.

"Good." I was an expert at lying, because given half a chance *Doctor* Sean would have had me on a sofa, checking my vitals and making PT and medication suggestions. Thank god for Finn and his dad who were coming down the stairs. "Sean, these are my new housemates, Cam and his son Finn."

Sean shot me a look implying we'd talk later, but Cam and Finn didn't get that face when he turned to them. "Hi, Sean from next door, nice to meet you." He extended his hand, which Cam shook, and then Finn. "We've come over to swim, are you joining us?"

I expected Finn to jump all over that, as he seemed so excited for the pool, but instead he shrunk into Cam's side. He didn't know Sean at all, so I could understand his reticence.

"We really have to think about studying," Cam murmured, and I could see Finn weighing up the pros and cons of the situation from a nine-year-old perspective.

"Can we maybe swim first, Dad? I'm okay. I'll work later. Promise."

Cam's expression was a study in patience, and now it was his turn to think things through from his *adult* perspective.

"Thirty minutes," Cam finally offered as the beginning of a negotiation, but maybe Finn was still nervous, as he didn't even make a counteroffer, just darted back up the stairs to change. I headed into the kitchen to put more coffee on, which left Cam and Sean in the hallway, and *please god, don't mention the migraine.*

"... so yeah, I moved next door, Eric went over to Brady's because the kids have their home, and when Leo, Jason, and Daisy decided to get a place near Daisy's school we sold it. All about moving on and starting the next stage of our lives." Cam listened attentively, but he shot me a look that I couldn't decipher as Sean rabbited on about everything and nothing. "Then Adam said he was looking to buy somewhere, and I thought it would be cool to have him next door, you know." He patted my shoulder, and I shrugged him off. I never even considered what it would be like to have an ER doctor living next door, but so far it had been offhand comments, and surprise visits to see how I was getting on.

The only good thing about the visits was that he always brought Mia with him as a distraction, and boy did Mia love me, my cookies, and my pool.

"Great," Cam said, just for something to say. "It's a lovely house, and we'll be very happy here."

"Is Mrs. Cam joining you?"

"No."

Sean turned to get down mugs and raised an eyebrow at me, and unspoken were questions that I genuinely wasn't going to answer. "A Mr. Cam?"

"I'm in the middle of divorcing my husband."

"I'm sorry." Sean lined up the mugs and poured coffee, adding cream for him, me, and Ash, before checking with Cam. "Creamer? Sugar?"

"Black is fine."

Then, armed with coffee Sean and I headed outside. The thirty minutes for Finn's swimming passed slowly and I expect it was more like an hour. Mia had only swum a little while, and then she'd made Cam her own personal project.

"Who you?" was how it started.

"I'm staying here." Cam crouched down next to her, and she stared at him in confusion, then glanced at me for my explanation.

"Yes, he's living in the house," I began, but she wasn't listening, instead she planted her butt by Cam and proceeded to babble at him for some time. He took it all in his stride, showing an interest in her doll, and the picnic she'd brought with her to make a party. Even this little, she had an innate ability to talk to people, not that anyone would understand a lot of what she was saying. Still, Mia was not shy, and Cam was perfect with her.

Perfect. Heart meltingly cute. Was there anything sexier than a man who loved kids?

He sipped from a tiny cup with pretend milk, even faked eating a plastic cookie and making suitable yum noises as he did so. Then it was time for him and Finn to head indoors.

Mia wasn't entirely happy that her new grown-up party participant was going indoors and would be out of sight and made her irritation clear in the mini-meltdown that was only avoided when Ash pointed out a bird. Still, she clearly missed Cam.

You and me both, Mia, you and me both.

THE REST of the day was quieter after Mia and her dads left. I caught up on emails, filled in some department medical forms, cleaned the kitchen, slept two hours on the sofa, and then headed for the kitchen to make dinner, only to find Cam already in there rummaging through saucepans. He looked at me all guilty.

"You want the kitchen? Sorry."

"No, not at all."

"I was going to think about making dinner for us."

"All of us?" I asked doubtfully.

"No sense in there being two of us working on different things." He smiled then, and glanced down at the pot in his hand. "You like chicken parm?"

"Is that a trick question?" I couldn't help the smile, because chicken parm was way up there on my list of tomatoey cheesy chicken goodness. The last time I'd had a good chicken parm was when my mom had stored away six portions in my freezer after I'd moved in here. She'd said it was my favorite, and that she'd made it with love, even as she'd hugged me and cried because I wasn't going to be living at the end of their drive anymore. It was telling that I was so damn lonely at first that I ate chicken parm six nights in a row. What Cam made might not be like Mom's but the thought of the simple dish being created so it was edible, as opposed to what I made, had my stomach rumbling.

"It's what I was going to make for us, but I was going to make extra for you, only I'd understand if you didn't want me to do that."

I eased myself onto a stool at the counter. "I'd love that —my cooking skills are... limited. Pasta mainly."

"I'm happy to cook for us all every night I can," he said, and then stared back down at that pot, and I got the impression he thought he'd overstepped.

"What if I pay for all the food, and you cook it, if that is genuinely something you really wanted to do. I mean, I *can* cook for myself."

He glanced up at me then, and he seemed shy. "I love cooking, and I need to feed Finn anyway, and it would give me something to..."

To think about? To do? I kind of wish he'd finished that sentence, if only because it gave me the opportunity to stare at his lips and his eyes, without being noticed. He really was a handsome man, sexy, and yes there was pain in his expression, but when he smiled he was utterly perfect for me. Square-jawed like a freaking classical hero, with lashes so long they would've made my sister envious, thick and black, and framing dark eyes. His lips were kissable, there was no other way to describe the effect of him being in my kitchen. Day two of him being there and I was thinking about his lips.

I needed to get out more.

I leaned on the counter and rested my head on my

hands. "Maybe you could show me so I can make it for myself."

He shot me a glance, "Share my old family recipe you mean? I'm horrified you asked."

Was he teasing me? I thought he was teasing me, but I didn't know enough to call him on it, and I could feel my cheeks heat.

He cleared his throat. "So, you take the chicken…"

I found out I had a new kink, and it was enough to have me not moving at all for the time it took for him to make dinner. Observing Cam cooking was like watching cookery porn. Plus, I also got to stare without coming off as creepy. My libido had been missing for so long—meds, pain, sheer inability to get off—and two days with Cam and I was waking up like a flower in spring.

We ate at the kitchen table, and I filled all awkward silences as if I couldn't bear them. Most of it was nonsense, but I talked a lot about Mia, and she was easy to talk about, because I loved her. Finn made us all hot chocolate, which was apparently a thing for him and his dad, and then he disappeared into the living room with his tablet.

"He's a good kid," Cam murmured, "It's been hard."

"I bet."

"Do you want kids one day?" Cam asked.

I gestured at himself. "Maybe once I did, but right now I have enough on my plate looking after myself. I have eight nieces and nephews and I love spoiling them, and Mia, plus friends' kids, so I'm happy with that."

The thought of taking on more responsibility for anyone other than just myself was overwhelming. I didn't even have a career anymore, and no idea of what I wanted to do next, let alone have kids.

"What about you? Do you want more kids one day?"

My question caught him off guard. "I never planned on having kids at all, not at first, but my cousin Daria found herself pregnant at fourteen, and I kind of stepped in. The adoption was final when Finn was one, and I got the most precious gift anyone can have."

"Does Finn talk to his mom?" I worded that very cautiously because I didn't want to offend Cam, or say something wrong with labels that would cause upset. "Sorry, you don't have to answer."

"No, it's okay. Daria passed away just after her nineteenth birthday—overdose. She was one of those kids who wanted to experience everything at too young an age, and it all went horribly wrong. Her parents disowned her when she was pregnant, I took her in, was there when Finn was born, and I never wanted him to go anywhere, so now he has me. He knows it all, none of it is a secret and we talk about her often with pictures and everything."

"That's sad for him."

He sighed. "I think deep down I always wondered if I was enough for him, and then I met Graeme when he was two, and I had this stupid fucked-up idea that what I needed was a husband to make this family I aspired to." He knuckled his eyes, "No that's wrong, it wasn't fucked-up at first."

What was it about this kitchen and this man that made me want to listen to him all night? Still, it wasn't fair to push him when he was vulnerable. "You don't have to tell me any of it."

He glanced at the closed door between kitchen and living room. "Graeme was clever, rich, a catch for any guy, let alone someone like me with a toddler. I did everything for Finn, and I thought so long and hard about letting Graeme into my life that I talked myself into it without even thinking. I didn't see the signs, and with hindsight I can tell you that he never had an interest in Finn apart from the photo opportunities. He twisted himself into my world so smoothly, and I had stars in my eyes."

"I'm sorry."

"It is what it is." He shrugged but I could see the pain in his eyes. "I was vulnerable, I mean the construction industry was hard hit, we had a couple of jobs that went badly. I was close to shutting everything down, stressing about money and paying the mortgage, all of this with toddler in tow. Graeme was in Cali for a six month contract, and my company were working on a house next to his. When I did a site visit I met him and I was naïve and I bought into his shit. He promised us the world, and all I had to do was move to New York, marry him, and he could provide a secure future for Finn." He sighed, and I could feel the bone-deep pain in the soft exhalation.

"But you loved him?"

"I think I did. I wouldn't call it lightning in a bottle, or passion beyond everything, but it was stable and secure at first. Until, of course, it wasn't." He paused for a moment then forced enthusiasm into his voice. "Tell me about the house. Nick said you haven't lived here long, right? Sorry if that is intrusive. Tell me to get lost."

"It's a short story. I shared a place in the center of town with other firefighters before the accident, but when I came out of the hospital I ended up in my mom and dad's converted garage. It meant I was close by for help, had family there all the time, worrying about me, and loving on me. Which was why I needed to get away, find some independence and claw back some of how I needed to be. It was hard-won, but I would come here as a friend for barbecues and things, when I was out of the hospital. Then Sean moved next door, Eric left to be with his partner, and Leo, he's the cop, him and his partner found a new place and decided to move out. I jumped on the house like white on rice, used up most of an inheritance I had from my grandparents, and here I am, in my own place."

"It's a lovely house, solid, dependable. I like it."

"You can stay as long as you want, you know. If it gets to the six months and you still need somewhere…"

"Thank you. I'll bear it in mind."

"Is it weird that even after just this short time of you being here that I can't imagine it just being me in the house again?"

"Is it bad that I immediately think Finn and I have taken over?"

"You're not at all. It just gets me thinking, and maybe when you leave I'll advertise for a housemate—preferably someone with kids, or a dog, anything to brighten the place up. Sometimes there's too much silence." Somehow I'd leaned in closer… so close. And he'd moved a little, and like magnets we were being drawn together, and I could imagine kissing him.

"Please Google me, if you haven't already." Cam stood and put his mug in the sink, the cozy bubble of our conversation destroyed in a second.

"I said I wouldn't—"

"You need to understand."

And then he left to sit with Finn, and I guess it was the end of our day together, and the chance of a kiss was gone. Probably for the best, after all nothing could come of it. Still, I felt unaccountably sad.

Chapter Seven

Cam

THE KNOCK on the front door wasn't heavy, but it was enough to startle me out of the newest homeschooling sub list of what I didn't know, that I'd entitled *Math*.

I hesitated to answer, for a million reasons.

What if it was someone from New York who'd already found out where I was and wanted to get some kind of soundbite from me?

What if it was Frederickson, or hell, any one of the hundreds of people Graeme had hurt.

Or the FBI wanting to question me again?

There again, it could be someone for Adam who didn't know who I was and then called the cops on me and…

I was losing my shit over a simple knock on the damn door.

Well, I wasn't some kid who couldn't answer the freaking door, so I padded into the hallway and opened it, ready to tell whoever it was that I wasn't Cameron Hastings and/or Adam was asleep and could they come back, depending on who it was. Only this visitor was someone who wasn't going to be leaving anytime soon, and abruptly my former best friend, Finn's godfather, was slap-bang in the middle of my life, in person.

Nick.

"Cam," he murmured.

I tensed because this was the moment he hit me, or lectured me about all my shit, told me I was a loser, that I'd not listened to him, let him down, left him when he was at his lowest, and broken our friendship into tiny pieces. I expected him to laugh in my face and admit he'd been joking about the job and the place to stay and how could I even think he'd want to help? All of that negativity slammed into me and my stomach hollowed. Nick and I had been friends for so long that I'd once imagined we'd be close forever, but one wrong decision in marrying Graeme had taken that away and made it an impossible thing.

The guilt and fear over what I'd done were all-consuming.

"Nick, I'm sorry—"

"Thank god you're both here safe." He stepped right into the house, forcing me back, and then grabbed me into a bear hug, rocking me back and forward, and after the initial shock I sunk into the hug and we held each other as if we would never let go.

He might hate me later when the recriminations began to fly, but for now he held me and made me feel as though there was a way back for us, and I wanted to cry like a freaking baby.

"Dad!" I heard Finn shout. "Let my dad go!" Finn shoved between us, and I wriggled free of Nick as my son situated himself squarely in my defense. I placed a hand on Finn's shoulder to reassure him.

"It's OK, Finn, this is Nick, remember?"

Nick went to a half crouch in front of Finn and then grinned up at him, the smile so wide that his dimples popped. He'd always been a good-looking man, but when he smiled the whole room lit up.

"Finn, hey, I'm Nick."

Finn was mute, but his hands were in fists at his side.

"I'm your dad's oldest friend." He glanced up at me, and the smile didn't slip a single inch.

"I remember who you are, but you weren't in New York with us so you can't be a friend," Finn accused. That was his definition of friend. He saw everyone who'd left us to deal with everything on our own and had told me, after a particularly brutal day at his school that friends stayed, and he didn't have any friends.

"I'm sorry," Nick murmured, and I could see the pain in his expression. He'd wanted to be there, but I'd told him to fuck off. Yep. I'd *actually* used those words. In my defense, the conversation had happened when I was still in denial mode, and he'd backed off with a promise to always be there for me and Finn, but I'd never told Finn all of that. Why didn't he explain to Finn that I'd told him to stay away?

Because he's a good man. He's protecting me with my

*son. After all this time he's looking out for me, and for
Finn. Time to step up.*

"Uncle Nick wanted to be there. He asked me if he
could come, but I wouldn't let him," I admitted, and Finn
frowned at me in confusion. "It's okay," I added, and after
a moment I saw Finn's shoulders lower a fraction,
although he was still on alert.

Nick smiled again. "Wow, Finn, I bet you hear this all
the time but you've grown so big since I last saw you. Did
you know I'm your godfather?"

"Yeah, I know. I remember you a bit, and Dad told...
him." Finn had stopped calling Graeme Papa a long time
ago, well before everything had begun to implode—I'd
never noticed. Finn's hands were relaxed, but his innate
curiosity about the world around him, plus the dash of
confidence that he didn't get from me, meant he was able
to push past being angry and move right into question-
land. Although he still didn't move from his protective
stance between the two of us.

Finn sighed and I wondered if he was doubtful about
the godfather connection. Why would he believe that when
I'd never told him the full story about Nick, or how we'd
lost touch. Yet one more thing I'd fucked up. "I used to
call you Uncle Nick I think."

"You did, yes, and that sounds perfect." Nick shook the
offered hand with solemn attention, then half-hugged Finn
with a laugh. The last time they'd met Finn was little and
into everything, a happy kid full of sunshine, who didn't
know any real anger or anxiety. Now he was different, and
I was the one to blame for each and every one of the small
things that had changed. Of course he didn't remember

Nick clearly as a person, just as an idea, and after I'd gotten so angry with Nick and cut him out of my life… well I'd cut him out of Finn's life as well.

"Dad?" Finn was looking to me for more than reassurance. He needed to know that he could trust Nick and he wanted me to tell him. Whatever had happened in the past, there was no one I trusted more than Nick.

"Call him Uncle Nick." That was my way of saying, yes, you can trust him, and my heart hurt when Finn didn't relax immediately. He'd seen me make mistakes when it came to knowing who to trust, and it had to have been crossing his mind that this was a day the same as any other where I could fuck up. Finally, he nodded, and stepped out from between us and Nick was allowed close to the Cam/Finn team, but I could tell it would be a long time before he was part of the trusted inner circle. If ever.

"It's good to see you, Cam."

Nick pulled me into another hug, and this time, the tears I tried not to let escape burned my eyes.

"And you," I offered with feeling. "We should talk about what I did—"

He talked right over me as if he wanted to avoid talking. Maybe he was saving that discussion for another day.

"I wish you'd let me come to New York when I found out." He didn't let me go. "I hated that you wanted nothing to do with me."

"I didn't want you there," I admitted.

He shook his head. "I don't understand."

Because I ghosted you when you needed me, accused you of ruining my life, told you that you meant nothing to

me, that I wanted to marry Graeme, and that my life was
absolutely fine.

"I couldn't let you see me like that." *I was ashamed.*

There was a major pause then, while Nick was trying
to find words, and I was waiting for them so I could
explain what I'd done, but in the end he just fake-punched
my arm.

"We have stuff to talk about." I caught him glancing at
Finn in the quickest move ever.

My heart sank. He wanted to *talk.*

I reached past him to shut the door, catching sight of
the beautiful brand new scarlet Ford F-150 on the drive,
and then herded Finn into the living room.

"Are you okay with him for real, Dad?" Finn asked as
soon as we were out of earshot.

"Of course I am."

"He's not like… *Graeme*?"

"No, I promise you."

Finn moved in front of Nick again. "Don't you hurt
him!" he stated fiercely then, back straight, he hugged me
before he sat on the sofa closest to the kitchen, and didn't
open his tablet, crossing his arms over his chest. "I'll be
right here if you need me, Dad."

Nick went into the kitchen after nodding his
understanding.

I pressed a kiss to his soft hair and then ruffled it,
smiling as he wrinkled his nose at me. I could never love
anyone as much as I loved my son. He was my everything,
and I would've done anything to keep him safe.

"Love you, Finn-Bar-Boodle-Bod."

"Love you, and stop calling me that, I'm not eight

anymore," he sighed, and I picked up the tablet and opened the cheap case so it came to life before I handed it to him.

"But you'll always be my Finn-Bar-Boodle-Bod," I teased, and he thumped me in the side. "Play your game, I'll be okay."

My exhaustion had been replaced by cautious optimism by the time I followed Nick into the kitchen and pulled the door shut, and my instincts had settled on apologizing for everything and trying to explain everything. I placed coffee mugs on the table, and sitting opposite him I got my first proper look at Nick for over five years. His temples were grayer, but then he'd been going gray at sixteen, so that didn't surprise me. He didn't seem close to forty, but both of us were heading that way if I rounded up thirty-eight to the nearest ten. The lines of grief that had once seemed etched forever into his expression had eased, but six years had gone since his husband Danny had passed away, and maybe he'd come to terms with the grief?

How would I know?

He was quiet, watching me, searching for god knows what in my expression, and I flushed hot at his perceptive steel-gray gaze.

"It's so good to see you—"

"You paid for my rent—"

We spoke over each other and he inclined his head for me to carry on.

"Somehow I'll pay you back for the rent here." I stiffened my stance and waited for him to tell me it was some ridiculous amount of money that I would never be able to pay back. He didn't have to say a word, but he bit his lip, and I remembered he only did that when he was attempting to hold something back. Great. Now I was indebted to a man who should've been hating me and not throwing money at me. I gathered my thoughts quickly. "I don't plan to stay long in San Diego, I just needed to have a destination, and somewhere to stop, but I'll make sure you have all the money first."

"Jesus, Cam, enough with the money. I like to think you came here because of me and that you want to stay."

"I might not be able to stop even if I wanted to."

He leaned forward. "If the media find you here then you move to my place because I have a shit ton of security."

"I can't do that to you, Nick—"

He waved off what I was going to say. "What's the point in having all my money if I can't help you? I'm thinking the bedrooms on the top floor, you can have those and then you'll be together, unless you think Finn wants to share with one of the boys? I'm not digging, but maybe he might need you or he might need them? There's a bathroom up there, and one of the rooms has this awesome balcony with views over the ocean—"

"Woah, stop. One, our friendship…" *is weird, wrong, over?*

He sighed and held out a hand with the palm upward. "It's forever. Remember?"

I curled my fingers into my own palm where I had a matching silver scar. Seven years old and we'd pledged as blood brothers forever. That was before I'd fucked up, and before he'd become public property. Rising from journalism through breakfast television, to anchoring his own show. He was a household name, and not just locally after his show had gone national.

"What do you think your viewers will say when—"

"Cam, stop," he said firmly, and I did what always happened when Nick got bossy, I subsided and let him talk. "I can handle myself," he summarized. "But that's not why I'm here, I wanted to give the details of the vacancy that I thought—"

"I don't want charity."

He frowned, seemed affronted and then shrugged. "There's this foster home, more a community halfway house that I do fundraising for. They're in the middle of a renovation and their contractors have been called away." He couldn't quite meet my eyes then, and I didn't have to know him to suspect he was leaving out the reason the contractors had left. "It's ideal, but as I said you'd need to talk to Bernie, she's the manager there, and she'll want to know you can do it. Her number is in the file, call her in the morning."

"Thank you."

"I just got your foot in the door, it's up to you what you do with it."

Grief swelled inside me, followed by anger and regret. "Nick, we have things to talk about—"

"We don't need to do that tonight. It's all too raw, and you look like shit, Cam. Get into a rhythm here, okay? And when you're ready, call me? Adam has my number. Come for dinner—we can get some beers, watch the ocean, sort things out for real."

"You must hate me."

"Fuck you, Cam, for even saying that. I could never

hate you." His eyes brightened, and there was the old Nick, the man with his emotions just below the surface. Only he was naïve if he thought a beer and an ocean view was going to fix everything, and my heart cracked a little more. He was doing all of this for us, but things were still broken in a way that might never be mended.

"Thank you."

He shrugged as if it meant nothing, when his help actually meant everything.

His cell vibrated. He picked it up and glanced at the screen. "I need to get back to the kids, but promise me you'll visit when you're ready, so we can fix things." He stood quickly, and walked to the front door, and I realized that was his way of saying we were done for the night. Maybe he was right to do that, my head was already spinning with everything as I followed him. He went straight to the truck, pulled out a cardboard roll, plus a heap of folders. He handed it all over, along with two suspiciously new-looking cell phones balanced on top.

"Before you say you can't take them, these are just old phones the kids had replaced, okay? With new sims, completely wiped for you both to use." A limo pulled up at the end of the driveway, blocking the entrance. "Talk to Adam about Ringwood—it's a good place to heal. I have to go, my car's here."

Huh? What about the truck?

Nick stopped by the shiny Ford, then tossed back a set of keys, which I caught on reflex.

"On loan, definitely not a gift, or something you can't take because of some weird-ass no-charity hang-up. Get a job, make my godson happy. Hell, make yourself happy, and text me when you want to talk."

I returned his wave as the car left the cul-de-sac, and stood there like an idiot, plans, folders, and keys balanced in my arms right by a brand-new high spec truck.

What now?

Chapter Eight

Adam

CAM CAUGHT me as I was inhaling the last of my cereal.

"Nick was here last night," he launched right into avoiding what had happened. It seemed as if we weren't talking about the almost-kiss, or the exchange of vulnerability that had us leaning in so close. "You were in bed, I answered the door…" He had a lost expression.

"It's your house too, you *can* answer the door," I teased.

"Yeah, sorry. Ignore me. He's set me up with an interview at this place called Ringwood, said to ask you about it?"

"I volunteer there with some other first responders, work in the gardens, even done a bit of construction in my downtime." I realized what I'd said. I wasn't a first responder any more, and I needed to rephrase that big time —maybe to other *people* or maybe just *friends*. "I know that we're always looking for help—is he asking you to volunteer as well?"

"No, this is paid, I think." He frowned as if it hadn't occurred to him that it was anything but a paid position. "Nick said they were looking for a project manager, and I have a meeting today at ten for an interview and trial." He looked down at a cell phone on the table in front of him, and pushed it with a finger. "It's been a long time since I worked construction."

That didn't sound good. We needed someone there who knew what they were really doing, because I was out of my depth mopping up the issues that the previous contractors left behind.

"You gave it up?"

"I married Graeme, left the business here, you know that. Then there was no point in starting anything in New York because I was able to be the stay-at-home dad until Finn was old enough that I could one day get back out to work. It was the way I was able to do it, to raise Finn with someone always there for him." He sounded defensive but he didn't need to be. I'd seen a ton of families where the dad did everything for the kids, and I didn't see anything wrong with it.

"I'm sure it's like riding a bike." He glanced up at me, confused. "Construction I mean, or at least I hope it is for you." Coffee hadn't kicked in yet and I needed to stop talking. Only I'd said something right because he smiled at me and it was a perfectly ordinary smile, but I noticed the way it lit his dark eyes and smoothed his worry lines. On reflection, there was nothing ordinary about his smile at all.

We ran out of small talk, and when Finn appeared at the kitchen doorway, searching for his dad, I took myself out of the kitchen and gave them space. I headed back upstairs for my second stair climb, stretching out the exercise and then heading for my bedroom to get on with the yoga part of my day. I'd normally have taken my mat down with me as part of my up and down stairs part, but the thought of sweating and huffing and puffing in front of my sexy new houseguest was a big no. I unrolled the mat, then sat in my best attempt at lotus position, and began the breathing exercises. I couldn't get into all the positions I was supposed to—rebar to the spine was enough to put paid to some of the stretches for my back, but I pushed as much as I could, whimpering in the locust pose, and near tears for the downward-facing dog.

I lay back, completely spent, staring at the ceiling and concentrating on small muscle movements until I was loose enough to attempt to stand. Rolled onto my side, then to my knees, I then used the bed to get up, ready for a shower, and to face whatever the day threw at me, starting with a walk in the park to the café, and then back home to unload the dishwasher.

Living the life, Adam, living the life.

I made it all the way downstairs after my shower, in board shorts and an old FDSD shirt, and caught a glimpse of scarlet that I hadn't noticed before. Opening my front door I stared at the brand new truck, and then closed the door, opening it one more time just to make sure I wasn't seeing things. I couldn't drive a car right now, and there was a truck there that hadn't been there when I was having my headache from hell last night.

"It's Nick's," Cam said at my side, and added a long-suffering sigh. "He left it for me to use."

"Cool," was all I could manage. It wasn't every day I woke up to a huge truck in my drive, left there like a really awesome gift.

"Is it okay on the driveway?"

"Of course, I don't have a car," I waved at myself, "for obvious reasons."

"You couldn't get an adapted car?" he asked, then flushed scarlet. "Shit, sorry."

"It's fine. It's on my list of things to look into as soon as I'm back on my feet for real." I didn't let on that it was actually way down the list because the thought of giving in to that was not on my radar. I glanced at him and then did a second take. He was wearing the smarter dark pants he'd bought and a short-sleeved shirt in a soft blue, plus a darker blue tie, and it didn't matter that these were bargain shop buys, he looked very different to yesterday. Gone was the stubble, and he'd tamed his hair from the loose waves.

Also, he was wearing glasses, and hot, smooth-shaven men in glasses were my absolute weakness. There I was, standing in my hallway, staring at the hot man who quirked an eyebrow and then offered a tentative smile.

"Not smart enough?" He fiddled with the tie and frowned down at himself, nibbling his lip as if that was going to help.

Danger. He's nibbling his lip, he's wearing glasses, he has a dimple.

"No," I forced out after a pause, "you look great." Sexy, glasses-wearing, hot dude. "Professional I mean."

"What is this Ringwood place like? Is it big?"

"It's sprawling, and Bernie is a star at making every penny stretch."

"That's Bernadette Summers, right?"

"Yep, Bernie to staff and volunteers."

I turned at a noise on the stairs, and Finn was there, staring at me, looking a hundred kinds of annoyed.

"Dad—" he began.

Cam interrupted whatever he was going to say straight away. "I have to go and you have to come with me, Finn."

Finn mumbled something under his breath, circumvented where I was standing by some distance, and then stood beside his dad with a mutinous expression, making me think he didn't want to be going with his dad. He could've stayed here, but then I saw the way that despite his expression, he gripped his dad's hand and looked nervous. So I wisely stayed quiet. They left soon after, the big truck backing off the driveway, and I was so lost in watching that I never saw one of my neighbors, Gina, approaching from my blind spot, being the front bushes, weighed down with not one but two casseroles.

"Hey, gorgeous," she called, and if I could have moved fast enough then there was every chance I would have hurried inside and pretended I hadn't seen her.

"Hi, Gina," I acknowledged. She'd taken to dropping food at my door every week, but this wasn't new as she'd had a thing for Eric and had gifted him with many a tuna casserole before he'd moved out. Now it was my turn, and as much as I liked tuna casserole on a typical day, Gina's concoctions were anything but normal.

Who in God's name makes tuna casserole with added sweet and sour sauce?

"I made you these," she said and placed them on the porch. One thing about Gina was that she never asked to come inside, happy to sit on the porch and chat about everything and nothing, and for the most part I welcomed the distraction of her company, apart from the weird dinners she brought with her.

"Who's the hottie?" she asked, and sat in the chair by the chaparral broom, a clash of bright purple and scarlet in her hair that somehow only she could pull off.

"Huh?"

"Tall, dark, and sexy with the kid?" she elaborated and I winced at the description. Poor Cam being summarized as that.

Wasn't that what you were thinking?

"Cam, he's staying here for a few months."

"Friend of yours?"

"Friend of Asher's."

She rested back in the chair, rocking it up on two feet and miraculously not tipping it over. "Gay? Bi? Interested?"

Jeez. "I have no idea Gina. So what's in the dishes?" I was as good at changing the subject with her as I was avoiding any talk about how I felt, and she fell for it.

"I had this idea you see. I know you love tuna, and everyone loves maple syrup so…"

I lost myself in hearing about how maple syrup tuna with falafel and scallions was a thing, and that it tasted even better in a mushroom sauce, and stared out at where the truck had been parked. I couldn't help but wonder how Cam was getting on at Ringwood, and why I was abruptly so invested in the lives of two total strangers.

And why it wasn't all about the glasses and the dimples, but also the pain in Cam's expression, and the way Finn clung to his dad. The story behind their matching dark eyes was a story that I wanted to buy into. I couldn't help the way I was wired to want to care for people, and I actually felt as if helping Cam and Finn might end up helping me.

Chapter Nine

Cam

"THIS IS WHERE WE'RE GOING?" Finn asked in horror.

I didn't react with my usual defensiveness because I knew that we could have been rolling up to a mansion with a dedicated games room for him, but he'd still act as if it was the worst place in the world. I should've taken it as a good sign that he'd gotten his sass back after a good night's sleep, but I couldn't handle it this morning because I definitely hadn't gotten much sleep at all.

Thinking about Nick swam in my exhausted mind alongside the almost-kiss with Adam, and those were only the surface worries. Every time I'd rolled over I could remember yet another part of the trial, or my marriage, and I was about done with feeling so destroyed. Hence the lack of sleep.

It didn't help that a Google alert had poked its way into my emails with details of a new article mentioning my name, and I had the worry about this interview today. It had been years since I'd actually done construction, slipping into the role of manager at a young age, and then of course, into the role of being a dad after that.

Finn was grouchy, and he'd been determined not to like anything we'd done today from the minute he'd woken this morning and when he'd asked if he could swim I said no and reminded him that I had an interview.

"For real? This place?" he said again.

I snapped back to the present, and stifled a yawn. Lack of sleep could be ignored if there was enough adrenalin coursing through my body but I'd really pushed the limits and was paying for it now.

"Yep," I answered after double-checking that this was Ringwood House. A midsized repurposed strip mall, it had all the sharp concrete feel of a build from the seventies but it was softened by planting and with windows full of hand-drawn pictures. I assume those had been drawn by some of the kids who passed through there, and I imagined if I examined close enough that they could tell stories that I would never be able to imagine. The center was part of the county's fostering structure but was independently owned and run by Bernadette Summers, and today I had to come across as capable and experienced.

But I was nervous and tired. So damn tired.

"Why did I have to come with you?" Finn slumped dramatically into the luxury leather interior of the Ford. "Can I stay in the car?"

"You're not staying in the car. You're coming with me. It will be fun," I lied.

"But I like it in here, it's so…" He didn't finish the sentence, but snuggled down into the cool leather of the beautiful truck. I really needed to get my own truck, because arriving at potential job sites in Nick's expensive loaner wasn't the look I was going for, and was an in-my-face reminder of a life I'd rather forget. No wonder Finn felt safe in the car when it was everything he'd become accustomed to in his old life. He'd have to get used to an old, barely working truck, because that was all we could afford, and it was going to be part of the new improved Cam Bellamy. A solid, stable vehicle screamed expert tradesman.

"I could have stayed at the house with Adam," Finn reminded me, and unspoken was the word *pool*. I wanted to remind him that he clung to me like a limpet as soon as he saw Adam, but that wouldn't have been right. He didn't need his worries or fears to be pointed out to him when he was living them.

"We don't know Adam very well."

"I could just stay in the garden, I wouldn't have to be *near* Adam. Anyway, you said he was a nice man."

He had me there. "You're only nine."

"I'm nearly ten," he muttered under his breath.

He didn't want to stay with Adam, he was just arguing for the sake of it, but the thought of leaving him at the house, and then maybe someone finding out where we were, then threatening him, or hurting him... I shuddered. I had this instinctive feeling that I could trust Adam, but if I lost Finn then I'd have nothing, and I didn't really *know* Adam.

Finn narrowed his eyes, and played the concerned son card, something he didn't pull out very often. "You look tired, Dad, so maybe you shouldn't be working. We could go back home and swim, and you could have a nap, and then we could play games."

"I *have* to do this interview, Finn, I need to earn us money. You understand that, right?"

Money had never been an issue in his short life, and he'd been used to me being at home all the time, but now he had to accept that I needed to work to keep a roof over our heads. He'd had a stay-at-home dad since he was little, then he didn't; we had enough money to waste it on anything we wanted, and now we didn't. Those truths were what we had to accept.

I was explaining things to Finn while attempting to keep him out of the loop of the tiny details of our circumstances. I never wanted to explain why his daddy had been arrested or why his rich friends had stopped calling him. He knew the basics, that the man he'd called his second dad was in prison, he was aware of what the media was saying, but I knew the entire picture was fractured for him at a very basic level. Not least of all our move across the country from a bitterly cold January New York to this San Diego version of winter which was chilly, yeah, but not anywhere near east coast levels. The fact we were here was my fault. I accepted that and cut him slack after everything we've been through— too much slack— but today I needed him to understand this was important to me. Our counselor back in New York had pinned me with a stubborn gaze and told me in no uncertain terms that I had to show Finn a certain amount of vulnerability otherwise he would never understand what I was going through. Only, the horror of letting Finn know it all was making my chest hollow, and I couldn't do it.

But maybe it was time to let out a little of the worry in my head? Just enough for him to want to help me now. "Can I tell you the real reason I wanted you here today?"

"Sure." He sounded doubtful and stared down at his sneakers. Maybe the counselor was right, in that he didn't know how I felt about everything, and I needed to be honest. Today seemed to be a good time to start with something small, even if it was a half-lie.

"Thing is, Finn, I'm scared that I'll mess up the work because I've forgotten how to do this building thing."

Finn stared at me as if I were a specimen under a microscope, and I saw the moment that the tension in him eased and his confidence flooded back. Abruptly, everything felt wrong, I shouldn't have been putting my fears out there for everyone to see, and I could feel the weight of the counselor's advice pushing down on me. Surely, me exposing how I felt meant that Finn would push his own feelings down. That was wrong and I even opened my mouth to explain that I'd been joking, but he beat me to it.

"It's okay, Dad. I've watched all the videos on YouTube and I can help if you get stuck."

Then he climbed out of the car and waited for me, his shoulders back and his gaze watchful, and I felt like the worst dad in the world.

"Finn, I'm sorry. I know this isn't the best situation, but I'm nervous and I need you to be on my side here." I offered him a fist to bump, hoping he'd accept the gesture, and after only a moment's pause he pressed a fist to mine.

"It's okay, Dad. You've got this." Finn pushed the door shut. "Let's go, and then after, we can go home and swim."

I stared at Ringwood House with its wide frontage and a front yard that was more parking area than decoration. Objectively, I could see the bones of the three stores that had been knocked into one and recognized the type of fancy portico that held the faint lines of an older sign. Last night I'd read everything I could get my hands on about this place. Nick had written an essay for the site, and because he was a celebrity, it was linked from the front page. He'd written so passionately about it, and from the news articles I'd seen, he was involved in a lot of fundraising alongside Governor Lester's family, which I assumed had some bearing on me being taken on as a contractor for this job.

Nick had probably vouched for me, and I knew that all my background checks would come back clean, but I still felt like an impostor being here. I'd apprenticed to my dad, a strong man who'd shown me the right path in life with lessons I'll always remember. He'd been the kind of dad who'd always known the right thing to say at the perfect moment, whereas I was this floundering father with a failed marriage and with a former husband in prison. I'd lived a gilded life in a cage of my own choosing, and in doing so I'd lost the last few years with Finn. I needed to get that back now, and stared up at the first step of what I hoped would be our new start in life.

The approved plans for expansion that I would be project-managing consisted of an entirely new wing with bedrooms and baths, a near industrial-sized kitchen, plus several smaller breakout rooms. The work would take a minimum of six months, and it was more than I'd ever taken on in a very long time.

"What now?" Finn asked as he stared at the building.

"We go in, talk to the manager and then we'll find you a corner to sit with your study books and tablet while I talk to her. It will be fun."

He rolled his eyes at me. "Will it though?"

"We'll make it fun."

Mumble mumble mumble was the only reply I got. He seemed to have lost his initial enthusiasm for helping me out.

I pressed the buzzer, facing the camera.

"Cam Bellamy for Bernadette Summers," I announced, and the interior door opened, a woman walking toward the gate in the security fence.

"Hello, can I just check your ID?" I passed my credentials and the covering letter through the gate and she stood back and checked them, then buzzed me in and extended her hand.

"I'm Bernadette Summers, call me Bernie," she said and shook my hand enthusiastically, then Finn's, waiting for the gate to shut and lock behind us. I recognized her from the website. She looked taller in real life, and that was the weirdest thing to focus on when she was asking me questions. "… so you'll get a pass, and there is a side entrance with two gates for staff, which is manned twenty-four-seven. We have vulnerable kids here and some of them have families who would rather they weren't under our protection. I'll need you to sign off on the information used to run your background checks and so on, but Nick has already put the groundwork in so I think we can safely say you can start as soon as it all comes through."

Nick had expedited background checks? How long had

he been planning this for me? Was it possible it had been the very first day when the shit had hit the fan? The same day I'd told him to go to hell and leave me alone? Guilt warred with relief, and I only realized I'd spaced out when I snapped back and saw Bernie staring at me.

"I'll sign what you need," I agreed. "First of all there is something you should know." I pulled out my cell phone and opened the browser, passing it to her with the page I'd found that summarized the case. She read it carefully, and I waited with bated breath.

"Thank you for sharing that," she murmured. "It can't come to our door, you understand?"

I pulled back my shoulders. "If there was any chance of it, then I would leave."

She looked at me with concern. "Wait here a moment, please."

Shit. Shit. I wasn't going to get this job.

She wasn't gone long, and then she urged me to sit before taking the chair opposite me. "It's all good. Nick has promised any extra security should there be an issue."

"He did?"

"He says he has our back, and I believe him." She peered at me over her glasses. "You must be very good friends."

I swallowed hard. "Yes." What else could I say?

By the time we were done I had a provisional start date, dependent on criminal check. Then, I found Finn sitting where I'd left him, but he wasn't on his own, a skinny kid with messy hair and a wide smile was chattering on about books, and I knew my son well enough to know that he was relaxed.

"Hi, guys." I watched them both look up from the books in their laps.

"Hi, Mr. Bellamy," the other kid said, as soon as I was close enough. "I'm Micah," he extended a hand for me to shake, and I took it very seriously. I doubt he was any older than Finn, but he had a confidence that made me smile. "I live here with my mom, she's Bernie, and I was saying that me and Finn can be friends if he likes."

I glanced at Finn who gave a subtle roll of his eyes, and a small shrug as if he didn't care that this boy wanted to be his friend. Thankfully, Micah didn't catch the reaction, because he wouldn't understand it for what it was —fear in Finn that he was given things for them to be snatched away.

Finn was quiet, and we were all the way to the truck and belted in before I began the difficult chat that was asking him how things had gone without me being there.

"That wasn't so bad, right?" I summarized.

"You were a really long time," he said, and threw me a look of exasperation.

"I'm sorry. Next time you can come with me—we'll set you up with a table in the shade where I'm working for you to study at. Anyway, seems like you were making friends with Micah."

"I don't need random new friends, Dad. He was too friendly and it was weird."

"You don't know well enough to say that—"

"He went on and on about the beach."

"There are good beaches here, Finn. We can go—"

"I don't like the beach, anyway, there's sand and *everything*." He rolled his eyes so bad that I thought they might roll out of his head. "I had friends and you made me leave them and I *really* don't want new ones." His shoulders dropped. He *did* need friends, kids who wanted to know Finn for the wonderful person he was under all the fear and nerves, and not like the old ones he'd had at St. Luke's who based friendship solely on net worth.

"I didn't *make* you leave," I began. But that wasn't true. He hadn't been given any choice in heading west, because *I* was the dad and *he* was the child. Still, that comment wasn't a new one, and I needed to address it, whatever the consequences. We hadn't talked about Graeme since we'd left New York, not in detail anyway. "We had to leave, you know that, right?" I rested a hand on his knee.

"I don't want to come here and have lessons. I don't want a new friend. I don't want any of it." He ignored my question, tilted his chin, my stubborn, beautiful dark-eyed boy, and I was lost for what to say to him.

"I know. I'm sorry." I felt defeated, lost, and knew that he wavered between needing me and blaming me, but one thing was the same; ever since we'd left home and arrived in San Diego he'd stayed close to my side, and followed me everywhere. Even if it was just to shout at me for the things I'd done wrong. I was the one who'd married Graeme, I was the one who'd turned a blind eye to things I should have called my husband out on, and I was the one who'd ended up putting my son in the way of things he should never have seen. Like the arguing, and then the cold silences. Or his *other* dad being dragged from our home by the FBI. He had every right to hate me, and if only I'd walked away with him when everything had started to go wrong then he'd have had the life of a normal kid his age, and not have had to battle the same fear as I did.

In a flurry of motion he was there, hugging me, and goddamn it I let all of that show in my expression. "It's not your fault, Dad."

There was no hostility in his tone, he'd slipped from angry to resigned in a moment, and then he stepped back, held my hand, and leaned into my side.

"I love you, Finn-Bar-Boodle-Bod," I said, because those were the strongest most affectionate, yet simplest words I could offer him.

"I love you too, but stop calling me that."

Chapter Ten

Adam

NOT THAT I was waiting for them to get home specifically, but I knew the minute that the truck turned into the drive, and I already had the ice-cold lemonade out of the refrigerator, along with snacks. It felt good to have another purpose outside of dealing with life in general. Since the last of the kids had passed through the program I'd been waiting for *something* and the lift in my mood when I saw them arrive home was encouraging. I didn't rush to open the door though, and waited for them to come into the kitchen before I said hello, as if I had only just noticed them.

"Hey, how did it go?"

"I start as soon as my background checks come back, which they'd already started courtesy of Nick, next weekend maybe." He sounded incredulous as if it was the biggest surprise of his entire life.

I worked out the dates in my head. "I'm there on Saturday with the guys, we volunteer when we can."

I couldn't help but notice the quick flick of his gaze to my leg and up, and I knew what he was thinking, that if I was indicative of the quality of the volunteers then things were going to be shit. I refused to feel hurt, because he was right to think the worse. Yes, Eric would be there, but he'll be on call and Sean would be there but his ability with a hammer was nowhere near his abilities with people as a doctor. And Leo was an idiot who didn't take things seriously, so the team as I liked to think of it, was somewhat lacking in a lot of areas. Never mind. We'd cross that bridge when we got to it and I would ignore his visible concern and pretend I hadn't seen it at all.

"Snacks?" I nudged the plate of cookies and indicated the tray of lemonade, and after a brief glance at his dad, Finn clambered to sit at the counter and helped himself to a cookie, his wobbling hold on the lemonade jug precarious, but he did manage. I noticed that Cam didn't try to help him, and so I didn't either. It was one of those dad things where Cam knew his son had to be trying new things. Or something.

"Can we go swimming, Dad?"

"After the school work." Cam sounded distracted, and I realized he was staring out of the window. What he was staring at I didn't know, but he seemed to be miles away in thought, and I wasn't going to interrupt him to ask about the studying. Of course Finn was school-aged, and I knew for a fact a new semester was underway, and I guess at some point Cam would find a school?

"What are you studying today?" I asked Finn, and took the stool next to him, grabbing a cookie and nibbling at the chocolate goodness.

"I have spelling and stuff," Finn sighed dramatically, "and *then* we're swimming."

"What kind of spelling?"

"Hard words. Big hard impossible words, in a grid of other ginormous words that Dad made up *for no reason*."

"I didn't make anything up, kid." Cam took a seat and poured a drink. "It's part of the curriculum that I'm following, and you sailed through the last lot because you're a genius."

"Daaaad," Finn whined, and then got a calculating gleam his eyes. "What if I do two of the long words and get them all right, can we stop early to swim?"

"Five words, in sentences, and the history project, and then we'll call it a day."

"Three and I'll do notes for the project and give you half my cookie?"

Oh, he was good, I couldn't help smiling, but Cam had his homeschooling teacher face going on, and there wasn't going to be a compromise.

"I'll get my own cookie," he snatched one before Finn could stop him. "Five words, one project, and then swim."

"You're the worst teacher in the world," Finn grumbled, but it was good-natured for the most part.

"Where are you planning to study?"

"In my room?" Finn said, but looked to his dad.

"I have a desk you can use," I interjected before Cam could come out with some sentence about imposition, "a whole study actually. Come on, I'll show you where it is."

I left the kitchen, limped all the way to the office door before realizing neither of them had followed me, but I gave it a moment and at last Finn appeared with his backpack over his shoulder, two cookies balanced on a plate, and a full glass of lemonade dangerously close to spilling. He stepped into the office, Cam close behind, and I gave them the ten-cent tour.

"There's a computer if you need it, I can set you up a profile, paper, pens, desk, chair. I don't know what else you'll need? A whiteboard? I don't have one of those."

Finn tipped his bag and corralled the contents inside, a couple of reference books, notepaper, his own stash of notebooks in different colors, and a calculator, then tidied them to one side and climbed into the chair that the guys had left here. It was a comfortable chair and my favorite place when the pain was bad—watching movies on the computer was easier than sinking into the sofa and not being able to get back up.

"Is that you?"

One thing I'd forgotten was the last remaining evidence of my career I'd left on show, a photo of my graduating class with me on the right side of the group who'd all gone through much of their training with me. I left it on the wall as a reminder of what I'd worked at to become a firefighter, and to keep me focused on my PT. Of course, the moment that they'd told me I was done, the aim of the PT wasn't to get me back to the firehouse. Instead, it had become a focus just to be able to walk. I wasn't going to remove the reminder of what I'd done though—I deserved to have that pride still.

"Yes, a long time ago," I said, although in reality it had

only been two years even if a lot had happened between then and now. "So, is this okay for you?"

Finn cast an eye around the room as if he was assessing the suitability of the solid wooden desk and super-comfortable chair, plus snacks, a drink, and a computer. Then, after a few moments he nodded. "Thank you."

"Are you sure this is okay? We can always set up in the kitchen?" Cam pressed a hand to my arm, maybe to get my attention, maybe to underscore his sincerity. Either way, his touch was warm and welcoming. I caught his honest gaze and got lost in his dark eyes, leaning into the touch. He blinked, and broke the spell. I pulled myself together and leaned on the doorjamb as far away from him as I could manage given the small space.

"My desk is your desk." I smiled, then headed for the kitchen before staring for a while at the remains of the cookies on the counter, and calling myself an idiot. The last thing he needed was me mooning over some weird connection that was due to proximity and lack of anything close to sex in over two years.

Sex? *Don't think about sex.* I'd only recently gotten to the point where I could get myself off with my hand and generous amounts of lube, but that pinnacle of tensing when I orgasmed pushed me over the edge into muscle spasms. I could easily imagine getting off with another person involved and the hot, sexy, lust leading to a messy, uncoordinated, painful *ouch*. But now, the thought of sex, and of Cam pressing me into a bed and taking what he wanted and I was getting hard...

Calm the fuck down.

I cleaned up, poured myself another drink, then with the rest of the lemonade back in the refrigerator, I padded out to the garden and down to the pool, taking my chair into the shade, and checking the time. It was eleven a.m., it was Wednesday, and I had no freaking idea what I was going to do with the rest of my day. I still had one more stair-climbing objective to cross off my busy list, I had a ton of books on my Kindle, a complete season of a new Netflix show about angels and demons, plus I had the biggest of decisions to make about my career, and the survivors program. So many things to do, but all I could manage was to sit here and stare at the light reflecting from the pool.

I heard the bushes rustle, and knew my silence was about to be broken, readying myself to give Cam or Finn a smile that said everything was okay.

"Hey, here's my little brother sitting here feeling sorry for himself."

I sighed dramatically. Erin wasn't known for her subtlety, and my sister finding me sitting in the shade in the middle of the day was opening up a big can of worms. Like the rest of my family, Erin had been at my bedside, crying and hugging her long-suffering husband Austin, when they'd told us that I might not walk again, but as soon as the doctors marked that down to a maybe, she'd been the one on my back with PT and forcing me to make a "*goddamn fucking awesome future life plan.*" Her words not mine.

"Fuck off," I replied firmly, but I did smile up at her as

she dragged her favorite chair out of the sun and into the shade.

Her hair was as copper-red as mine, her eyes the same green, but that was where the similarities ended. She had our mom's willowy beauty, and had a kind of peace about her that I envied. She was a mom of three, happily married, and with a degree in fine art that had manifested into a career in design that she fitted around her kids. I loved her for her drive, and her happiness, and her kids, but she was also the annoying big sister who messed with me on a regular basis.

"What are you even doing out here?" she asked, and moved the chair a little more so she was fully in shade.

"What are you doing here?" I asked with fake irritation, and glowered when she reached over and took my lemonade.

"Charlie needed new shoes, and I was out this way."

"You're lying."

"Okay, okay, Mom sent me, but in my defense Charlie did need shoes," she said, and drank the entire glass, slurping and making a big show of wiping her mouth. She didn't have to say anything else because those three words explained everything. Mom had cycled back to being worried about me again, which was a regular thing. After all, her other three kids were all *safely* and *happily* being okay.

"Don't tell me you left her in the car? You do know that's illegal, right?"

"Pfft, she's in the house making friends with the hottie's son."

"Huh?" I'd lost the thread of the conversation while

consigning worried mothers to the pile of things to deal with later.

"Sexy McSexy Cam and his cute-as-a-button son."

"What about them?"

She flicked my forehead and sighed. "How come we didn't know about the man with the beautiful swoony dark eyes and the adorable son who apparently live here?"

"They're only here for six months—"

"Why only six months, and did you notice Cam's a fine-looking man? Boy, those shoulders, not to mention his ass," she whispered.

Yes, I had noticed his ass, and his arms, and his hands, and eyes, and the way his hair fell over his eyes, but I wasn't going to let Erin know that, so I stuck to the sensible part of her question.

"It's just a temporary thing, until he gets back on his feet."

She leapt on that so fast I didn't have time to blink. "'On his feet'? Oh, why? What's wrong? What happened?"

"I'm not at liberty to say," I teased, but there must have been a serious part of me showing, because she subsided back into her seat and relaxed.

"So how goes the PT?"

I could've lied. Told her that everything was going well. I could have even hedged around the fact that I'd had another migraine, because then she'd worry about me having another seizure, and that would lead to her moving in or something as dramatic, or maybe an intervention from her, and my brothers, Saul and Luke. They'd already done it to me twice. The first was when I'd been released from hospital and Saul had found me in the bathroom with a bottle of pills. The second was after I'd refused to leave the house for a week.

Never let it be said that my siblings didn't care for me with deep affection, or that I didn't appreciate what they did, but sometimes on days like this when I'd been feeling kind of okay, I didn't need them to be asking me questions that dug into my psyche.

So I didn't lie, but I cut it all dead. "Okay, hard, but positive. How's planning for the big sixty going?"

As eldest son, Saul had stated that he was in charge of Dad's upcoming sixtieth celebrations, but we all knew that it was Erin who was working out the logistics for it all.

"We have the caterers booked now, put the deposit down, and his friends are planning some kind of cop thing that we will never understand. I told them that as long as we got the speeches out of the way and it didn't interrupt the eating side of things that they could do what they wanted." She shook her head in exasperation, then pushed back an errant curl that had fallen over her eye. If I left my hair to grow long it would have had the same curly spring to it, which was why I kept it short. I secretly loved that my friends at sixty-three called me Red, but I drew the line at them finding any reason to sing songs from *Annie* at me.

"Uncle Adam!" Charlotte-Anne, aka Charlie, dark-haired like her dad, leaned down and hugged me hard before stepping back with a grin on her face. "We're swimming," she announced and yanked off her T-shirt to reveal a swimsuit beneath. She let her mom spray her with sunscreen, and it was only when he moved a little that I saw she'd brought Finn out with her. He looked wary, trunks on, but a T-shirt covering his chest.

"Hey, Finn." I sketched a wave, and he gave me a half smile, his eyes wide as Charlie grabbed his hand and tugged him to the pool. There was no avoiding the Williams women when they wanted to get on with doing something.

"Come on, Finn, last one in is a loser." She jumped, tucking her knees up, and barreled into the deep end, the splash reaching Finn and causing him to wince. The words to reassure him that he didn't have to swim if he didn't want to, fled, when he went to the edge and sat, before easing into the water. He hadn't exactly jumped with abandon, but I could see the smile before he ducked under water.

"Look, I have a real reason I wanted to see you. Emma's at an overnight party, Harper's staying with Saul, can I leave Charlie here for the rest of the day, so Austin and I can work on baby number four?"

I groaned, because I did not want to think about my sister and brother-in-law and what they got up to in bed. Some images I just didn't want to give room to in my head.

"Jesus, Erin, not fair. You know you don't have to ask, but..." I trailed off ominously, and she groaned, because none of us agreed to anything without putting a deal on the table. "In exchange, you tell Mom you saw me and that I'm fine."

She pouted, but didn't argue, because she knew a good deal when she saw one.

Charlie let out a whoop as she splashed Finn, who

ducked under the water again. This was natural, kids in the pool messing about, and I found myself putting too much weight in seeing Finn happy and just being a kid.

How could a boy who'd only been in my life a day or so, have dug so hard into my soul?

Chapter Eleven

Cam

ONE WEEK at the house and I stopped looking over my shoulder expecting the media to congregate in the front yard. Not that I wasn't being vigilant, but there was no sign of being tracked down, no new online articles that spoke about me as anything but a footnote. In fact, the articles had trickled to a stop, given Graeme was in prison and I was nowhere to be found. The last mention of my whereabouts was a statement that my beleaguered counsel, Jim, had leaked where it implied that I was taking time to process—in Maine.

Why Maine I didn't know, but it was a long way from California, and for that I was grateful. He was the only one from my old life who knew where I was, and he was happy to keep my secrets. He'd pointedly added to the issued statement that I was filing for divorce, and that I was taking time out for my son. That article had been part of a weekend spread about Graeme's case, but since then, nothing.

And, believe me, I searched Google every day.

Nick had texted me last night, a simple, friendly *hey*, that I'd responded to, and that had become a more detailed exchange of texts. We hadn't dug too far into what had happened, but if I had any hope of meeting Nick halfway I had to be honest with him and admit I missed him badly.

So, that was yet another thing making me worry, and my thoughts were getting too full to keep worrying, particularly when I couldn't stop staring at Adam. Somehow he'd insinuated himself into my thoughts as well, but in a pleasurable way. He was kind, and smiled, and despite his physical issues he never once complained about pain or ignored Finn whenever my son asked a question. So far this week he and Finn had discussed dinosaurs at length, plus they'd even covered being a firefighter, although I noticed that Adam had changed the subject quickly when they'd gotten to that point.

Finn was still defensive and cautious. It wasn't as if he'd changed overnight, but I could see the taut edges of him relaxing a little and wondered if that was something to do with me. Was I feeling safer? The last thing I wanted to do was relax into this house, but it was the first time in a long time that I felt different.

I sank into homeschooling, plus researching the kind of project management details I needed to brush up on before my first day at Ringwood. The homeschooling side was going okay. I could manage history, and I found out new things that I'd never known before, I also consigned the curriculum to the trash when it became obvious that the history they expected Finn to know was way too basic and revisionist. I wanted Finn to think for himself about why he was part of this world, and the journey his ancestors had taken and why. He wanted to go way back to talk about dinosaurs. We compromised for the most part, but researching our family tree was a good way to access the past, and the impressive wall chart we had with family that went back to Scotland, was right next to the dinosaur identification chart that he'd insisted we hang. Adam had told us his family was originally from Ireland, and laughed about having red hair, and freckles. When he laughed I got hard, which was a shock. I couldn't recall the last time I'd been turned on by a laugh.

When I'd checked that it was okay with Adam to pin things to his board all he'd done was dig out pins, and join in with a heated debate about an Elaphrosaur, a rare dinosaur identified in Australia that had been in the news. I backed away then, because it seemed as if Adam had a knowledge of dinosaurs that I would never have.

He was also good at math and pretty hot with science, and he didn't seem to leave the house much and appeared to love that he was able to be included, even helping Finn with questions. We'd settled into a routine in the last couple of days, breakfast, study, lunch, study, swim, dinner, second swim, bed, and it suited Finn who relaxed into the space he was in and had even taken to asking Adam questions without Adam offering information first.

There were no more deep conversations that nearly ended in kissing. Although last night had been close, because we'd slipped into spending time just talking after Finn was asleep. We'd get a drink and sit on the patio, never going too far from the house in case Finn needed me, but so far he had settled into a sleeping pattern that I envied. I was still waking up on the hour, every hour, plagued by dreams and impossible thoughts, and worries, but the late night chats with Adam seemed to settle me enough to at least fall asleep in the first place.

"Hey." Adam placed his mug on the small table and then relaxed back into his chair, completely at ease with me. He hadn't had a migraine since that first day, but I noticed the little things. He managed the world around him so that it made sense for him. He had a list of things he achieved every day, and that included unloading the dishwasher.

"How was the project?"

"Thought you'd want to see it." I passed over the essay that Finn had written on the Elaphrosaur and Adam read each word, and when he'd finished he was smiling.

"That's a really interesting summary," he announced, and I was filled with pride as much as I had been when I first read the couple of hundred carefully written words. "And his handwriting is tidier than mine. We should do a field trip to the Nat."

That brought back memories of my own childhood, with the school visits to the Natural History Museum. I'd loved the exhibits, the packed lunch, and the pocket money I'd had to spend on whatever I wanted in the museum shop. I recalled I'd bought an eraser in the shape of a shark, because who didn't need one of those. It had been my treasured possession until the end of fifth grade when Nick and I decided to use it in an experiment to prove that erasers burned. We'd proved it burned for sure, when the small wastepaper bin fire set off the school alarm and landed us in detention, much to my dad's horror.

"That's some smile," Adam commented, and I pulled myself out of the memories.

"Oh I was recalling the school trips to the Nat."

"So you're from around here originally?"

Had I not mentioned that? To be fair I hadn't told him much at all, and right now staring up at the stars I felt the urge to talk about what used to be. The urge to connect to the past had gotten stronger every day we lived here.

"I was born about twenty miles from here, and didn't leave until I…" No, that was not where I wanted to go. Talking about why I left Cali wasn't on tonight's to-do list, because I was in a good place. "I went to school with Nick, it's how I know him, and I was thinking about the day he nearly burned down the science lab."

Adam shot me a look of disbelief then huffed a laugh. "Nick I'm-a smooth-TV-personality was a pyromaniac?"

"Well, not exactly, but he was the one who pushed the boundaries. Everyone knew he'd be something in the future, because he was always larger than life, and a show digging into other people's pasts is kind of perfect for him. I remember he could get anyone to spill their secrets, even me."

"I've only met him a couple of times, at charity events, he's friends with Leo's dad, the senator I mean."

I stared at him blankly, because I seemed to recall him mentioning a Leo, and I think he was a cop? Or a firefighter? I couldn't remember the facts.

He laughed again. "I forget you don't know these people, but you'll meet Leo at Ringwood, because he's one of your volunteers, along with..." he stopped and shrugged, "there's too many names to list. Leo and Jason, Eric and Brady plus the kids. Then Sean and Ash, plus Mia. I tend to live vicariously through their lives. It's so hard sometimes."

He spoke with such conviction and then he looked awkward as if he'd revealed things he hadn't meant to and then he changed the subject.

"Anyway, are you looking forward to starting at Ringwood?"

"Mostly," I hedged. Okay, so that was another conversation stop—I was getting good at that, and I needed to elaborate, otherwise my reticent ass would cause issues. "I remember the first day I worked with Dad. He was a carpenter and he taught me everything I know. That first day, I think I was six or so, and he just handed me soft wood, a dull knife, warned me to be careful and then told me to carve into it. I didn't know what to do then, but I managed to get a feel for the grain, and made a miniature carved-out pot. It wasn't anything amazing, but Dad was proud, and in that single moment I felt as if I could create the world." I smiled and relaxed back in the chair. "I just have to get that same feeling back to take with me to Ringwood, and I will be fine."

"You sound as if you and your dad are close."

"We were, he passed away when I was eighteen. He found out he had cancer, and was gone in a week. I was left with the business, and a grief so great..." I didn't want to talk about this tonight, not when I'd started to relax and push away the pain in my head. Now it was his turn to change the subject, and he chose the one thing that he knew would make me smile.

"Talking of creating the world, how is Finn getting on with the homeschooling?"

We talked for a while, the night growing chilly but I could see he was cold, and guessed that it wasn't the best place to sit for aching muscles. I called time by saying that I was tired, and we headed back into the house and the warmer kitchen. He rinsed the mugs and added them to the dishwasher, I tided up the chocolate and wiped down the surface, and then there was no other reason to stay down, even though it was only nine, and I was too wired to go to bed.

He stood from the dishwasher, and I saw him wince, crossing immediately to offer a hand, which he ignored. The wince became a smile after a moment, but the pain didn't leave his eyes.

"My lower back, it gets tight because it's compensating," he explained when I kept staring.

"Can I help?"

"You *really* know massage?"

"Enough to get by." Before he could say yes or no I nudged him until he was leaning against the counter with his back to me and I could assess where he was tight. I knew nothing about major back surgery, but if I could help with gentle pressure on the tension in his neck then that was one thing I did know. Graeme had carried a ton of tension in his shoulders, and I'd researched enough to help him relax, but with hindsight maybe I wouldn't have helped at all if I'd known the stress was due to stealing from vulnerable people's pension funds.

I kept my hands on top of his T-shirt, felt my way around his lumbar region, and he was tight.

"Will it cause an issue if I press here?" I laid gentle fingers at the very base of his spine, just above his low-hanging shorts, and he shook his head.

"The muscle damage is high in my shoulder, in the middle, on the right."

That explained why he would sometimes lean that way, which would cause an imbalance and stress to the supporting muscles.

"What does your PT do with you?"

"The man is a monster," he griped, but it was good-natured, "but he's warned me about posture." He sighed. "I just forget sometimes."

I guessed there would be scars, but that wasn't what I wanted to see, right now it was all about loosening the tension, and I smoothed my fingers over the material and worked on the knots with gentle pressure. At first he tensed and pushed back against me, but I bent closer to his ear and murmured for him to relax. After a short while I could feel the knots loosen, the tension in his lower back ease, and I worked my way up his spine, learning the paths there, not resting on the raised bump of scars, and then reaching his neck. This was where he held most of his tension, and I smoothed the pale, freckled skin, leaning forward as I concentrated on warming him and releasing the strain. He sighed, and turned to face me, testing his neck by moving his head slowly from side to side, just once.

We were so close I could see the darker green in his iris around the pupil, striations of forest in the jade; as he leaned in, and I leaned in, and if I moved a tiny bit closer I could have kissed him.

"Cam?" he murmured, and it was a question of sorts. A why, and a how, and an opening to talk. But I couldn't do this. I couldn't be open with anyone yet. Certainly not the man who tugged at my heartstrings so hard.

I pressed a hand over his shoulder. Then I knew I had to leave.

I couldn't give in to the temptation to kiss the man. We barely knew each other, and Finn was my priority so I had to back away. "Good night, Adam."

"Wait," Adam asked, and I couldn't move from the doorway.

He took the two steps toward me and pressed his hands on my shoulders, and then he tilted his head and kissed me.

"It's just a kiss," he whispered against my lips, and then stepped back, and coward that I am, I ran.

Back in my bedroom I couldn't shake the way he had stared at me as I'd left. His expression was one of shock, and pleasure, and desire, and I couldn't handle that. I wasn't lusting after my housemate, the man I paid rent to, the one who'd offered us a safe place. I wasn't letting another man into my life when I had Finn to consider.

I refused to.

Chapter Twelve

Adam

SLEEP IS FOR WIMPS.

At least that is what I tried to tell myself, because last night had been one long mess of sleeping, not sleeping, dreams, wishes, and desire, all mixed up with the all-pervasive nightmares that yank me sideways. I didn't have nightmares of being trapped, or of the pain, or the fact I was a few minutes from bleeding to death, it was a recurring image of not being fast enough, of not getting there in time.

Of Ben. Of the child in the car dying when I could've done something about it.

In my worst nightmare I almost got him out, but people behind were pulling me away, and even as I fought and struggled to get to Ben I knew I wouldn't reach him. I felt a fury so intense at those moments, hating the faceless people who stopped me, and I always woke in despair.

So, exhausted, I sat on my bed, trying to stretch out

some of the tightness that was threatening to return, and attempted to shove the despair and anger back into the box it had escaped from.

Only, as I went down to breakfast, all I could think about was Cam, and the kiss, and the regret that I hadn't stolen even more kisses when I could've. I'd felt such a bright connection to him as I'd touched him, and I could have held him longer, and then who knew what would have happened?

Certainly not anything too physical, because the thought of sex, of even getting anywhere near acting on attraction, was terrifying. *Who would want me anyway? Not able to fuck. Not even able to walk sometimes. Pain. Migraines. Thank fuck the seizures have stopped.* I need to get out more and stop spinning fantasies based on nothing more than meeting someone who wanted to talk to me.

But kissing would have been okay.

Of course, there was also the accepting side of me who understood why he didn't want to kiss me. Whatever his current issues or worries, I was the last person in the world who could be anyone's strength right now. The attraction had to be one-sided, because my broken body wasn't capable of offering the physical elements that went along with the temptation and desire.

So why did I kiss him? Am I some kind of masochist?

"Morning," Finn interrupted my destructive thoughts as soon as I stepped into the kitchen. He was working his way through a huge bowl of cereal, his tablet propped in front of him and an animated battle between starships on the screen. I couldn't see the details because he shut it down, but it wasn't done to hide it, more that he knew that the tablet at the table was forbidden by his dad and I was an adult of note.

"Morning." I poured myself the first coffee of the day and settled at the counter on a stool, peering at Finn over the rim of my mug before yawning behind my hand.

"Are you tired?" Finn asked with nine-year-old innocence.

I was going to deny it, but the caffeine hadn't kicked in yet and I yawned again instead. I could explain that his dad and I were talking until past midnight, but that was opening a can of worms that led right to the kiss. "Just a bit."

"You should go to bed earlier." He shoveled in a mouthful of crunch, and grinned at me at the same time, then chewed it fast because he wanted to impart some extra wisdom. "That's what Dad says, anyway." He was such a miniature Cam, and not just in the way he looked, but they had that serious expression in their eyes, and that flash of absolute responsibility that kept their lives straight. When the kid in Finn burst through the control it was with a light so brilliant it was blinding. He was funny, and sweet, crazy about *Star Wars*, a good swimmer, and he loved his dad to forever and back, his words not mine.

It seemed to me that Cam needed to be easier on himself when it came to Finn, because under the worry was a normal kid and it was this Finn who was beginning to reassert himself.

"I'll have an early night tonight," I reassured Finn, who nodded as if he was proud of my decision. Bless his heart. "Where's your dad?"

"Outside, on the phone with Uncle Nick, talking about work I think."

"I'll take him some coffee."

"Good idea, he's very sleepy as well."

I had to hide the smile as I poured more coffee and then headed outside, finding Cam standing with his back to the house, staring out over the yard, his hands pushed into the pockets of some board shorts. I admired the way he held himself, his broad back straight, legs spread slightly, his dark hair damp from the shower, and Erin was right, his ass was fine, not to mention the muscles of his calves, and the way he filled out a pair of cheap shorts.

"Morning," I murmured so I didn't startle him, but it didn't work because I've never seen someone move so fast as he spun on his feet to face me, hands out of his pockets and one of them on his chest.

"Jesus," he said on a breath, "you scared the shit out of me."

"My bad." I held out the coffee, then sat on the same chair from last night. I saw the moment the surprise vanished and was replaced by caution and maybe some regret, and I didn't want to see either of those. "So last night's almost-kiss," I dived straight in.

He took the other seat, but he didn't slump back all relaxed, he was on the edge, and balanced forward poised to make a run for it. "What almost-kiss?" he asked.

"Are we really pretending it didn't happen?" I was disappointed.

"Okay... what about the almost-kiss?" He sounded sad, and that gave me hope. Did he think I was going to tell him it was a mistake or something?

"Any chance we'll do that again?"

He shot me a surprised glance. "Fuck, no."

Well, that was direct. I guess I should've been grateful that he didn't give me a spiel with thirty reasons why kissing me was a bad idea. My stomach sank, but I wasn't going to assume this was a personal issue with me, that I was so broken that he could never want to kiss me. So I did what I did best—I lightened the situation.

"Okay. Yeah, I get why you wouldn't want to." I threw in a fake laugh just to be sure he understood I was being self-deprecating, but all he did was frown. "Anyway, it's just kissing."

He blew out an exasperated breath, so I hadn't lightened the situation enough because he was still in serious mode. "I'm not here long, and it doesn't matter what attraction I might feel, Finn is my priority."

Oh. So…

"So you *are* attracted to me, despite all of this," I waved at myself, and he was pissed, but I wasn't sure if it was *at* me, or *because* of me.

"Look, Adam, we haven't even known each other long, I don't want to be talking about this. Anyway, it's never *just* kissing, and you have to know it's wrong."

"It's too right to be wrong," I said with dramatic flair and attempted a shimmy in the chair, but fuck, it hurt although I never let him see a moment of my pain.

At least I'd made him smile, and I sensed a tiny spark of that same connection from last night, but we weren't going to be allowed to step further into what was next when Finn joined us and started talking about what he and his dad were doing today—mostly swimming and playing board games.

For now I had time to kill, so I took a book and spare sunscreen, and went to sit by the pool. I'd lost my edge if I couldn't even flirt enough to get kisses. It used to be that I could get whatever I wanted with a smile and wink and some of that cute charm that went with the red hair, green eyes, and freckles.

"We should talk." Cameron stalked down the path and took a chair, turning it so he was diagonal to me.

"I thought we'd covered it all." I gave him a smile to soften the words. "I wanted a kiss, you said it wouldn't be just a kiss, and then I said we were too right to be wrong."

He muttered a few curses, and then leaned forward in the chair, clasping his hands and leaning his elbows on his knees.

"I have a son."

"Yep."

"And a past."

I closed the book, which I hadn't actually managed to read any of, and fixed him with my best casual look.

"So do I."

"And an uncertain future."

I gestured at myself. "Likewise."

He sat back, exasperation in every line of him. "It's not the same."

"I bet if we talk long enough we could come up with a ton of reasons why we shouldn't be kissing."

He cursed again and ran a hand through his hair, gripping it tight as if to anchor himself.

"Even if I was attracted to you, I have Finn—"

"You're *definitely* attracted to me," I flirted, and fuck knows where that had come from. I genuinely thought my flirt gene had been crushed in the rubble of the bridge.

"Are you seriously messing with me over this?"

I let out a snort of disbelief. "Life's too short." Oh god, and now I was lying, when in actual fact I was lost in my head with the weight of all the serious shit I was coping with. Was I addicted to pain meds? Was I in actual pain? Did I have a career? Was there a future? Would I ever fall in love?

If only he knew.

"How about you tell me more about you," I changed the subject quickly.

"What about me."

"Well, I didn't check up on you, so tell me about this guy you're married to."

"Wait, you didn't check the story?" He looked horrified, and I wondered if maybe I'd messed up. Perhaps he thought I'd checked and what I'd read meant nothing to me. I needed to fix that.

"I'm waiting for you to tell me. So, make me understand why I can't kiss you, and tell me everything."

Chapter Thirteen

Cam

THIS WASN'T how I'd expected this conversation to go. I'd only come out here to explain why I wasn't able to lower my barriers. I'd assumed he'd searched my name but hadn't understood the full depths of what I'd let happen. I just wanted to put him right, so he could back off.

But he wanted to know everything? God. How far did I go back? Right to the moment I met Graeme and fell head over heels, or the time Nick had told me he didn't like Graeme and I'd chosen my new lover over my best friend, or the moment Finn had told me he hated his other dad and I hadn't listened? I wasn't ready to reveal that much of me yet, even if Adam's open and understanding gaze invited confidences.

"I'm not sure where to start."

"You just said that because you want me to say you should start from the beginning," he teased. I wasn't going back there, but I could talk about the night it all went to shit, enough so that he understood.

"No, I meant… it doesn't matter… I guess, I can start that night when he hadn't been home in five days. Even though that was the new normal in our marriage, I was getting worried. I mean, we'd fallen out of love, but he was still my husband. I called him, and no one picked up, so I left a message, then texted after a while, called his office, just in case he was working late there. Nothing. My next thought was 911 but he'd always come home before, so I didn't think it was an issue for the cops."

"Did you call them after all?"

"No. I could imagine him not coming home, *ever*, and when I did I was equally hopeful and angry and I actively avoided calling anyone for help. I suspected he was having an affair, and for him not to come home then he must have chosen to spend time with his latest *whatever*. This meant he'd chosen another family over me and Finn. I wanted to confront him, I wanted to say that the last two years of us trying to make things work hadn't worked and that I knew he'd been seeing other men. But I couldn't say that to an empty house—I needed to say it to his face." I scrubbed my eyes to stop the emotion from escaping.

"It's okay, Cam."

Okay? It was far from okay.

"Graeme and I hadn't shared a room, or a bed, in a very long time, so I had my own room. I checked in on Finn, then went to bed because I guess I didn't even expect him back. Only I couldn't sleep. I was hungry I think." I closed my eyes to recall everything clearly.

"So, I headed back downstairs and into the kitchen and

I remember opening the fridge, staring inside there for a while just lost in my own thoughts. I never heard a sound. When I shut the door, I looked up and I saw Graeme, just standing there by the back door, white as a sheet and covered in blood. I didn't understand, I thought he's hurt himself. I remember feeling compassion, fear, and then as quickly as I saw him, the door slammed open and the FBI arrived. Everything was over that quickly."

"What had happened?"

"Murder." I paused to let that sink in, but Adam held my gaze steadily. "Graeme had been investing money he didn't have, lost thousands of dollars of other people's money, and someone had come after him, followed him back to our house, where Finn was asleep upstairs. There was a fight, a knife, and Graeme killed a man. I never even knew him." All the soundbites spilled out of me, without conscious thought, and I exhaled sharply, then settled my breathing. Adam reached out and laced our fingers, and I didn't even stop him.

"Fuck," Adam murmured, and I squeezed his hand to let him know I appreciated the sentiment.

"His defense team built him up as this perfect husband, painting me as a man who wanted a million things that he wanted to give me. Private education for a son who wasn't even his, vacations, cars, that kind of thing. I was the trophy husband who used him for money." I shook my head. "I never wanted any of that, I needed a husband who loved me and wanted to be part of a family. I thought that was what he wanted, too." I snorted a laugh, because that was the only reaction I could let myself feel. "They said he killed the man in self-defense, and when Graeme offered passwords to bitcoin accounts as part of a plea bargain he got seven years in prison."

"Are you..." He frowned and didn't finish the question.

"Am I what?" I prompted. I expected him to ask me something about marrying Graeme, or if I had regrets, but he didn't ask anything like that.

"Are you waiting for him?"

"Fuck no." I tempered my reaction as soon as that burst out of me. "I filed divorce papers, I'm never letting him anywhere near me and Finn again. He had no legal hold over me, I don't have anything of his. I didn't know anything. I just want to cut him out of my life."

"Oh."

"But that doesn't mean I feel free of him, or of what happened. He's a specter in my life that I just can't shake. So when it comes to kissing..."

Chapter Fourteen

Adam

Ah, so this is why he followed me out here. Cam evidently wanted to explain in a hundred different ways why he couldn't kiss me, and was looking for a way out of whatever it was I was foisting on him. He'd summarize that we should move on with being housemates and that we shouldn't add complicated layers of attraction to the equation.

I'd woken early and lost a lot of time in the shower staring at the tiles.

After last night I was in the need for some alone time to think and the shower was my safe place, with the added seat that Eric had installed before he left, for my benefit even if he didn't admit it. That kiss had been utterly perfect, and simple, stripped down to the barest of touches, yet I'd never felt a stronger connection to another person. I craved so much more, and even dressed and ready to head out to my parents' place, I was thinking up scenarios that resulted in more kissing.

Nothing more than that, because the thought of sex filled me with crippling doubts, but a few months of kissing would be good. Only... what if I'd made everything awkward? Just when I thought I might like having him and Finn staying there on a much longer basis I'd kissed him—or he'd kissed me—and now everything might be ruined.

"I get it," I said with forced brightness, and he winced. I never was very good at acting. "No, I really get it. I can't stand and kiss anyone for very long, let alone take it any further to sex."

His eyes widened, and I could have kicked myself for even mentioning the S-word, then, *fuck my life*, pity crossed his expression.

"Is it because of the accident?"

"What? Yeah..." Then it occurred to me that maybe he thought I wasn't able to get all riled up enough to have sex, and that was one misconception I wasn't letting him carry around

"Oh, I can get it up, I can get myself off." I realized how crude I sounded, and checked behind me in case Finn had crept up and was listening, then I lowered my voice as my cock began to harden. "When I'm getting close to coming I tense, and then when I lose control, it fucking hurts."

He swallowed, and gone was the pity, and instead there was something else in his expression and his tongue darted out to wet his lower lip, and through all of that he was staring at my lips.

Oh shit. He's going to look at me like this, listen to my most hidden secret, and then refuse to kiss me and I'll be left all turned on and wanting.

"I don't... I mean..." In a flurry of motion he stood, and I didn't need X-ray vision to check if he was as hard as I was, because he was in loose shorts and wore nothing to restrain his erection. It was right at my eye level as I sank into my chair, and I could...

He kissed me. It wasn't hard, but it wasn't soft, and god help me I pushed my fingers into his hair and held on tight. Then he backed away as fast as he'd started, and shook his head.

"What you do to me," he murmured. "You're like sin all wrapped up in temptation and need."

"Dad? Are you coming in?"

He wavered, indecisive for a split second, and then he stalked into the house.

As he'd said, Finn would always come first.

I FOLLOWED CAM INSIDE, at a much slower pace, yanking at my T-shirt and rearranging my erection so it wasn't quite so obvious. As soon as I stepped inside Finn was there asking me questions.

"Are you playing with us too? We saw you have Monopoly, but it would be better with three, so can you play?"

I'd have liked nothing more, but today was family lunch day. Even if it had become less about fun and more focused on everyone talking at me about what I should be doing next in my life it was expected I'd be there. I wanted to see everyone, and even though I felt the instinct to ask Cam and Finn to come with me, I held the words back. There was no way they were ready for the Williams family in full force. Maybe next week.

"I'm out today, back later though, so save starting any Monopoly games until then, okay?"

"Okay."

I *really* wanted to play board games with Cam and Finn, but Cam wouldn't look at me, and I was still turned on, and weirded-out by the conversation we'd had, plus the kiss. I needed time to process the back story with Graeme, the fact that Cam had kissed me, and how I felt about all of that. I hid in my office before I needed to leave, and wasted the hour messing about researching various important but ultimately useless future career options for a former firefighter with limited abilities.

By the time I left the house time was ticking and if I was late for the third week in a row then mom and dad would start up by asking me to move home again. I had my own place, and my independence had been hard won after the accident. So now I needed to get to my parents' place and show everyone I was fine so they didn't make me explain yet again why I'd moved away from the converted garage on their property.

Saturday brunch at the parents' house was a weekly thing, and when I'd been in the hospital they'd brought it to me as I'd lain immobile in bed, along with the rest of my family, including the kids. All I could think was that I was lucky I'd had a large private room, because adding in visiting firefighter colleagues, I needed all the space I could get.

I got Mom-hugs, Dad advice, talked with siblings and my nieces and nephews, and got to catch up with everything. Only in my desperate need not to be late, I'd made the mistake of getting there early, and that meant I couldn't lose myself in the crowd, but was instead front and center for a two-pronged attack from Mom and Dad.

"So have you made any decisions on your future this week?" Mom asked the first question after the typical comments on my limp, how I was getting on with the cane, and was I sleeping, and eating properly, as she passed me lemonade. I could ignore the question and change the subject, but she wouldn't let me in her usual kindly-but-persuasive manner. I couldn't tell them I was planning devious ways to kiss Cam again, because they'd start planning the goddamn wedding. I was the last of the siblings unmarried and without kids, and being gay wasn't an excuse to not fulfill my destiny of giving them more grandchildren. The pressure was real.

"The answer is the same as last week when you asked, I'm working out all my options."

She patted my hand. "Well, you know you don't have to decide now."

Then stop asking me what I'm going to do.

As usual, Dad chimed in. "But, you at least need to think about it," he interjected, and sat on the other side of me, putting an arm over my shoulders. "The best thing right now might be for you to fix on what you want out of your life, then you can move on. You have a degree—you could do anything."

My degree, after my years at Cal State, was in fire science, every second of it preparing me for a career as a firefighter, but of course it had a huge amount of science, and that was my strength. Still, it didn't exactly lend itself to any other careers that could be carried out by someone who lost days to pain.

"I don't know." I tried to shrug him off but he wasn't budging. This was different to all the other weeks, this was Dad pushing me just that little bit further.

Dad sighed, "It's like this, your mom is worried about you, and if you had a purpose—"

"Please don't give me a speech, Dad," I pleaded, and wriggled free to stand by the fireplace. "I *know* Mom is worried about me. Hell, I'd be worried about me. I *know* I need to find a purpose, I get that, I just don't know what that *purpose* is yet."

I wanted to go back to the point where Mom held me and told me everything was going to be okay, because it had felt safe there. But now Dad was saying that Mom was worried about me, and the last thing I wanted was to worry her. I loved my parents, and they'd been the rocks in my life for so long. From the moment I'd woken to find them by my bedside I'd seen the fear in their eyes. I could have died that day, and I'd seen that in the way they'd both cried. Even Dad, who refused to admit he ever cried.

"What can you do with your degree?" Mom asked.

Dad was quick to interject as if the two of them had a pre-planned script they were reading from. "There's a shortage of science teachers in schools, I read an article about it. All you'd need to do is go back to school for your teacher's credentials and you'd have a career just like that." He snapped his fingers as punctuation.

Teacher. I couldn't help wincing, because some people

were born teachers, but I wasn't sure that was me. I had this image of me standing at the front of a class talking about chemistry and knowing I didn't have any chance of keeping the kids invested. I'd worked with kids alongside Engine sixty-three, and of course I volunteered at Ringwood, and I seemed to get on okay with Finn, but it didn't matter how positive I was being, at the back of my mind all I *really* wanted was my old career back. I wanted action. I wanted to be out there in the thick of it, helping people, saving lives. Not tottering around needing a cane more often than not.

"That's not me." I leaned on the edge of the table to take the weight off my knee and crossed my arms over my chest. I could use the Williams' stubborn streak and show my parents that a role in a classroom wasn't my path in life, but Dad wasn't letting this go.

Dad snapped his fingers as if inspiration had struck him. "So work with little kids, go into schools and work on field trips, become a rep for Smokey the Bear or that kind of thing."

I didn't want to point out the issues inherent with Smokey the Bear as an outdated concept. The mascot was from a time when everyone was encouraged to believe that fire was a bad thing. This in turn led to suppression of fires back in the sixties and seventies, which resulted in the wood and scrub accumulating beyond normal levels. Using the bear was of its time, but in modern forest fire fighting, the message was thinking about fire's place in the ecological system, rather than considering all fire being bad. I knew I was the odd one out to see fire as good, but if the unpredictable goddess could be tamed then we might find more of a balance in the hills. Still, I didn't say anything because my parents needed me to lecture them on things that seemed counterintuitive.

"You want me to dress up as a bear?" I teased—anything to lighten the mood.

"Don't be silly." Dad sighed. "But you could go back to college, get your teaching credentials—"

"No, Dad."

"But you love working with kids—"

"No." I sounded as if I wasn't giving them a chance to offer up any ideas, but I'd looked into it and I wanted to be outside doing practical stuff that made a difference. My physical health was better, only one migraine, and that had been due to circumstances. I could swim, walk the garden, I was working on my PT every single day, add in yoga and healthy eating, and I was determined to fix this. I hadn't come over today to have my future path hammered out with Mom and Dad, who'd never completely understood why I wanted to be a firefighter in the first place. Not that they'd stopped me—they weren't that kind of parents—always fixated on wanting their kids to follow their own paths. For Erin it was into art and design, for Saul it was being a veterinarian, and for Luke it was finance and banking.

The rest of the family started to arrive then and finally we could stop focusing on me. The oldest Williams sibling, Saul, arrived with his family in tow, the twins, Riley and Grace, clamoring to tell me everything they'd done all week, Saul's wife, Caroline, hugging me and telling me about this person she knew who said that teaching was good, and had I thought of it? It seemed as if the family was fixated on me teaching my way out of a career I'd lost, but in the same way I knew I was a firefighter, I felt in my bones I would never be a teacher. The next oldest, Luke and his partner Melanie, arrived with Jaxon, Seth, and Aubrey, and out of them it was Mel who suggested teaching within two minutes of getting there.

Yep. Pre-planned intervention from the entire family for the win.

Erin was last as usual, her long-suffering husband, Austin, carrying in bags of something or other, and Emma and Harper trailing her. Charlotte came running in last, waving flip-flops.

"Found them! Uncle Adam, can I come over and swim with Finn again? He's fun." That was all blurted loudly in my ear as she hugged me hello.

"Any time, just get your mom to bring you over."

Erin hugged me. "How is your tall, dark, and sexy houseguest and his adorable son?" she asked loud enough so that the entire family heard.

"I hate you," I whispered into her ear.

"And I love you," she said in her normal voice and winked at me.

That was when the teasing started, and layer by layer my entire family peeled away information about my new housemates, until there were only a few secrets left.

Telling them he was hiding out after tragic betrayal was a big no, instead I told them he'd relocated to be nearer to family. There was not one mention of late-night chats or that stupid kiss, or the fact I wanted loads more kisses. The teasing lasted through dinner, and I could see the way my mom was staring at me with the perception she'd honed through raising four children.

"You like him?" she asked when we were alone for two-seconds as we passed in the hall.

I could never lie to her, but I wasn't ready to share these fragile new feelings. "Maybe," I offered, then pressed a finger to my lips in a *shhhh* motion. She nodded, but I gave it a few hours before everyone started calling me.

"Hey, you want a walk?" Saul asked when everything had been cleared away, and I agreed until I realized he just meant me and him.

"Are you big-brothering me?" I asked as we set out to walk the edge of the vast yard.

"Just catching up with my *littlest* brother," he teased. Then he was talking about the twins being at a party where there had been a bouncy house, plus cake, and went into detail about the technicolor clean up in the car on the way home, laughing and elaborating for me as he always had. We were the closest out of the four of us, always had been, maybe because he too had known as soon as he'd mended his first teddy that he wanted to be a vet. He was the one I'd consider talking to about Cam, but it seemed as if he wanted to fill our walk with so many words that even if I wanted to talk about the man who'd landed on my doorstep, I didn't get a chance.

"… and then I met Meg, she brought in a cat, a sweet thing who'd broken his leg in a death-defying leap from the garage." He stopped talking and looked at me expectantly.

"Sorry?"

"Were you listening at all?" He waited at the bench in the herb garden and gestured for us to sit.

"The twins did… something…there was a cat… or… " I winced as I realized I'd kind of tuned out, and Saul didn't deserve me to be halfway here in his life. He didn't seem pissed as he punched my good arm, not hard, but at least *he* wasn't scared to touch me unlike my friends and the rest of my family.

"I've met this woman, Meg—"

"What?" I interrupted horrified. He was happily married to Caroline and this was the first I'd heard about him meeting a woman. "What happened? What did you do?" I snapped.

"Huh?"

"Have you been having an affair?"

"The fuck?" He was wide-eyed and then he snorted a laugh and raised a hand in defense. "You genuinely think I'd do that?"

I shook my head. Of course I didn't, but the way he'd said it. "My head," I said and rubbed my temples which, had I'd done that in front of Mom it'd have engendered sympathy, but with my older asshole brother all it got me another shove.

"I have a *client*. Her name is Meg and she bought her cat to see me, she's happily married to this accountant, and they live down the street from me, but that isn't the story."

I waited for more.

"So, Meg was talking about finding the cat when she was out working, and bringing him home, only to find out he was the kind of cat who ignored the fact he only has nine lives. She called him Riggs, you know, after Mel Gibson in *Lethal Weapon*."

"Huh?"

"You know because all he wanted to do was to find ways to die, but that's me getting off the subject." He took a deep breath, then rummaged in his pocket, pulled out a note, and passed it to me. "She's a pyrogeographer, which I don't totally understand, but she did say she'd be happy to talk to you. It has something to do with fire, and she assures me it's not made up, so I guess you know what one of those is?"

Of course I knew what a pyrogeographer was and quoted from the article I'd read only a couple of days before in the latest issue of *Firehouse Magazine*. "They explore fires over space and time."

Saul snorted. "That sounds like a hippy-tripping shit fest."

"It's not, it's serious and fascinating and all about examining ecosystems historically, in the present day, and looking at how forces disturb habitats."

"Uh huh," Saul encouraged me to continue talking.

"It's looking at controlling burns and the effects on vegetation, understanding how things have changed over the centuries, and how everything is a balancing act, and how fire is just one part of controlling nature."

"You lost me at the first word," Saul teased.

"No for real, it's really interesting." I leaned forward, sketching words in the air in my enthusiasm. "They take historical data, and create fire lines working with the environment. Me, I was just the blunt instrument out there fighting the fires because as a people we've all fucked up so much."

He examined my face for a moment and then pulled me into a sideways hug. "You're a hero, you idiot."

I let him hug me for a while, even leaned into it—my family was never shy when it came to expressing emotion. But after a short while, as brothers, we needed to pull it to a close, and he shoved me away, carefully, and then wrinkled his nose.

"You stink," he lied.

"Not as bad as you."

We sniggered as brothers do, and then he was thoughtful. "Anyway, I told her about you, and she wants to meet you."

"Jesus, Saul." The last thing I needed was a pity meeting.

"I didn't tell her everything, just that you were measuring your options. She's got all these ideas, and she's excited for you to give her a call, or organize a meeting. Even if it's just out of interest."

"Did you tell her I was a freaking cripple?"

Saul's gaze hardened, "Fuck that crap, Ads."

"Well, whatever, it's true. I'll get better but I'll never be fixed."

He scowled at me. "Take the card, and stop talking shit."

I took out my wallet and placed the card inside it. "I will, thank you."

He muttered something about idiot brothers, and then when we started to walk again, my cane raising dust on the hard dirt, he changed the subject. "Anyway, back to the twins…"

Dinner was boisterous, the talk got louder, the jokes quicker, and I didn't have time to think about Cam or my life at all.

Probably a good thing.

Chapter Fifteen

Cam

ADAM ARRIVED HOME BEARING LEFTOVERS, and it was the perfect time to start a game of Monopoly. It was a nice change to play with someone who didn't pout every time they lost something, and I wasn't referencing Finn. Graeme hated to lose and he'd only played three games with me and a young Finn. I should have known from those that he was the kind of person who was out for himself, because on the last occasion we ever played a game, Go Fish! a few weeks after we were married, he threw the cards at the wall, called Finn an idiot and made him cry.

A kids' card game had made Graeme lose his shit.

That day had been the one where the scales over my eyes had begun to slip and we had our first fight. I told him that he would never again make my son cry. He threatened to hit me, I blocked him, but even then I didn't question it, not in our beautiful house, not when it ended with sex and him saying he was sorry, over and over, with tears in his eyes. He never attempted to hit me again, that was about the only good thing in our marriage, but he'd changed and his switch to belittling me, and blaming me, had been so subtle I'd barely noticed what he was doing. He'd been a master at gaslighting, making me doubt myself without me even realizing it, and by the time I'd really seen him the damage was done, with Finn, with my marriage, and even thinking about it now made me nauseous.

"Where did you go?" Adam asked, and I blinked back to the present, my eyes wet. Finn had long since gone to bed, and I was working out a few minor issues for my first day at Ringwood, and I kind of expected Adam to come and find me, but not to see me in mid-memory-meltdown.

"Huh?"

"You look a long way from here." He leaned against the desk and then reached over to capture an errant tear before cupping one side of my face. Was he going to kiss me? I didn't want to kiss him because it was wrong.

"I wasn't anywhere," I lied, and I instinctively pressed my cheek to the soft touch. I'd trusted Graeme and been left less of a man than I should have been, and in all of that Finn was vulnerable. I wanted to kiss Adam but should I even be thinking of that? What kind of man was I to start something that could hurt my son?

Adam's different. I'm not as stupid anymore. I know what I'm doing. Finn doesn't have to know about a single freaking kiss.

"Cam, you're crying," he said in such a gentle way that my chest hollowed, and he rubbed a thumb on my cheek wiping away tears, a soft rhythmic motion that made me want to cry all the more.

"I didn't mean to," was all I could think to say.

"Tears just happen." He closed in, the puff of his breath on my lips, and I was lost in his green eyes. "Don't stop them if you need them."

Heat fought inside me, I was lost in painful memories, but I also wanted to kiss Adam so bad that it hurt inside. Was it wrong to seek comfort right now? With all the mess in my life, and the fear, and worrying about Finn, and the job, and money, and the future, how could it be wrong to steal just a moment for myself? I covered his hand with mine as he smiled at me.

"Adam…"

"I know you said you didn't want to, but can I kiss you? Is that okay? Tell me no if you—"

I kissed him to stop him talking me out of it, moving at a slow pace so as not to break the kiss until I caged him against the desk, and eased him up to sit on the edge. He didn't stop touching my face, instead he placed his other hand there so he cradled me close, and then he wriggled to spread his legs, and I slotted in as if we were made to fit each other. He sighed into the kiss and tilted my head to deepen the taste, our tongues sliding and tangling and it was intoxicating. I didn't know what to do with my hands, desperate to pull him closer, so I settled them on his hips and kept the touch light. I still didn't know all the places that hurt for him but from the way he kissed, deep and with purpose, I had to believe I wasn't hurting him. We parted long enough for him to drop his hands to my shoulders, and then to my back, tugging me close, moving to the edge of the desk, and he was as hard as me.

"I want to kiss you so bad," he muttered, and kissed my cheeks free of tears and the tip of my nose before closing his eyes and sinking back into a deep kiss. If nothing else existed then I could've stood there pressed hard against him, lost myself in the kiss, and carried on forever, and that was a dangerous feeling. I didn't want to think, I just wanted to *feel*, but that soft doubt was at the back of my mind, warning me to be careful.

Then the kiss changed, Adam sighing into it, breaking us apart, still holding me.

"Where did you go?" he asked, but he wasn't angry at me, he was smiling and his eyes were bright with passion.

"There's too much mess in my head to do this," I admitted, and we rested our foreheads together. "I need to think about this."

"One more before bed?" he teased, and pressed a soft touch to my lips, I chased for more as he pulled back. "There." He released his hold on me, and he didn't push for more, or demand anything, and I had the paralyzing thought that maybe that was more dangerous.

Could he offer me something I'd never had with Graeme? Attraction that became more, lust that was edged with beauty? The kind of love that Nick had once had with his husband, Daniel, that everlasting, hopeful, beautiful, but fragile thing that I thought I'd never see for myself?

"Are you ready for tomorrow?" he asked, and I blinked back to him, aware we were pressed together and I was still hard, although not with the desperate need to fuck him over the desk, but something altogether more dangerous.

I cleared my throat and then stepped out of his loose hold, tugging my T-shirt down over my shorts. "As ready as I'll ever be."

He rested a hand on my shoulder. "You'll do great, and hey, I'll be there backing you up for what it's worth with all of this." He gestured at himself with his free hand and I hated that he even said that, but I knew he wouldn't be ready for me to tell him to stop. That was his self-deprecating way of getting ahead of anything people might think, and I'd seen that defense mechanism in the mirror.

I'm not clever enough to have known what he was doing. Look at me. I'm a carpenter not a finance expert.

Hell I was a boss at making people ready for when I failed them. I just didn't like seeing that in someone else.

Adam shimmied off the table, wincing, taking my help when I offered it, and then he limped to the door.

"And off I go with the endless journey up to bed. Sleep well. Eric has a day off and is picking me up early so I'll meet you at Ringwood?"

He's not coming in with me? Why did I feel so abruptly disappointed? After all, I was a big boy who could get to a worksite on my own. I think I'd gotten used to him being around, and I felt calm in his company.

"Okay, that's cool." It *so* wasn't cool at all.

"I have to check in with the station, I'll see you at Ringwood."

I nodded as if I understood, and then without moving a muscle I strained to hear him slowly make his way upstairs. Only when he was at the top and I heard his door shut did I follow.

Because I swear, the way I felt at that moment meant

that if his door had been open and he'd been waiting for me, I'd have been in there for more kisses so fast that he wouldn't have stood a chance.

———————

BERNIE WAS WAITING for me to arrive and that meant I didn't have to listen to Finn mutter under his breath about homeschooling, being there all day, or not being able to swim. He was polite in front of Bernie, and I welcomed the interference after I'd had a really bad night's sleep.

Those kisses? They'd messed with my head, and I'd had to stop myself from finding Adam this morning and kissing him awake. I was addicted to staring at Adam's soft lips, wanting the touch of his hands on my skin, and thinking about things I shouldn't have been thinking.

Proximity. That was all it was. Stupid, fucking, frustrating proximity.

"Eric is here today so if you want heavy lifting then you need to get to it, because he's on call. Poor guy is covering a lot of shifts." Bernie was waiting for me to comment, and I wished I remembered who Eric was because I was sure I'd been told what each of the volunteers did. How was it I recalled all of that, but not whether Eric was a firefighter or a cop?

This was a serious contract and could be the first of many, and I needed to pull myself together.

"Sorry I was thinking about the job," I lied.

She seemed pleased and didn't call me on my woolgathering. "I was just saying, Adam and Eric are volunteering, but Eric's on call."

Not that this made anything clearer, but I could see from her expression this was serious.

"Oh, okay," I said with what I hoped was the right amount of sympathy, and I must have gotten it right because she nodded as if my single word summed up whatever she was implying.

"You can go straight through, but would your son like to stay in with me? We have a couple of kids his age—"

"It's okay, ma'am, I want to stay with Dad," Finn murmured at my side, and gripped my hand. That was *not* what he'd said in the car when he'd spent twenty minutes telling me that he didn't need to be there today, and that he was capable of staying at home with the pool and his tablet. *So not happening.*

"Absolutely," Bernie was enthusiastic in her response. "You'll learn a lot at his side I'm sure, but we have cookies and milk in the main kitchen if you need a break from all that hard work."

Finn deflated when he heard the words "*hard work*" in juxtaposition with "*cookies*" and his grip loosened. I knew what he really wanted to do was give in to the lure of the cookie, but he'd have to get over the nerves first.

"Thank you, ma'am," I spoke for him because he was now half behind me and I didn't know what to do for the best. Did I make him speak? Did I get him to respect Bernie for her maturity, or ask him to thank her for her kindness?

I didn't fucking know anymore.

"Well, if you change your mind. Your background checks came back fine, so we need to get the final health and safety forms done, and then I'll show you around." It was only thirty minutes before we were released to investigate the actual site we were working on, but I could sense that Finn went from cautious and needy to clingy to plain bored in that small space of time. We saw dorm-type rooms, two beds in each, bathrooms, rec rooms, and checked in on a group of kids, six of them, working on craft projects. The feel of the place was one of hope, leaflets everywhere, sheets were pinned to a notice board in the main admin office for events from pottery painting to a trampoline park visit, but it was the fundraising artwork that caught my attention.

A year ago I could have pulled out my phone and donated money without hesitation, no questions asked, pulling on the vast resources I'd had access to as the husband of a Wall Street mover and shaker. In fact, I'd worked with several charities back east, but every single one of them had politely asked me to move on when Graeme's shit had hit the fan. It was something when a charity wasn't interested in a person's help because of what their husband had done, but I understood that the implication I might have had something to do with high level embezzling would make them nervous.

I'm so fucking understanding of why people didn't want me. Maybe I should have gotten pissed and demanded that they trust me.

I missed working with the charities, I missed the friends I'd made. Scratch that, the friends I *thought* I'd made. I knew that places like Bernie's got limited funding but the remainder would be raised through events, and she must have spotted me staring at the huge thermometer that was only a third of the way full.

Two hundred kids passed through the doors of Ringwood annually for emergency and short-term shelter, and Ringwood mopped up the shortfall when the county-run facility was at capacity, which according to what Nick had explained was a daily problem. Ringwood was part of the national model for the protection and care of abused and neglected children, and used animals in therapy—they were cutting edge and he pumped in as much money as he could, but one man couldn't run something this huge on his own.

"We're down on funds compared to this time last year," Bernie murmured sadly, "it's the economic climate, so many people without the spare money to donate. Adam and the guys did a couple of charity events, but it's never going to be enough for what we want to do. It's only through private funding that we're able to undertake capital projects like the extension you're here to complete." She ushered us through a final door and out into the vast backyard.

"It's a big space out here," I offered, and she nodded. I'd seen it in the first walk-through, but actually being there knowing I'd be working on it was overwhelming for a moment.

"We have a volunteer, Brady, Eric's partner, who leads the kids and other volunteers in yard work, but as you can see it's a work in progress." With a practiced eye, I identified that the backyard would have once been the loading bays for the stores, plus more parking, all of it bordered with secure fencing. It was asphalt but there were painted markings for basketball, baseball, and even a track of sorts with small jumps for bikes. None of it appeared permanent, as if someone with a spray can had come in and decided to paint lines. The other half, though, had been turned into a real yard, lots of gravel and plants, no grass as such, but it was cared for. "We have sports and recreational tools, opportunities and guidance, to help the kids address the circumstances that brought them into foster care, and another project to redo the sports area, and create a small skate park, with some hang-out space, for the older longer-term kids. One day."

I forced down my instinct to offer my time at no cost, because that would've been financial suicide for me, and I had to put Finn first. The money I earned here would pay Nick back with interest and leave us enough to head to Montana and that remote ranch I imagined would be our home. Still, I could take a look at a couple of the smaller projects in my breaks—that wouldn't take money, just time.

Bernie stopped at the far end of the buildings. "This is it."

I'd seen detailed photos of the construction close up. Excavation was done, as some of the construction of the two floors, but mostly it was an unfinished shell. There were supplies being piled to one side by a giant of a man while Adam sat on a bench and watched, and when Bernie called out, they both turned to face me. I caught Adam's gaze and fell into his wide welcoming smile, but I knew I had to be professional.

"This big man here is Eric. Eric, this is Cam and his son Finn."

I immediately extended a hand to Eric who wore a CalFire T-shirt stretched over his wide, muscled chest.

"Eric," the giant said, and his grip was as firm as his muscles indicated. He looked as if he could bench press me and Finn combined, and it hit me that he must be on call for the fires in the hills that raged and spat and ate up acres of brush, so no wonder he looked exhausted. I'd watched the reports of the latest conflagration, the Low Pass fire, on the morning breakfast show, staring at the map as they showed it had bypassed a town. The report had shown a hell on earth, and I couldn't imagine being one of the people having to fight it. The newsreader had been keen to point out that unusually warm and dry conditions coupled with powerful wind gusts had ignited a spate of winter wildfires. The summary was that California didn't even seem to have a specific fire season at all any more but had a year round problem.

"Thank you for the work you do," I blurted.

Eric gave me a smile. "You're welcome," he murmured, and backed up a little.

"This is my son, Finn," I added.

Finn dutifully shook Eric's hand, and then it was time for me to do something proactive, balance Finn being bored and having to do schooling outdoors, with meeting and managing new people, plus recall if I could even do construction anymore.

"So," I began and then failed to make a full sentence at all. Adam, Eric, Bernie, and I, stood in a weird face-off for a few moments and I knew we were all waiting for someone to talk first. Only when it started to feel uncomfortable did I pull up my big boy pants and decide to take control of the situation. "You want to bring me up to speed?" I was talking to Eric, but he gestured to Adam.

"It's all him," he said with another smile.

"Okay cool. Do you want to run me through where we're at?"

Adam nodded sharply, then turned and stumbled but sidestepped my outstretched hand when I'd gone to steady him. I knew what construction sites were like—full of trip hazards, and I didn't want him to end up with another migraine, or to fall.

"Careful, Adam," Eric warned.

"I'll show you what we've done so far." Adam ignored Eric, avoided my reach and indicated I follow.

I did, and took in everything as I walked. Neatly organized supplies sat in rows, and there was an old picnic table with nails and screws, power tools at one side of that, and a small generator. The tools were padlocked to a metal post, which I guess had at one time been part of a fence, and there was also a row of hard hats, and a sign about health and safety.

Adam started to explain. "So this is what I organized, but when Nick suggested you'd come in to work on this I decided not to touch anything else, and feel free to change anything you need to."

His words were even, and it was a long way from the reaction I'd expected. I'd imagined he'd feel pleased that he didn't have to volunteer and take on the headaches that went with what I was going to do—awful things such as suppliers letting us down, or the weather turning on a dime, or just general fuck-up'dness that could lead to any sane contractor tearing their hair out. In fact he seemed different today. Yes, he smiled, but he seemed brittle and defensive, and I couldn't understand. Was this me seeing a part of him he wanted to hide? Forewarned about a man with secrets was forearmed. Not everyone was out to get us but I couldn't help worrying.

"It all looks really good," I murmured with appreciation as I cast a professional eye around the space, not wanting to give away that I was fishing deep for the instincts I'd once had. I refused to be overwhelmed, but there wasn't much I could do to avoid the rising panic.

I hadn't worked construction for six years, and fuck... could I even remember what I was doing?

"So what now, boss?" Adam asked. I glanced at him, my gaze locking onto his, and I was lost again in his green eyes. *I need to stop staring and forget absolutely having my hands on his milky-pale skin, tracing each freckle with my fingers, kissing him.* "Cam, are you okay?"

I wanted to joke about not knowing what the hell I was doing, but that would've been the worst way to start. I cracked my neck, stretched my shoulders and then nodded. I could do this. It was second nature, and the scent of the wood reminded me of Dad, and organization and construction was in my blood. *I can do this.*

"Finn, you want to sit at the table?" It was in the shade, he had a book, and notebook for notes, and a list of questions I'd spent all last night writing. Added to which I'd made his favorite peanut butter cupcakes in Adam's pristine kitchen, and I hoped he'd at least give me a smile. Instead, he sat but stared up at me with mutiny in his expression. I couldn't deal with that battle as well as look professional right now. "Okay then, let's see where we're at."

Chapter Sixteen

Adam

THE LAST THING I wanted was to appear weak in front of Eric, but I'd already nearly fallen once, and when I hurried to follow Cam to the table I caught my foot on fucking nothing at all, and almost fell on my ass, with only Eric's outstretched hand stopping me from face-planting.

"Are you okay, Red? Should you even be here today?" Eric asked, and there it was—the single thing that I didn't want to hear. That incessant question from Eric, which he asked me every goddamned time he saw me, took me from pretending to be okay to not giving a shit who saw my grumpy side.

"I'm fine," I snapped. The last thing I needed was for Cam to hear Eric and ask the same question, because for some reason I didn't want Cam, who'd been in my life for such a short time, to worry about me, or to think less of me. Maybe I should have rethought helping today, but I wanted to see Cam working with his hands, so I could add another layer of sexy to him.

It would've been just my luck for me to kiss a hot guy, and all he wanted to do in return was nurture. Where was the hot and messy sex, him throwing me down on the bed and devouring me? Not that I'd be up for that. Hell, even considering sex made me shrivel inside, and not only because of the scars, but the pain. What kind of man couldn't even handle a bit of rough, freaking sex? So, sex aside, if I fell over, all I'd end up getting from Cam was fucking pity, particularly after the migraine incident, and I wouldn't get any more kisses. So I needed Eric to stay cool and not mess this up, and it put me on the fucking edge and colored everything with worry.

With Cam being brought in to project manage the extension my informal job as volunteer site manager was a redundant position. Which was half great and half shit, because I'd researched and written notes, and I'd even drawn up a plan for how to approach this entire thing. Not that anyone knew I'd done that, but still, I'd put the work in. Objectively, I knew Cam was there in his capacity as an expert tradesman, and I was okay with all of that if it was only me and him. He was a good guy, and he deserved the break. But Eric seeing me losing something else made all the old doubts creep in. I bet Eric pitied me, and now I was pitying myself, and it was a shit cycle to fall into when I'd been doing so well. I *knew* I was only a volunteer, but I'd enjoyed having the responsibility in front of Eric and the guys, because it made me think they saw me succeeding at something.

Shit. I should just leave before I get even more morose,

and take it out on Cam and end up losing one of the only
bright things I have going on right now.

"You don't have to do this," Eric commented. Eric
commenting on my health, or asking me if I was okay, was
pretty much his default setting when he started with the
guilt trips. It was probably the thousandth time since the
accident, maybe more, and I was getting sick of being
asked, even if he asked in such a way that it sounded as if
his heart broke every single time. He'd been my mentor
when I'd joined Engine sixty-three, I'd been hurt on his
watch, and as a result the relationship we had now was
sickeningly complicated. He blamed himself for not
stopping me, I blamed myself for being stupid while
knowing that I'd done the right thing. He was always
wanting to check on me, I just wanted him to back the fuck
off. It was a lose/lose.

"I'm fine," I muttered through gritted teeth, with as
much calm and patience as I could muster to make Eric
think everything was okay.

"So what happened with the other construction
company?" Cam asked as he leafed through the plans and
came across my project list. I wanted to reach over and
grab my schedule from him before he waved it and
declared it all wrong, but he nodded in approval and
placed the papers back with the plans. "They seemed to
have a handle on things. What went wrong?" Wind gusted
into the yard, the Santa Anas letting us know they were
there, curling around the corner of the building and lifting
the paperwork so that Cam had to place a hand on them to
stop them flying away.

My stomach sank—the winds had grown in strength

from a mild breeze to sizable gusts over the past hour, and that was a factor in the spread of the fires in the hills as strong downslope winds would blow through the mountain passes in SoCal. It used to be that, post-Thanksgiving, the fire risk would lessen, but it seemed as if one fire fed the next, and the next, and it was a year round issue just waiting for the next fire and hoping it wasn't a bad one. The thought of Eric out there fighting fires for the entire year was horrifying. Eric tensed, then he pulled out his cell to check the screen—he was on reserve call as were all the firefighters in the district, but he'd only had one day off since his last heavy shift. He was supposed to have three days clear, but I knew better. Hot, dry, sustained, and gusting high winds meant the National Weather Service had issued a red flag warning for most of Northern California's interior, as well as Southern California. I hated that he was leaving to go into that, but I *knew* it was what he was born to do.

"I need to…" Eric began.

"Sure," I said.

"Can you…?" He waved at the construction, which included Cam, and I nodded.

"Go."

Eric left with a murmured goodbye, and I watched him stride across the yard to the admin building, breaking into a jog and vanishing through the door.

"What's wrong?" Cam asked. "Is he leaving?"

He was going to ask me questions about Eric, and then that would lead to talking about fire. But I didn't want to talk to Cam about the fire, or fighting the fire, or being on call for the fire, or in fact *anything* to do with fire. It used to be that it would have been me going with Eric, keeping people safe, taking on Mother Nature and hoping that we would win. I missed the danger, and the camaraderie, and the purpose I'd had in life, and abruptly I felt like my strings had been cut. I sat on the bench, the phantom pains and the real pain tugging at me and leaving my chest tight. I didn't want to talk about the fires, and I didn't want to be asked to elaborate about how I knew, or why I felt the icy dread trickle through me or the spike of adrenaline that left me shaky, so I did what I did best—handed over enough information to appease the listener and then changed the subject—something I'd gotten very good at since the accident.

I hated that I was being so fucking miserable, because he was seeing a new side to me, but how else was I going to handle my messy thoughts. Just when I thought I'd made progress, I was destroying everything.

"The Low Pass fire could shift direction with the wind change, Eric's on call, he had to leave. So what was your question about the construction company again?"

Cam appeared confused at my abrupt change of subject for a moment, then pulled himself back to the paperwork. So much for any connection we might have had, because he wasn't going to want to kiss my moody pouty face right now.

Pull yourself together, idiot.

The plans detailed two levels, the bottom one having a new kitchen layout with an extra area walled off as a quiet space and another for arts and crafts. On the top floor were two more bedrooms, plus an extra bathroom, and the whole thing would make the currently L-shaped house into more of a U. The entire project might have appeared daunting, but we had blueprints to work from, and I knew how to read them mostly, and all the labor was free.

I just liked having something I could achieve. That was all.

Cam hmm'd and then anchored the moving plans with his phone on one side, his hand on the other. He had strong hands, and my neck tingled from the reminder of how he'd helped with the knots in my back. He hadn't even moved my T-shirt out of the way, yet I had a ghost memory of him as if he'd run his fingers over my bare skin.

He hmm'd again, and I snapped back to what he was hmm'ing about. "Well, they had a clear plan, the foundations were dug and filled, so what happened?"

Oh that? I could answer that one as best I could.

"I don't know for sure, but I assume they'd offered to do the work at a low price as a way of giving back, but when the chance of work came up that actually put food on the table, they left. It happens." I could've made a long list of projects at Ringwood that were half done, or plans that hadn't been implemented. The place relied on volunteer work, and no doubt even though he was hiding out, Cam would've been the next person to leave as soon as a more lucrative offer came to his attention.

But that would mean him leaving the house, and I didn't want him to go. Not yet. Not until we'd found out where *us* was going.

"So you rely mainly on volunteers?"

"Yeah, we have a pool of people, Eric and the guys at Engine sixty-three is one group, although this time of year they're exhausted and on call and mostly not available. Then there's Leo and his cop friends, all of whom are just as pushed at the moment, working crime, and backing up on the fires, and doing all the other cop-type things that keep them away. And of course I have Sean, but he and his medical teams deal with the fallout from everything, fires, crime, and just the everyday stuff. I really should think about looking for volunteers outside my first responder friends."

"I'm going to try very hard not to go anywhere until this is finished," he promised with passionate commitment, then he pulled the plans around, and placed stones on the corners to stop them moving, before putting my list front and center. He pointed at the far corner. "Can you tell me more about what the planner wanted to achieve in all of this?"

"Two floors, bedrooms with shower rooms, private areas, and the biggie is the kitchen."

"I meant, can you give me an idea of what we're trying to achieve." He tapped the plans. "There's no door between the existing buildings and this extension, which makes me think they want a separate entrance, is there a reason for that? Does the entrance need complete privacy? Is it for the more vulnerable kids who need isolation and peace for some reason? Or is it maybe for the older kids to start working on their independence? Or a new project completely from what is here already?"

I blinked at him. That was one hell of a long list of questions. "The concept is a space for the older kids…" I took a step closer, ignoring the pain in my hip, and leaned on the table. "Counseling, quiet spaces, independence skills, medical support."

"So, we're talking privacy, but with a community feel as well."

"Yeah."

More by luck than judgment I ended up close enough to Cam as he talked about raising walls that I could stare at his brown eyes without coming off as creepy. Cam was gorgeous, six feet of sexy hotness, with an ageless face and a gentle smile, and I knew what it was like to kiss him, taste him, to want to get naked with him. He was tired today, gray smudges under his eyes, but the rest of him was constructor-gorgeous, in the way he filled the jeans and the T-shirt. Hell, he even made a hard hat look sexy. Plus his grip on project progress was steady and perceptive. I shouldn't have been staring at him as if he was dinner and I was starving, because that was dangerous.

"I want to apologize," I blurted.

He side-eyed me. "What for?"

"If I was off before. It's just that Eric can go over the top with worry sometimes, blames himself… never mind that, I just wanted to apologize before you think I'm unhappy you're here." My hand brushed his and something passed between us as we stared at each other. It was only a gusty blast of wind that snapped the connection.

"It's okay."

He smiled at me, then bit his lip as he stared at the plans. I was transfixed by the way he frowned, and how his brown eyes widened and then narrowed as he contemplated what he had in front of him. He was so serious and all I wanted to do was reach out and cradle his face to kiss him.

"There need to be more small spaces, with windows, so a kid can sit in peace but also not feel like there was no way out, like…" he glanced over at Finn who was buried in his book. "… a den," he finished. "If we move this door here," he made some marks on the plans, "we can form three separate quiet spaces, put in some shelves, get some soft chairs or bean bags, a socket for chargers, I don't know, but it sounds like the kind of place a teenager might like?"

"You're already focusing on that kind of level? Shouldn't we get the work on having the structure done first?" I was confused, but also mesmerized by the way he was looking at the building plans—as if he was invested in what we were trying to do, and not just some ad hoc builder who was filling his spare time.

He glanced up at me and the thoughtful gaze was replaced by a glimmer of excitement. Clearly, he loved talking about this kind of thing, and I couldn't take my gaze off his expression-rich features. He smiled a lot as he talked, his eyes sparking with enthusiasm, and he used his hands to underscore his points. "It's important at any stage to think about purpose at the same time as form. Imagine we read from these plans and made cupboards in all these spaces and we were lazy and just did what the architect thought would suit the staff for storage. I mean, who *needs* storage when I can create a space with a window that means the area floods with natural light and where a child can sit and think about everything. Like a den, a special secret place for a kid where the world can't reach them."

He was so impassioned, and I stared at him, willing him to carry on talking, but he must have noticed me staring, and I had my mouth open, so he'd assume I wasn't getting any of it, but I did get it, and he was right. He dipped his gaze and I could see he was embarrassed.

"That's a cool idea," I encouraged him.

"I'm getting ahead of myself as usual, who is the person I should be talking to if I want to make changes?"

He was asking me? "Uh, we have approval for the structure, I guess what we do with a closet, if it needs a window then there will be planning implications." He frowned then scribbled a note at the end of my list.

"I'll get onto it," Cam said.

I couldn't help the tug of disappointment that this was actually my job, or at least my area of responsibility until Cam had arrived. It was just one more thing I was losing control over, and it wasn't Cam's fault, but I hurt from sitting on the hard bench, I hurt when I was standing, and my normal meds weren't kicking in. I didn't want to have to pull out the big guns, the Vicodin left me spaced-out, and Cam needed me to pass over all the information I had on this project, but if I didn't take them then by the time we were done I wouldn't be able to walk.

He stepped away to check out the construction and I took the time to pop the pills as secretively as I could, aware that Finn was watching me.

"Do you have another headache?" he asked, and I nodded as I screwed the lid back on and pocketed the pills. "Dad says that if you close your eyes and try to relax all your muscles then you can get rid of headaches without taking tablets."

"It's a bad headache," I lied. It was crippling, breath-stealing pain in my ribs, and it radiated down my arm as far as my elbow. "Anyway, what are you studying first?"

"Algebra." He leaned toward me and whispered. "Who even uses algebra?"

I could tell him a hundred ways I used algebra, from splitting my burned recipes for four into sad little meals for one, or working out MPG in my car, but I recalled the days of math lessons, and being his age, and not understanding *why* I had to learn any of it.

"Yeah," I wasn't agreeing, but I wasn't disagreeing, and he could take that single word any way he wanted it.

"Three bananas and three bananas and two apples and one apple is nine, right? I mean I know that three-plus-three-plus-two-plus-one is nine, I'm not stupid, but Dad keeps marking it as wrong." He threw a glance of frustration at his dad, and drew a big nine in his notebook, followed by a ton of exclamation marks that made his book seem as though it had been attacked by ants carrying sticks. "He's gonna make me do math for hours and hours every day, I just know it."

"Actually, in algebra, you can't mix apples and bananas," I murmured, and he side-eyed me.

"Huh?"

"Yeah, actually the whole point of algebra is to collect same things into groups to make sense of them." I wasn't talking on his level, I could see that in his confused gaze. "So, you count the bananas as one thing, and the apples as another. So the answer can only ever be six bananas and three apples. It won't ever be nine."

He raised an eyebrow and I could see the way he was

studying me, as if he was attempting to measure the truth of my statement.

"Dad never said that." He stared at his dad's back. "I bet he doesn't even know that. So for real it's not nine?"

"For real." All I could think was wait until he had to deal with As and Bs instead of apples and bananas, it would blow his mind.

"Hmmm." He found an eraser and rubbed out the original answer, plus the exclamation marks, and then wrote in *6 bananas* and *3 apples*. "I don't get it," he admitted.

I threw him a smile. "You will one day."

He let out a noise that was half snort of disbelief and half sigh of annoyance. "Dad keeps saying I'll understand everything one day," he said softly.

Cam was heading back, which stopped Finn talking, and the meds weren't softening any of my pain yet. If he asked me anything else I'd have to make explain—lie to him—and just the thought of yet another weak-assed excuse made me feel sad, confused, and pissed.

Everything hurts so much.

He moved so quickly I didn't have time to say a thing, and then he was behind me, his hands working their magic on my neck and upper back, and I began to melt as I had the last time. If only this would lead to another kiss I'd have been in heaven, but Finn was *right there.*

"How are you getting on, Finn?" Cam asked as he worked on the tight muscles.

"Is the answer six bananas and three apples?"

"It is."

"I don't get it," Finn muttered, but I wasn't paying

attention to their banter about how Cam didn't really get it either, and how he'd prefer making a fruit salad, because Cam had magic hands, and with the meds kicking in as well, I was just about ready to fall off the bench and sleep on the ground. Maybe if that happened then Cam could kiss me awake.

"I need to find a way to keep you," I thought, or said, because he chuckled, and I never wanted to kiss him more than I did at that moment.

And goddamn it but it was the sexiest chuckle I've ever heard.

Chapter Seventeen

Cam

TONIGHT WAS the first night being home that I hadn't fallen asleep on the sofa. I was exhausted, juggling the physical work on site, for the most part on my own, plus the homeschooling. At least I hadn't had to drag Finn with me every day, because Adam stayed at home for much of the week, and I'd gotten to the point where I felt okay leaving Finn with him. Adam was beginning to get more involved in the homeschooling, and when he covered some of the more intricate parts of the grade-five curriculum, I could have kissed him.

The fact of the matter was, I could have kissed him every time I saw him for a ton of reasons. Maybe because he was cute, or disheveled, or I had my hands on him, massaging knots, or it could have been when we sat and watched kids' movies with, or without, Finn. The inevitability of kissing him was in direct proportion to me trying to avoid situations where it could occur.

Like, who knew that watching Adam wiping down the counters was sexy?

He made everything he did seem sexy, and I felt a mix of lust and admiration that swirled inside me and sucked me down to a place where all I could imagine was touching him. Today was a day off, and it was also the day we met his family for the first time. This was officially our fifth Saturday living with Adam, and I couldn't say no again, not when he asked me to go with such huge puppy dog eyes, nor when his sister Erin and her daughter ganged up on me and insisted.

I could have said no, focusing on not wanting to muddy the waters of our relationship, but it was Adam's dad's sixtieth birthday, which meant it would be an event I could hide away at. Or at least that was how I thought it would go, but the minute I stepped into the sprawling ranch-style house I was dragged into the Williams family chaos. I was thankful when his mom guided me into the kitchen with a comment about prepping vegetables, which turned out to be a thin ruse to quiz me on everything from Finn right through to Adam. Finn came with me, sitting on a stool close by my side as I chopped carrots about as awkwardly as a person could, while trying to field the quick-fire questions. I didn't know that before the rest of the extended family arrived, plus friends, there would be a more intimate dinner—if ten adults plus kids could be called intimate, and I think it put me on the back foot, because the questions just rolled right at me and I didn't have time to get out of their way.

"How is Adam doing?"

"I don't—"

"We worried about him, all alone in that house until you arrived. Bless you for being company for him. So how are you getting on with him and the migraines?"

"Well, I—"

"They're horrible aren't they. Debilitating. But it's like no one in this family appreciates that I stay up all night overthinking for them. You understand that as a dad, right?"

"Well, yeah, I—"

"It's nice to see Adam smiling though."

That was how it went on. I wasn't actually sure my purpose was to answer questions, but to listen to Adam's mom explain what she felt about everything. She didn't seem to be doing it with any kind of malice, her questions held an edge of relief that maybe I would've been able to stop if she said anything that wasn't right. When she asked about his cane, she answered her own question, and when I nodded at her assumption he was doing okay, she stopped cooking for a moment and let out a sigh.

The break gave me a chance to talk to Finn who nibbled on raw carrot and swung his legs on the stool. I knew Adam had a ton of nieces and nephews, Charlie plus five other girls, and two boys, and the noise level in the game room was intense. Too loud for Finn, it seemed.

"You doing okay there?" I asked, and scooted another piece of carrot his way. He caught it and nibbled on the edge as he nodded that yes, he was fine. I'd always wanted a ton of kids, or two at least, even thought about another adoption, or in the first flush of love with Graeme, maybe even surrogacy, but none of that was ever going to happen. Graeme hadn't had the capacity for loving anyone other than himself, although he'd put on a good enough show to get me to fall for him.

"Yeah," he offered after a moment.

"You want to go and be with the kids?" I asked.

"Nope."

"You might have fun."

He glanced up at me with a serious expression I'd grown used to. "But who would look after you, Dad?"

My heart cracked, and every sorrowful thought that I held back flooded me so fast that I dropped the knife I'd been using.

"It's okay," Adam said with a laugh from behind me, laying an arm over my shoulder. "I'll keep an eye on him for you. Go find Charlie."

I could have shrugged Adam off, but Finn's serious expression shifted in a moment, and he wrinkled his nose and then smiled.

"Cool," he announced, and hopped down off the stool, scampering around me and Adam, snagging another piece of carrot and then darting through the door where the kids were congregated. For the longest time I didn't move, frozen in place and waiting for the earth to open and swallow me whole.

"He loves you so much," Adam's mom murmured, and pressed a hand to my arm, and I came back to awareness with Adam's arm still over my shoulder. He was my strength at the moment, and I leaned into him.

"Shit," I muttered, and turned in his arms, taking his silent support and letting him hug me.

"I need to check on the..." His mom left us in the kitchen, and the hug lasted so long that I realized it couldn't have been good for Adam to be standing like that. I eased us back until he was by a stool, then moved a little so I could help him sit, and not once did I let him go. He stroked the length of my spine with a consistent rhythm that lulled me, and stopped the grief from taking hold of my heart, and then he eased away and cradled my face, kissing me with a whisper of a smile.

"Are you okay?" he asked.

I stared into his beautiful green eyes, and lost sense of where I was. I rested my hands on his hips, and closed my eyes, inhaling the scent of him and thinking I'd never smelled anything so wonderful. "I'm good," I lied.

He caressed my face, ran his hands over my shoulders, and I desperately wanted to sink into his hold, if only to give in and let someone look after me. He kissed me deeply, and I melted into everything that the kiss promised.

"I doubt you're *good* at all," he murmured against my lips. "How about we go and *really* meet my idiot siblings, and you can help me by stopping them from asking all kinds of stupid questions about my future. How about that? You want to be my hero?"

Did he know how much he'd done for me? I wasn't anyone's hero, but he was mine. I straightened back and away from him, and helped him down from the stool without even realizing it, until once more we stood near each other. This could be the moment we kissed—right after he'd taken my world and clicked it back on its axis so it could spin for the rest of the day and I could be strong.

"I know it's the wrong time, but I could fall for you," I blurted.

He blinked, then gave me a soft, secretive smile. "Well, that's a good thing. A *very* good thing."

We kissed again, in his parents' kitchen, as if some invisible thread pulled us together. The kiss was soft, a gentle touch of our lips, and I closed my eyes at the intensity of need that washed over me and burned into my soul. Only when the kisses fortified me was I ready to try to be his hero. Of course, the minute we walked into the main sitting room, his mom threw me a glance filled with compassion, one of his brothers sniggered, his sister beamed the widest grin, and the other brother was sharing confused looks with everyone. Not to mention Adam's dad raised an eyebrow at us and smirked.

Then I realized it was because we were holding hands.

The rest of dinner was a study in chaos, and I loved every minute of it, bantering with Saul about baseball, arguing with Luke over the best brand of olive oil, and putting up with a myriad of questions from Erin who was determined to wheedle my entire family history from me. Adam was quieter around his siblings, but he didn't stop smiling, so I guess it was just what he felt happy doing. They quizzed him about a career, and that was the only time he tensed, but for the most part he seemed relaxed and happy.

I didn't know how much they'd been told about my time in New York, but buoyed by the love in the room, I wasn't unhappy to know that Saul had googled me and announced that it was all bullshit. I'm not sure what he meant by that, but I didn't get to ask because Finn, Charlie, and Jax, the oldest of the cousins, decided that they wanted to build a den in the backyard, and could they go. Why in hell's name did I decide that was a good moment to get emotional I didn't know. Maybe it was relief that Finn was interested in going out and doing kid-type stuff, or that he was smiling, but whatever it was, I sought Adam's hand under the table and held on hard, catching his mom's gaze, and offering her a rueful smile.

"You never stop worrying about them," she said as soon as they were gone with the rest of the cousins following. "Even when they're heading for forty."

"Thanks for that, Mom," Saul muttered, and grumped about age and wisdom.

Every single adult descended on the kitchen to help clean up. Adam and I were on boxing duty, working on leftovers that would be taken home by various family members. I just hoped that the dessert option of a sinfully rich tiramisu was going to be heading back with us.

"We get first dibs on dessert," Adam mumbled around a mouthful of cream he'd scooped up from the rim of the now empty bowl. I couldn't help myself, no one was looking our way, so I kissed him, my tongue darting out to taste the cream. Then I stepped back because, hell, that was overstepping, right?

"Break it up," Erin teased before snagging the empty bowl and heading back to the sink.

It shouldn't have worked with so many people in such a tight space, but somehow it did and amidst the chaos everything was being cleared, and then it was time for the rest of the family to arrive, and this time the entire event with extended family, all ended up in the yard, and the cake was enormous.

By the time we left it was nine, the kids had subsided

into silence, sprawled around the television watching a movie and eating whatever snacks remained. Finn made it to the truck, climbing into the seat and nearly falling back down, buckling himself in and yawning. I was pleased that tomorrow was Sunday and we all got to sit around and do nothing because I was exhausted from so much talking, and listening, and joking.

"I'm sorry, but could I get some help?" Adam hovered at the passenger door, leaning on his cane. He looked tired, but there were none of the telltale signs of a headache, and he was smiling at me. The truck was high up, and between us, with my hands on his ass—thank you very much—he was up there, and he snorted a laugh as I got in a final squeeze.

Something had changed today. I wasn't shoving him away, or closing doors, I was wondering what he tasted like, and what it might be like to see him under me, or over me.

What would it hurt to have sex with no pesky emotions involved? He knew I was leaving, and both of us deserved some relief from our lives. Just sex. That was all.

"Ready to go home?" I called back to Finn, but when I heard nothing I glanced at my son. He was already asleep, slumped against the door. "Might have to carry him in," I said, wondering how much longer he would allow me to hold him when he was sleeping. I loved those moments when he curled next to me on the sofa and slept on me, and I would miss it when he was too old to sit with his dad.

"You might have to carry me in as well," Adam murmured.

I turned back to him. "Are you okay?" I couldn't stop

the worry that filtered into my words, and I kicked myself when his smile dimmed a little. He'd been flirting and I'd shoved my feet right into my mouth. I leaned over and kissed him back into that needy flirty space. "I can carry you too," I whispered against his lips, and there was a heated promise in my words that he picked up on, because the shadows slipped away.

"I'll hold you to that."

It didn't surprise me when, not that far into our journey he fell asleep as well, so it was just me and a soft rock station for company, my son sleeping in the back, my... friend... sleeping next to me. The roads were quiet, only me and a couple of other cars in my lane, and I lost myself in humming to an old ACDC song, indicating to avoid a broken-down truck, slowing as I passed a car that had pulled out, and for a second when I looked over I had to take a second glance.

The white-haired man driving, staring back at me, looked like Simon Frederickson, but before I could check he'd accelerated away, passing my turnoff.

I'm seeing things. Why would Simon Frederickson be on the same road as me, in San Diego, at this random time of the night?

I'm seeing ghosts again.

I knew I was stressing about things that I had no control over, a frustrating lack of progress on the divorce, plus a small article about the case in *The Washington Post* had a ton of hateful comments attached to it. People wanted to know where I was hiding with all of Graeme's money. Some said they'd find me. Others said I would get what I deserved.

I can't let it hurt me. Or Finn.

Today had been hard on Finn, meeting a family, making friends, taking a step in a new direction. I hadn't realized how much responsibility he was taking on for me, and that made me feel like shit. I knew he was protective, but to stay in the kitchen with me when he could have gone and played with the other kids, was eye-opening. I'd been naïve to think that I was being strong for both of us when he was invested in looking after me.

Things were going to change. Finish this job. Get Finn caught up on missed schooling. Have a no-strings affair. Stop imagining people from New York had tracked me there. Then find this mythical ranch in Montana where Finn and I could live in peace.

Simple.

Chapter Eighteen

Adam

I woke when the truck pulled onto the drive, the familiarity of turns and bumps pulling me out of sleep. At first I couldn't make sense of things, the remnants of the promised headache that had started at the barbecue were enough to make me feel confused and out of sorts. Not to mention the intensity of that kiss in the kitchen which had destroyed me from inside out.

"Hang on," Cam ordered me, then carried Finn inside, reappearing a few minutes later and opening the passenger door, holding out his arms to help me down. I moved enough to know that my back was paying me back big time for ignoring it today.

I shouldn't have pushed so hard, but I wanted to be by Cam. I wanted to show I wasn't completely broken, and maybe look a bit sexy.

Yeah right. I left sexy under a concrete bridge over a year ago.

"Okay?" Cam asked, and moved closer, a concerned frown creasing his forehead.

"Of course," I reassured him and even added a smirk, which I hoped wasn't more of a grimace. He helped me down, and as soon as my feet touched the ground I knew I was heading for a bad night. We headed for the house, but it was slow going, and only when he'd taken the boxes from the car and the front door shut, did I breathe a sigh of relief.

"Finn is out for the night," Cam explained as he piled the containers into the refrigerator, pulling out two bottled waters, and placing them on the counter. Was he telling me that to suggest that we had time to kiss, or flirt some more? I wished I had the energy.

"Great." I picked up the bottle, but it slipped through my fingers and fell to the floor because I had misjudged how much pressure I needed to hold the damn thing. Brain misfires like this happened sometimes, and I was frustrated, because I was exhausted and *had* been horny, and wanted to be normal so I could have more kisses. "Fuck, shit, fucking shit," I yelled at the offending bottle as it rolled under a stool where I would never be able to reach it.

Silence.

Cam stared at me, then crouched to pick up the bottle. "It's okay," he said.

"No, it's not," I snapped, and then leaned on the counter and gave up trying to stand upright. I might as well give up trying to look sexy or flirty when all I wanted to do was go to bed and do fuck all except take meds and attempt to sleep. How had it come to this, why had I gone under that bridge, why did I let it happen to me? Why did I have to be a hero? The darkness tugged me under and then he was there, at my side, stroking my hair.

"Adam, you didn't let anything *happen* to you," he said.

God help me, had I said all of that out loud?

"Let's get you upstairs. Do you need meds?"

"In my room." I was mortified, exhausted, drained, and all I needed was water and I could close the door on today, and the rest of my goddamned life.

"Come on then." He put a shoulder under my arm, and while there was no way he could carry me to bed the way he had Finn, he supported me up every single stair and took me to my bedroom, digging in the medicine box I pointed to. He found the painkillers, shook two into my hand and offered me the water he'd shoved into the pocket of his jeans. As he sat next to me on the bed I wanted to make a joke, I felt the urge to say something sexy, or snarky, anything to not end this day, but there was nothing left in me to pull out.

"Night," I murmured, but he didn't move even though I'd dismissed him.

"No goodnight kiss?" he teased as he stroked my hair.

I moved. "Yeah right," I sighed, and couldn't breathe as pain shot from the base of my spine, down into my right leg, and I yelped. Fucking pain.

"Okay then, we'll leave the kisses for tomorrow. Lie down and I'll make you feel good," he was teasing again, but my tight control broke.

"I can't fuck!" I snapped.

"Shhh," he said with urgency, and glanced behind him

as if he expected Finn to be standing there. Well fuck him and his sexy eyes and his assumption that he could *make me feel good.* "I never said anything about…" He scrubbed his eyes. " Let me get your clothes off."

I wanted to argue, rail at him, tell him to stop, but all too soon I was naked except for my jersey boxers, and he was bound to see the snake of scar tissue that ran from my shoulder to near the middle of my back. Another inch to the center and I would have been paralyzed by the rebar—I needed to be thankful for small mercies, or at least that is what they told me in rehab. I'd wanted to kill anyone who'd said that back then. Sometimes I still felt that way.

"Now what?" I demanded, because I'd rather he got angry at me and left than to see him staring at me in shock.

"Lie down," he encouraged me, and helped me to get comfortable. The meds hadn't kicked in yet, but I must have missed him finding lotion. "My hands might feel cold," he warned, and then he was massaging the muscles that were tight with pain. I shifted to bury my face in the pillow, swallowing the hurt when all I wanted to do was get him to stop. He pressed and smoothed slowly, and something began to shift, between him and the meds the tension was easing. Not that he had magic hands for real, nor that the meds were strong enough to fix everything, but I could feel myself relax. He ran his hands from my shoulders to the base of my spine, working each tiny knot, staying away from the scar, as far as I could feel. Although the sensation of warmth spread everywhere, and I didn't know which way was up as he pressed kisses to my skin, and when I turned my face from the pillow, he would kiss my lips, or my nose every so often.

"Did you know you have a million freckles?" he asked as he kissed a trail from my mouth to my shoulder.

"Mmmm," I replied, which was the absolute limit of what I could say. I felt disconnected, and loose, and so tired.

"I could kiss a freckle every second and still be here in a hundred years," he whispered, and kissed a little lower, his hands still moving. "And all this pale skin, we'd look so good together in bed, I can imagine licking you and sucking, leaving tiny marks against the freckles."

I shifted a little, because that feeling of need returned. It wasn't an inferno, but it was a bright spark in the pain, and even though I wasn't capable of a damn thing, he was taking the time to love my freckles, and for that he got the win.

I wanted him to do more.

I wasn't sure my body was capable.

"It's been a long day," he murmured, and pressed yet more kisses, chuckling when I squirmed to get comfortable. Despite the pain and the meds, my cock was showing way more interest in some action than my body could ever deliver on.

"Too long," I whispered back. "I'm sorry."

"Hang on." I felt the bed move as he got up, and then the subtle shift in air as he left the room, and even though I wanted to be disappointed, I knew I had a tough hour or so of my body unknotting itself and I wanted to be alone. I was not surprised he left, because the snake of scarring, even though they'd tried to keep it minimal, was enough of a reminder of what had happened to scare me, let alone anyone else.

"It's okay," I told the empty room, and moved to get more comfortable, already missing Cam's hands on me.

"Back." Cam climbed back on the bed, only this time he lay next to me, and rolled onto his side so we were facing each other. "Just wanted to check on Finn, he's dead to the world."

"It's been a busy day," I offered after a short silence, because I genuinely thought he was there to talk to me, and that he wasn't going anywhere. Selfishly I wanted him there, and when he reached out and smoothed a warm path on my back I wanted him touching me as well.

"Luke talked to me, when you were with the kids in the yard."

"Luke? Whatever he said, he's an asshole big brother who needs me to be well enough to take him down," I snarked, although I didn't meant it. Luke was the idiot in our family, the joker, the one who kept the rest of us sane. It was a standing joke that we were all shocked he'd managed to snag Melanie and then managed to keep her, and not only that was now dad to three kids. A good dad.

"He said I should ask you what happened that day, so I can properly know you."

"Why would he say that?"

Cam chuckled and leaned over so he was even closer to me and I could stare into his eyes.

The accident had been the end of things for me. I was never going to pass physicals to get back on the engine, not in my wildest imagination, not even if there was a freaking miracle that magically fixed my back. Battalion Chief Emmet Lewis had explained my options and aside from desk work, which I would have to reapply for after a while, there was nothing for me. He hadn't been telling me my options as my friend, even though I respected him, and he considered me a good firefighter, I'd been the one to fuck up. He'd been blunt in his assessment of what the shape of the rest of my life might look like.

"He asked me how I was," I began, and realized I'd started in the middle of a conversation. A breeze moved the drapes, and Cam pulled the covers over me. Just that small thoughtful caring touch had me closing my eyes tight and counting down from ten. "Sorry, I was thinking about the final meeting with Chief Lewis."

"Your boss?"

"Yeah. The one who had to give me the bad news and when he asked me the polite stuff, y'know, how was I and all that?"

"Yeah?"

"I had to be honest, and I told him I was about as good as I can be considering everything had changed. He understood where I was coming from, and then I summarized it for him, which I could only do because I'd had hours of therapy. I said that there was a before in my life and now I lived in the after. I remember he nodded at me, and I recall feeling my counselor would be proud." I huffed a laugh. "I'd seen so many doctors, surgeons, shrinks, that I knew what answers to give, and even though I'd raged at them all…"

"You ended up thinking you had to look at everything in black and white."

That was more insightful than I'd expected, and I gave him a tight smile. "So he said to me that he needed to understand that final day. Even with the reports in front of him, even with all the evidence, he still had to get me to repeat everything and for the first time I actually clinically examined it all." Pain stabbed my chest, a phantom reminder of the recklessness that had destroyed my career and nearly taken my life. "Why didn't these supposed *experts* talk to each other when they all wrote the shit down? Why did I have to tell people the same fucking tragedy of a story all the time?"

"You don't have to tell me."

God knows I wanted to take that and run, but there was so much understanding in his gaze, and he'd seen his own shit, made decisions that maybe he regretted as well, and I wanted him to see the real me. I knew the meds were helping loosen my tongue, but he couldn't know that, and so I wondered exactly where to start because I expected Cam to judge me. I knew it was the entire point of me telling him, and what Luke had meant about knowing me.

"I want to."

"Do you need to sleep?"

"I won't, not for a while. But you don't have to stay."

He snuggled even closer, and I felt safe and protected.

"I'm not going anywhere."

"Engine sixty-three was called out to a car wreck. A loaded semi had aquaplaned on diesel in the rain, and went sideways into a bridge support. The driver was out and assessed as ambulatory, able to walk, you know."

He smiled again. "I know what it means."

"Sorry." I was so tired even if the remainder of the memory was a sharp knife to the heart. "A Lexus collided with the truck, impacting the damaged bridge support and embedded in it, trunk-first. The mom was easy to get out, and once we had her free our lieutenant said we should hold back because the bridge was unstable." The cold, hard fact was that the concrete had been under strain and the rebar was protruding at crazy angles around the car.

I left out that the mom had been hysterical with fear; her family was in the Lexus, a husband, a kid. I didn't mention that Eric had had to hold the mom back even as he assessed the scene with the same practiced eye as the lieutenant. I'd known we had to do something, but everyone around me was being so careful, thoughtful, counting steps and judging who should live or die, as the bridge cracked at a crazy angle and two people were trapped in the car. One of them a kid.

"The engine descended on impact as it should have done, likely occurring with the first collision into the back of the truck," I cleared my throat, because I was slipping into acting as if I were giving an official report. "Only, dashboard and plastic snapped and embedded itself into the husband's thigh. He was pinned and losing blood, and the lieutenant ordered Eric and another firefighter to get him out, but it was clear I had to stay with the mom, but the kid was in there, and we could hear him crying."

"Oh shit, Adam, that must have been horrific." He was pale, and I considered he was maybe imagining Finn in a car, and I knew that if it had been Finn, he would have done the same thing as I did if he'd been able to.

I flashed back to the day—Maury, the tall skinny paramedic on scene, the same guy who teased me relentlessly about burning food, had given me that look. *The older male is not good* the look said.

I cleared my throat of the emotion which threatened to strangle me.

"In black and white, the dad was by far the easiest to retrieve. We could hardly see the kid under the crushing weight of concrete and the rebar that pierced the car. But we all knew he was alive, because he was sobbing." A person, any age, trapped in place, and firefighters helpless to get them out, was only one of the many parts of being a first responder that could break even the strongest of people. Or make them stupid.

"We got the dad out." I closed my eyes again, reliving the small win. I knew what was coming next, and could feel the bile rising in me, and the stress pushing and poking at my temples. I should try to stay calm and state facts but the emotions in me were too much to hold in. Unspoken were many things for me to cover.

A month before the accident our company had been at a structure fire in an apartment block, families locked behind doors we couldn't open, and in my nightmares I hear someone pleading for help and hoping they would still shout, because when they went quiet I knew I couldn't help them anymore. I felt a failure that was greater than my own need to live. Eric and I had scratched and kicked at the doors at that fire, wielding axes, pulling at bricks, the O2 in our tanks low, but we hadn't been able to get in. The single positive in any of that horror was that the victims had suffocated from smoke long before the fire reached them. I wasn't going into details of past events that fed into why I'd felt so helpless at the car accident—I was raw with going over and over it, and Cam didn't need to know everything.

"I needed to get in to save the kid, and the lieutenant ordered us to wait for back up, but that bridge wasn't stable and we could hear the crack of concrete, the groan of it. It's sentient. The weight shifted, the crack widened, and the car was being crushed even further. The noise was deafening, and I don't mean like a stadium after a touchdown, this was like the earth was opening up and swallowing us whole."

Cam's eyes were bright with unshed tears, and I fought my impulse to tell him he didn't need to know anything else, and that he should go.

I cleared my throat. "When the dust settled from the latest shift in the road support, the kid had stopped crying. I could see a narrow point of ingress, I didn't even think. I didn't demand backup, I didn't run things up a chain of command. I was the smallest on the team, but even with only being five-ten it wasn't easy to get in." My shoulder ached, sense memory of metal tearing through my gear. "I shoved off my jacket, the helmet, and I got far enough in that the kid could see me. He was crying, but not screaming or loud, just staring at me wide-eyed with silent tears, and a cloud of dust was all around us. I couldn't breathe, all I could think was that I needed to get him out."

"Adam, shit—"

"I reassured the child. Ben. I reassured Ben. He reached out a tiny hand, which I grasped. At least the straps holding him into his seat had been easy to undo, and I gripped him, turned when I got caught trying to back out, shoving the kid out through the small hole, watching as he got stuck."

"But you did get him out."

"I did. We did. The lieutenant was there, Eric and the guys stretching in for us like the kid had been trying to reach me. They had hold of me, they pulled but I was stuck and the car shifted. I braced myself as the rebar came dangerously close, gave the kid enough time to get free. Finally he tumbled out, popping out like the cork from a champagne bottle. I scrambled to follow, the guys tugging, and I felt a hundred feet tall. I'd given the kid a new chance at life. He'd be okay. And then the car shifted." *The concrete, the car, my entire fucking world.* "I don't remember anything else. The rebar pierced my side, close to my spine, the weight of the concrete had crushed my shoulder. I had operations, therapy, talked it out, hugged it out..." *Time to look for something else. Stay positive. There is light around each corner, and new opportunities behind every door. Blah blah, ad infinitum, fucking hell.*

"I'm so sorry," Cam whispered, and gathered me close without moving me too much. I buried my face in his hair.

"You know what the chief said to me? It's kind of funny really." I eased back so Cam could hear properly. "He said that if it was any consolation he would have done exactly what I did. It was possibly the most honest thing I heard in all of it. But it wasn't going to change a single thing. Ben visited with his parents. They'd moved away, back to the mom's family in Ohio, but they came to see me before they left. I was Ben's hero apparently." I snorted. "Some fucking hero."

I waited for him to use the H-word as well, but he didn't. Instead he slid even closer so he could kiss me, and then he smiled. "I would have done the same thing, for what it's worth. And for Ben's mom and dad, for Finn and other kids like him? Thank you."

Well, that was new. I really wanted to kiss him, hard, messy, and to try to connect, but the meds had finally done their work and I was sleepy and my thoughts uncoordinated.

"You have to know I really want to make love with you, but the pain is so bad. I wish I could even think about sex without it hurting," I murmured, and that was my last conscious thought.

Chapter Nineteen

Cam

I COULDN'T SLEEP, thanks to a mix of the powerful emotion in Adam's words, plus not being able to get Finn being in danger out of my head. I hadn't been lying when I'd said I would have done the same thing. As a civilian I would have become a have-a-go hero, but for Adam it had meant losing everything.

"I wish I could even think about sex."

Me too. It had been a very long time since I'd been in any kind of headspace where I wanted to sleep with anyone—*sleep* being the misnomer when what I *really* wanted to do was have sex.

Any kind of sex I could get with Adam, who desperately wanted the same thing. Could we be intimate? Was it even something we wanted to do?

Graeme and I had stopped any kind of intimacy long before the night everything had fallen apart. So, yeah, no sex, and I had never betrayed our marriage—never wanted to. And there it was, my thoughts spinning out of control to the point where I accepted I was a useless dad, a terrible husband, naïve…

I eased away from Adam, who huffed in his sleep and shifted a little, but didn't wake. In the soft light of the lamp I could make out the scars on his back, pathways of pain that tracked from his shoulder to his spine, but I also saw every one of the freckles scattered over his pale skin. His dark red hair was bright against the white pillows and I knew how beautiful his green eyes were. All of him was perfect.

What now? I'd put myself into a spiral where I wouldn't sleep, so I rolled off the bed, and padded out to the hallway, checking on Finn and going in to fix the cover over him. Ever since he'd been tiny he had been a sleeper who moved around a great deal, losing the covers, ending up hanging off the edge of his bed, and I'd grown used to tucking him back in, and kissing his head. Then I had nothing else to do, and I didn't want to go to bed, which left going downstairs and making a hot chocolate. I took it out to the patio into the cooler night air and sat back to stare at the stars. There was light pollution here, the same as anywhere there was any concentration of habitation, but it was less so than New York, although I could imagine the haze of smoke from far-off fires and how hard it must be for Eric, and how that was what Adam used to do.

I couldn't imagine him in danger again, wanted to keep him close and look after him as best I could.

Just for the rest of the six months. I'm not staying here.

But what if we did stay? What if we didn't leave San Diego? I owed Nick a visit, if only to talk about repaying him for whatever I could. The homeschooling was good, I felt safe here with Adam, as if this could be some kind of new normal. If I tried hard enough I could forget all about Graeme and what he'd done, because there were no journalists at the door, no one asking me what I'd known, or what I thought. There had been more articles, but not one of them mentioned Finn and I being in San Diego—we were safe here.

I could sneak in kisses and maybe even more.

Inspired, I fired up my laptop, and began to research broad keywords about experiencing pain in sex. At first I found a ton of sites where pain was the objective, so I amended it to chronic pain, sex, and various other keywords until I found a website that was a lot more. The article on the site went straight into explaining about anxiety, and anticipation, and the cycle of pain, and before I knew it I was sucked into clicking all over the place searching for advice. I knew Adam was anticipating that sex would be painful, but what kind of relationships had he had before? What did I know about him? Did he top? Was he even into anal, or was he all about a hundred other ways to have fun times? He was a former firefighter, all grumbly toppy male, so how would it sit now that he maybe wasn't able to do what he'd done before. I liked to take charge sometimes, only not in the way the first websites I found wanted me to do. Although the idea of restraining Adam so he wouldn't move and hurt himself was appealing in ways I'd never imagined.

What was it that made Adam tick? What made me the person I was, and how could the two mix? Anticipation of pain was a catalyst for anxiety, or so the latest website repeated, along with feelings of not being a real man, or expecting failure as a partner. I clicked on a link for same-sex, and then again on a link about physical limitations. Most of it wasn't applicable, but there were points of insight that gave me my eureka moments. It was okay for Adam to feel conflicted, that was part of him and he was entitled to feel worried, and still feel arousal at the same time. He'd said he got himself off, that when he tensed it hurt, so how could a partner help him in that? First off by not getting frustrated, or to judge, any kind of physical next step was about us as partners, rather than him versus the pain.

"People have internalized the idea that 'real' sex includes penetrative sex," I read out loud, and scared myself. *Idiot.* "It's not all about that," I told the empty room, just to hear my voice again. There was all kinds of sexual intimacy, and sex was whatever felt good, or right. I could carry on kissing and massaging, and I'd have been happy with that because in a way it gave me the escape clause. Adam wanted to take the next step and he was beyond frustrated that it was yet another thing he didn't have control over. So how did I balance both? And was it up to me to help make it happen? Did I want it to happen? I was still married by law, but…

I wanted Adam in bed with me so bad it was an impossible thing that had lodged inside me. I wanted to hear his sighs, and kiss him everywhere, and bite marks of possession, and I wanted it all.

And then I found the link that made everything make sense. Now to make notes for the next time we were alone.

. . .

UNFORTUNATELY, alone time was at a premium, and the next time we were both awake and able to do more than snuggle on the sofa and kiss, it was five days after I'd done all my research and that was five days too long. I had all these ideas of things I wanted to try with Adam, anything to make him feel good, and the more I thought about them the more excited I grew. I'd stopped at the store on the way home from Ringwood to pick up massage oils, lube, extra pillows, and I had moved everything up to my room a handful at a time so as not to seem too suspicious.

"Time for bed?"

Adam straightened from where he'd been loading the dishwasher, and glanced at the time. "It's eight-fifteen."

"I know." I held out a hand. "Let's go."

He eyed my hand as if I was holding a stick of dynamite, and didn't reach out to take it. "What's going on?"

Okay, so he wasn't going to assume I had no ulterior motive and simply trust me, so I stepped into his space and caged him with my arms. Then I kissed him, and as usual he went pliant in my hold, his hands going up to link behind my neck, and he was hard against me.

"Come upstairs with me," I murmured against his lips, and took another kiss, tugging him from where he leaned as we kissed, and then taking a step back toward the kitchen door and bringing him with me. We made it to the stairs, and when we separated so we could take the first step he didn't ask any more questions. I hadn't explained what I was doing yet, but trust was a fragile thing, and I was honored that he'd bestowed it on me. "We're going to take this really slowly."

"I can't." He stopped about half way up, white knuckling the banister, and there was very real fear in his eyes. "I want to be normal, I want to go with you but what if…"

I cradled his face. "What if we just lie together and kiss?"

"Really?"

"That's how this starts, and you control it all."

"I can't do…"

"Come on, let's just enjoy snuggling."

He moved again, and at the top of the stairs he held my hand as I opened Finn's door a crack to check on him. He was dead to the world, clutching Fred-Bear and I loved nothing more than seeing him sleep so in peace. I carried on to Adam's bedroom, shutting the door behind us. For the next few hours I wanted no chance of being disturbed, and I wedged a towel under the door to make opening it difficult but not impossible. Just enough warning, plus I also had dad-ears when it came to Finn, and tonight wasn't about me, it was all about Adam so I intended to stay present and focused at all times.

He caught me to kiss me and I walked backward to the bed, helping him with his T-shirt, until I had my hands on his bare skin, and slid them down to help him out of his shorts, and then his boxers, removing my cut-offs and then taking care when I lowered us onto the bed. He frowned as we fell into the nest of pillows I had created, but didn't stop me as I eased him to his side and made sure every part of him was supported by softness. That was stage one, only I had to look for anything that might cause pain, and I felt around him for so long that he grasped my hand and laid it right over his cock.

"Do you want me to draw you a map?" he asked.

I smirked into another heated kiss, reaching for the massage lotion. It was scent-free, I wanted him to focus on me and my touch, and then I began to massage his neck, kissing him at every moment. At first he attempted to pull me closer, to grind against my thigh, but I stilled him and focused on kissing where I'd pressed, following the same procedure down to his nipple, pulling on the nub then soothing the skin with a kiss, sucking. Each time he moved I soothed him with soft shushes and whispered instructions to stay still. After a while, he stopped moving, and I praised the stillness with soft nibbles and sucks of skin, taking a long time on the 'V' from his hipbone to his groin, my nose bumping his cock just enough to make him hiss, but he didn't move.

I *accidentally* nudged it a few times, and every time his breath hitched I moved away.

"You're beautiful," I said with reverence, concentrating on a freckle near the trail of hair where it began to dip, worrying at the skin with my lips and tongue, and smoothing a hand over his thigh, down to the muscles around his knee, pressing at the knots, until he whimpered and then sighed into the touch.

Chapter Twenty

Adam

CAM WAS KILLING me one freckle at a time and he was so close to my cock, his breath warm puffs against the heated skin.

Please. Just suck me. Lick me. Send me over...

I tensed as my thoughts began to spiral, but he stopped me, pressing a hand to my belly and crawling up until we were face-to-face, kissing me deeply and silencing my fears.

"It's okay," he whispered, "breathe with me."

"Huh?"

"In through your nose and out through the mouth, with me."

"I know how to—"

"Shhh," he said, which was becoming infuriating because he wouldn't touch me.

"Shhh, yourself," I muttered, and he chuckled into yet

another searing kiss, our tongues tangling, my hands burrowing into his hair unbidden, gripping hard.

"In, out," he murmured, and then began another long path from my lips to my throat, and to each nipple. Heat was like an inferno in my groin, and from that alone I could have come, and I tensed again. "In, and out." He came back from another kiss.

This time I listened to him tell me how to be still. Face-to-face, we settled into a rhythm, staring into each other's eyes, and I focused on the dark striations, the patterns of his soul in his irises, and the way his lips parted with each breath. I didn't even register that, as we breathed, he was tracing a path to my cock, but when he began to move his hand, massaging with a light pressure, as we exchanged breaths, I registered a soft whimper and realized it was me.

"Cam," I murmured, and he smiled, but he never stopped looking at me, supporting his weight on one arm, and rolling pressure along my cock, my balls, behind, above, weight on my belly, my thighs, my hips. Holding me still as I tumbled towards the finish.

Press. Release. Press. Release…

Every muscle in my body was relaxed, every breath tuned to his, and when my orgasm hit me, he swallowed my cry, and kissed me through every moment of it, until I was too sensitive to his touch and I whimpered again. I'd never felt anything like this, and he moved against me, staring into my eyes then closing them when he came, his mouth slack and that final exhalation against my skin, it was the most erotic moment of my entire life.

We kissed, and he only left the bed once to grab a cloth

from the bathroom, cleaning me tenderly before setting an alarm on his phone and then climbing back into the nest of pillows, and holding me as close as I was comfortable with. I knew for a fact that in that one moment, I was falling in love with a man who was leaving.

And my heart hurt.

———

AFTER THAT NIGHT THINGS CHANGED. It wasn't so much that we had sex whenever we could, because being together wasn't as easy as fucking each other up against the wall—it was long and slow and gentle and everything I had never expected from anyone for the rest of my life. I had a connection to him that went deeper than skin and bone itself. We made love, and it spilled into my heart and it stole my breath, and it was everything to me. Every night we managed to be together— if I wasn't in pain, if he wasn't exhausted, if Finn didn't have trouble sleeping— it was more beautiful than the previous, and last night I'd come from just the breathing and talking, and from staring into his eyes and imagining his touch.

We didn't have much time for more kissing that week. Alongside time with Finn, Cam did a whole lot of sleeping, but that was due to the hours he was putting in at Ringwood, plus the homeschooling, plus this air of worry and fear he had buzzing around him, and selfishly I missed him being downstairs to talk to, or to make love as completely as we had.

Of course me having alone time meant more space to think about me and my future. I still had the number of the pyrogeographer Megan, and Saul had taken to texting me every day to tell me that I needed to call her. What kind of work did he think I could do? Yes, I was interested in pyrogeography, yes, I wanted to work, but going out onsite would be impossible some days.

Anyway, my first priority was to sort my health out. Right? So every day I texted back with a single word.

Soon. Maybe. Yeah. Okay. Or something like one of those. I wanted to concentrate on alone time with Cam so when it came to today, with Leo, Eric, and Sean volunteering with me, I had this irrational hope that every single one of them would call to say they couldn't make it.

Only of course, all three of them were overachieving alphas, and not one of them had decided to cancel. They were all very serious about their volunteering, and I think it gave them time when they could all be together. Not that they cut me and Cam out, but they were best friends and physically able, Cam was the boss, and I was… *god knows what.*

Lost. Floundering. Aching from my head to my toes. In love with my housemate and his son. Wanting more than I could have.

Getting my friends organized was like herding sheep. Sean had vanished somewhere, Eric was moving lumber around as though he was carrying matchsticks, but not putting it in the right place. And as for Leo? He was being an annoying asshole, and today I wasn't feeling very organized, or in control, or even remotely happy to be there with them. I knew I should've been over the moon to have more help, and I was pleased to see all three of them, but Sean was coming off an eighteen-hour shift, Leo had brought Cap with him, and Eric's eyes were red with exhaustion. Not to mention Cam was going to be onsite soon and I couldn't get the idea of him kissing me out of my head. I wanted to kiss him, and suck him, and love on him, so bad it hurt.

God. I could feel the heat in my face. I'd never had kisses so erotic, so perfect, so fucking sexy, and even now I was getting hard.

"Yo, Red! Leo!" Eric called from the storage shed. "Where do you want this!"

"Stop shouting," I muttered, but Leo heard me and patted my arm, all full of sympathy. I shrugged him off because I didn't need or want compassion, not when there was a chance that Cam might see.

Eric came around the corner, his arms full of lumber the weight of which would have taken a normal man to the floor, and Leo's black lab, Cap, trailing behind with a new-looking length of wood in his mouth. "I thought you would know where this should go."

Of course I knew. That particular marked wood, *A5* through *A9* would form the first of the interior walls that needed to be fixed in place—a job for today—so it should've been piled right where I was standing on the edge of the site.

"Red? Hey, Red? Earth to Adam?"

I snapped back to Eric and his load of lumber, and pointed at a space under the tree. "Sorry," I blurted, and Eric nodded, and there was such compassion in his expression that I regretted letting my mask slip. "Right there is good."

I watched Eric amble away for the next load of wood

and then I noticed a teddy decoration, with trailing hearts fixed on the entrance to the space we were going to be working in, and let out a sigh.

"That needs to come down, Leo," I said, and reached for the decoration that had appeared on the structure while my back was turned.

"No, you can't move him, he's good luck." Leo pushed me a little, but not enough that it would hurt or unbalance me, because he treated me as though I was fragile the same as Eric did. I hated that Leo was so gentle with me, and my irritation at that only made me more determined to clear this situation up, because I was a trained firefighter who knew my shit about fire safety, and he was a cop with no specific fire hazard training.

Okay, so that argument was weak—he was a good cop, with as much training as me in how to keep people safe, but I was hurting after yesterday's PT, and I was fucked off that I'd needed my cane today. So I understood that Leo was playing with me, the same as he messed around with Eric and Sean, but I wasn't in a good place, so he was annoying the hell out of me. Irrationally, I felt as if he was laughing at me—rationally, I knew he wasn't, but that didn't stop the knife of betrayal in my chest. Why didn't he move it because I knew what I was talking about? Why did he have to make me feel as if I didn't know anything?

"I repeat *five-oh* that this is a fire hazard," I pointed at the crepe paper dangling inside the frame where the doorway would be. From a technical and safety point of view it was blocking egress, and the fake hat balanced precariously on the top of the teddy was in danger of toppling to the floor.

"It's not really," Leo argued, and made the teddy swing back and forth as he poked it with a stick. I knew he was only joking but there was a force inside me wanting to argue for what I knew was right. What I wouldn't have given for the damn thing to fall on Leo's head, then maybe he'd have gotten the hint that the decoration was a fire hazard.

"It's as much of a hazard as your dog being on site."

"Cap is a good boy," Leo defended as he glanced around him, looking for Cap.

"Do you even know where he is right now?"

"He's around here somewhere, being a very good boy," Leo said, but I didn't feel reassured. I hadn't seen Cap in the last few minutes, and he could've been off somewhere doing anything. Last time he'd wandered off I'd found him digging up something he should not have been digging up in Brady's brand new vegetable bed.

"You should keep him on a leash."

Leo raised an eyebrow. "That is undermining his civil liberties as an American."

I couldn't help rolling my eyes. "Take the decoration down." I reached for it but Leo blocked me and grinned.

"But it makes the place look all cute."

"It's blocking the way and it can't stay there," I said with exaggerated patience in case he hadn't got the hint about the dangers inherent in paper and wood in a doorway.

"Uhmmm," Leo sighed, and did a slow three-sixty at the start of the timber frame which comprised a few uprights. "It's an empty space." To underline the statement, he stepped through the gap where a wall would eventually be, and bypassed the door altogether. Sometimes I hated smart-ass cops with their stupid cute dogs and their partners with sexy smiles.

I couldn't help looking at Leo and Jason together, because add in Cap, then Jason's cute-as-a-button daughter, and there was the epitome of perfect family. *I should be so lucky to find that with Cam and Finn.*

What is wrong with me today? I'm so fucking grumpy. Why am I even getting so riled up by one decoration? Why am I even thinking about Leo's family?

"But what if you want to use the doorway?" I should've been letting this go because any minute Leo would ask how I was and then I would have to kill him.

"I would... uhm... " He slunk back into the work area, bending at the knees and then changing his mind at the last minute and limbo'd his way under the teddy.

I ignored his attempt to lighten the situation. "Who even put it there?"

"Eric." Leo glanced at the waving decoration and then back at me, and he might not have meant it but to my broken brain there was a clear message. Eric the *firefighter* had placed the decoration in the space where the door would go, and he hadn't thought it was a danger. Whereas me, *former* firefighter, couldn't be relied on to have an opinion. Oh, shit. Self-pity strangled me, wound insidiously through my body and pulled at every aching nerve and muscle. *I will not let self-pity drag me down.*

I tugged at the teddy and it came loose easily. I tried to catch the hat tumbling after but my reflexes didn't keep up with my brain when it was my right arm I was trying to use, and I missed. Leo with his cop-honed speed caught it before the whole lot vanished into the site. Then he handed it to me without a word.

"Thank you." I was embarrassed and angry at a whole bunch of things. I headed straight to the first tree I came to, giving myself time to calm down while attaching the teddy there and hoping it stayed. I counted backwards from ten as I pretended to fiddle with the ties for the hearts. Leo was right; the teddy wouldn't have caused an issue, and the younger kids at Ringwood would have loved it. But looking out for the project was my default position because I wanted to be involved with the guys, and there wasn't much else I was able to do today. I could hold up wood, but not for too long. I could pass things, as long as they weren't too heavy. I could check the plans and make sure things were happening the right way, but I could only direct people by pointing. Leo shuffled up behind me, reaching up and holding the knot as I tightened it. I'd have loved to be pissed at myself for not doing that, but Leo was on a mud ledge and could reach higher. I couldn't blame a mound of fucking earth being in the wrong place at the right time.

"Yo! Red," Sean called. "Leo gave me these screws and I don't know what in Hell's name they're for? Is he fucking with me?"

Sean was currently staring down at his palm in confusion. Where had he gotten the screws from? Cam had sorted them all in the right bags and now Sean had two containers open and random screws falling to the ground.

"Put them back in their right boxes," I took one from him and opened it as wide as I could. "All of them."

Sean glanced at me. "For real? Leo said we needed them for—"

"Back in the tubs before we lose them." Jeez, Cam was going to arrive and find chaos, and who would he look at? Me.

"Leo said I needed to add them to a pile with the tartan paint, and I can't find that anywhere." He blinked at me and yawned, clearly not firing on all cylinders.

"Jesus, Sean, there's no such thing as tartan paint, he's messing with you," I ground out, hearing Leo losing his shit behind me as he fell to the ground, holding his sides as he laughed.

Sean stared past me at his laughing friend and then it dawned on him he'd been had, which resulted in a wrestling match by the large space, which was the start of the extra drainage system, and I hoped at least one of them would roll in. All three of them were idiots, but they were my friends, and I should've been joining in. Only if I had then Eric would've been careful with me, Leo would've asked me if I was okay, and Sean would've wanted to talk about my medication regime. I didn't want to spoil their fun so I left them to the fighting and laughing and headed off to find Cap, as an overwhelming desperate need to get away consumed me.

It didn't help finding Cap digging his way to the center of the earth in a flower bed, or that grabbing Cap upended me so I landed in said hole.

"Hey," Micah said from above me, falling to his knees and fussing with Cap.

He always ended up spending time with us when the guys were there, but he and Finn were best of friends now, and it hurt me that Finn wouldn't get to stay with Micah, go to the same school, go to prom with or without girls, and I added Finn's friendship with Micah to my growing list of reasons why Cam and Finn needed to stay with me.

"Whose dog is that?" Finn exclaimed, also from above me, which meant that Cam and him were back from the wholesalers, and there was me on my back in the flower bed.

"Whatcha doing down there?" Cam asked, and extended a hand to help me up, pulling me to his side and sneaking a quick brush of his lips to my temple.

"Checking the flowers," I deadpanned.

Finn had also fallen to his knees, petting Cap who was in seventh heaven, thinking Finn was just like Micah—another friend to join playtime.

"Here you are!" Leo bounded around the corner, and tossed a ball for Cap. "See, I told you I knew where Cap was."

All I could do was brush myself down and shake my head. Idiot friends.

"Can we get a dog, Dad?" Finn asked, grinning up at Cam as Cap barreled into him and pressed him to the dirt then dropped a ball on his chest.

"One day."

"But *he's* not around anymore, so we can now," Finn wheedled, although there was derision in the word *he* and I assumed he meant his *other dad.*

Cam softened, and tousled Finn's hair. "Maybe."

"How about when we get to the new place?" Finn singsonged the words as if they meant nothing and weren't stabbing me in the heart, then went back to playing.

Cam shoved his hands into his pockets. "Graeme was allergic," he explained in a low voice. "Otherwise we'd have had a dog years ago." I couldn't miss the regret in his tone.

"I'm sure Eric will let you borrow Cap if you wanted to." I watched as Cap ate a flower. "Or maybe you can find a sane dog instead." *Please borrow Cap. Please don't leave.*

After introductions were done, and the usual teasing happened over how Leo was a cop, and Sean was a doctor, and bickering over whether cop or doctor beat firefighter, we lined up to get our instructions from Cam on what we were going to be doing today.

Or at least the other three lined up. I took a seat on the pile of lumber Leo had arranged, to give myself a chance to rest before starting.

"Ignore me," I said when I realized all four men had stopped what they were doing and were staring at me. I couldn't bear to meet anyone's gaze, aware that Leo would be all sympathetic, Sean would be observant, and Eric would be sad. Not to mention I didn't want to see anything awful in Cam's expression. I didn't want to see any of that, so I stared at the structure beyond them and faced it.

If I couldn't see pity then it wasn't happening. Simple. After a short while of pretending to examine the extension, everyone returned to normal, and Cam began to explain what we needed to do.

"It's a good old fashioned barn raisin'," Leo joked, with an atrocious approximation of a country accent.

"Ass," Eric shoved him and Leo nearly ended up back in the drainage hole.

"Where do you need me?" I asked, before Eric and Leo began wrestling again.

Cam quirked a smile at me. "If you could partner with Leo—"

"It's okay, Red, we got this," Eric interjected, which led to him and Leo exchanging looks, then Leo and Sean exchanging looks, and then all three of them staring at Cam. They must have thought Cam would have assumed I was a liability, but Cam wasn't judging me that way at all. Still, I was stubborn, and stupid, and Cam was sexy and in charge, and I was in love, and I was a *goddam capable man*, and I'd feel like shit if I couldn't do *something*.

"He can do it," Sean backed me up.

"Thank you Sean, now where do you need me?" I repeated, and after a moment's pause Cam finished the sentence that Eric had stopped.

"So yeah, if you and Leo take this one…"

I moved to Leo's side, and Eric muttered something about being worried under his breath but I ignored him. I was more than capable of assisting the lift if I moved in a certain way. I wasn't a complete invalid, I just had to be careful.

We all listened as Cam explained with exaggerated patience what we needed to do. Standing with Leo, I was on the right side, Sean and Eric on the left. The bulk of the weight was at the sides, and Cam began to set up the ratchet system that would steady the weight as it moved. When the wood clicked into place, it was Cameron and Eric who used the nail gun to secure everything, and I took the time to sit again with a bottle of water.

"Everyone okay?" Eric asked everyone in general,

although he was very deliberate in the way he didn't look in my direction. I wasn't going to be sensitive about it, because I fucking hurt all over, I'd pushed myself too far. I was an idiot who should've known better. My PT would kill me for getting caught up in the moment, hell, from Cam's expression he was going to kill me as well.

Every one of us nodded, but I was the only one who was lying.

"Can we talk?" Eric asked when we were sharing water and laughing about nothing. Eric separated me from the group and moved a little distance away from them.

"What?" I knew I sounded belligerent, but I didn't want any more pity, or sad glances, or understanding looks. I just wanted to be normal again, and if I couldn't get back to what I used to have physically then I wanted my friends to understand me.

"I want to apologize." He glanced over at the building we'd just worked on. "I know what I'm doing, and I don't mean to do it. I just feel…"

"Guilty?"

He closed his eyes briefly and nodded. "You were my probie, my responsibility, and I should have stopped you, but it isn't just that."

"Jesus, Eric, what else do you want to lay on me?"

"I want to say sorry for not being able to get you out of the car in time, that's on me, I went into panic mode and I don't know what I was thinking—"

"What?" I looked at my friend in complete disbelief. "That's why you keep staring at me? Because you think I blame you?"

"Well, if I'd just gone with you…"

"Then we'd both be injured, and what's the sense in that?"

"I could have pulled you out quicker—"

"I was stuck—"

"If I'd yanked harder—"

"Stop!" I yelled, and I felt everyone's eyes on us so I held out a hand to stop anyone coming over. We subsided into silence, and then it hit me just how much Eric and I really should have talked instead of being stoic idiots. Both carrying pain for things that would never change and wasn't going to fix anything.

"Well, shit," Eric said miserably, but I wasn't letting things stay like this. I needed to take over this conversation and pull it to an end.

So I did what any firefighter would do to a colleague in a situation such as this. I fake-punched Eric in the chest and then shoved him. "Let's leave the past where it is? I could do with a friend who is just there as a friend. Yeah?"

And then I pulled the big idiot in for a hug, and we backslapped a bit before returning to the guys. I caught Cam's gaze, and nodded that I was okay.

And I knew I would be.

Chapter Twenty-One

Cam

THINGS WENT BACK to a quieter normal after the boisterous weekend with the volunteers. In the last few days, Adam had spent most of his time at home and didn't come to the site. He said he was busy with *things* but I know he was struggling with pain after the work we'd done, and it frustrated me that he was refusing any and all help. I wavered between wishing he hadn't assisted with the work and loving the way he smiled when he wasn't being treated like an invalid.

What must it have been like for a firefighter to lose everything that made him what he was? The clichés were there—he was lost, rootless, the entire future he'd mapped out so carefully had vanished in a single moment. But on the other hand he'd saved the life of a child, given that child a future he might never have had, and whatever the reason for putting himself in danger, he'd paid for the sacrifice part of the equation in full. Last night we'd made

love again, even slower than last time, and when he'd
come he'd buried his face in my neck, and I'd felt the
warmth of tears on my skin, but I didn't say a single word.
When we were apart I missed his touch with such a
ferocious ache that it didn't make sense when I balanced it
with the fact that I was supposed to be leaving.

Today he'd decided to come with us to site, chatting
with Finn in the car about a museum visit they were
planning, asking me if I wanted to go with them, setting a
date, and I had an incredible sense of rightness about
everything—as if the three of us were meant to be together
in this moment. With Finn studying, Adam decided to stay
with me, learning about woodwork, interspersed with
kisses.

"So I just do this?" Adam asked as he slid the two
pieces of wood together, grinning when mortice met tenon
and formed a solid joint. "That is so cool."

"And it goes here."

We were constructing the last of the cabinets that
slotted into the more awkward spaces, and the final one
went around the space where the huge refrigerator would
go. Then it was down to installation of the counters before
detail work, attaching doors, and making sure drawers ran
smoothly. Another three days and the kitchen space would
be finished before turning it over to the experts installing
ovens, stovetops, and the refrigerator, plus running final
checks on plumbing. I'd been working there a month now
and we'd achieved so much in such a short time. One
custom kitchen, plus homeschooling, plus whatever it was
that Adam and I were doing, and somehow we were nearly
a third of the way through our planned stay in San Diego.

I was going to miss Adam. Our no-strings exploration of what he could and couldn't do in bed was a mix of erotic fucking and muffled laughter, and I'd never had a connection like it. I think I'd mapped every single one of his freckles with my eyes, from the cluster on his hip, to the path that trailed over one shoulder and down his back. I tried to kiss every one, so that none were missed, stupid I know, but I wanted his skin to remember me. Then as soon as we were out of bed, as soon as I had any separation from him and his addictive kisses, I swung back to the fact Finn and I were leaving, and that it was only a matter of time before someone with an axe to grind tracked us down. Then there was the weight of everything with Nick because I still hadn't visited him, because I was a coward.

Yeah. My brain and I were one messed-up place.

On the one hand I had a man I wanted to be with, in a city I couldn't stay in, with a best friend I couldn't face, on the other hand I had the ghost of a man whom I wished I'd never met, and fear that I would put Finn in the way of exposure and ridicule.

At least the homeschooling was going okay, although Finn had mentioned last night that he wished he was going to school with Micah. They'd grown close, and it was good to see he had a friend who wasn't there only for what Finn could give him. They had a genuine friendship that I would be ruining when we moved on.

Last week as we'd been working on the kitchen carcasses, my favorite part of the process, the creation of something beautiful, working with wood, Finn had shown an interest in the work. I remembered standing with my dad, barely able to see over the table, watching him

working with wood and convinced that I was going to
learn how to do what he did. I'm not sure Finn was as
interested as I had been, but he was carefully concentrated
whenever he took a break from schoolwork to help me.
Until of course Micah was home and then he would
vanish.

Yesterday, I'd noticed Finn had taken an off-cut of
wood and small chisel, and was whittling away at the
wood at the lunch break, learning the best way of cutting
and the direction of the grain. Maybe he'd end up working
with his hands, maybe he'd be a paleontologist, which was
his current career aspiration, or a racing driver which was
last year's. Whatever he did I wanted him to be happy and
as far away from Graeme's name as he could be. That
wasn't too much to ask, right?

"Dad!"

I was so busy woolgathering that I didn't move fast
enough, the football smacking me upside the head, and I
pretended to collapse to the ground, rolling to lie on my
front, knowing that in less than a few seconds both Finn
and Micah would be jumping me. A few days ago they'd
painted a wall in the yard, along with a bunch of the kids
who were there temporarily, with more paint on
themselves than on the project itself. Today it was tag
football of sorts, which basically meant yanking me away
from current work for a break so I could be on Finn's
team.

It wasn't going well. Hence me lying flat on the ground
with Finn and Micah crowing about a touchdown. Since
when had I become the goal posts?

"That was sad." Adam shook his head from his chair,

phone in his hands, chilling after working alongside me all day creating the carcasses for the new kitchen. He'd been heckling me the entire game, a broad grin on his face as I was getting more bruised and battered. I'd have carried on getting pummeled on the ground if only I got to see that natural, happy smile again.

"I'm getting old," I grumped from under a mess of loud and muddy boys. How did they even get so muddy? There was literally no mud around that I could see.

The ball ended up next to Adam's chair, and he hooked it up, standing and then letting it fly way past the boys and me, causing them to scramble off me and tumble like puppies over each other to retrieve it. Some of the other kids came out, and thankfully I was able to call uncle on any more catching.

"Want me to rub it better?" Adam asked, but when he chuckled it sounded brittle, and I caught the wince as he sat.

"Have you hurt yourself?" He'd put some force into throwing the football across the large yard.

"I can throw a damn ball," he muttered, and I guessed it was best to let things lie after that. No person wanted to be reminded of things they couldn't do, and I also had this whole inexplicable twist of attraction that settled in my groin whenever he was near me, which made working uncomfortable.

I ran water over my hands, washing off the mud, and grabbing the dishcloth that Finn had *borrowed* from Bernie when he'd gone on his latest cookie hunt, then headed back into the extension, which now had walls, and windows, and a door, courtesy of the volunteers.

It was up to Adam whether he came in with me or not —he wasn't there to work, not really. He was an observer today, but so far he'd observed a whole lot of me working. I was in the kitchen area, working at the bench for a good ten minutes when he wondered in and stood next to me.

"Sorry," he murmured, and then leaned against the bench, close enough that I stopped working.

"It's okay." It genuinely *was* okay—he was dealing with much more than I would ever know or understand, and he had every right to be grumpy. With a quick glance through the window, where Finn and Micah were still throwing the ball, he then gripped a handful of my T-shirt and tugged me. I didn't fight the pull, and ended up in front of him, slotted between his legs.

"Will you kiss me?"

"I'm not sure that's a good idea, who knows where it will end?" Not that my traitorous libido was agreeing with my sensible comment. I'd been hard since I'd taken my first step toward him. The body wanted what the body wanted, and fuck the part of my brain that had any control.

"I disagree." He raised his arms and tangled his hands behind my head. "You know you want to." He was definitely using his flirty voice, the one that teased and scratched at my hindbrain and made me think impossible things. "I know I want to."

"I don't think—"

He swallowed my protest with a deep kiss, one that went from zero to sixty in a few seconds flat, and then there was no time for thinking, because he was exactly where I wanted him to be. I forgot all my good intentions about not doing this because I was leaving. I needed his kisses, and God help me, I wanted more. I sank even deeper as he pulled me closer, and I rested my hands on the table to support my weight. He groaned into the kiss and I reared back.

"Am I hurting—"

He wasn't letting me talk, taking his fill of kisses, twisting his fingers into my hair and tugging just enough that I got the message that he was controlling this kiss. Maybe I needed that—to be shown what he wanted and what I could do, and what he could take. There was so much for us to explore and I couldn't think—he was stealing my brainpower, and now it was my turn to groan into the kiss, because I wanted to taste more, the curve of his neck, his skin, the weight of him in my mouth.

"Micah, it's your turn!"

The call wasn't next to me, it was muted, so I knew it was coming from outside, but it was enough to break the spell that had held us together, because it was Finn's voice, and it was a bucket of icy water over my head. I eased back and at first he wouldn't release his grip in my hair, and then he reluctantly let me go.

"I had a dream last night," he whispered, "I was riding you. You were inside me, and none of it hurt, and it was the best fucking dream I've had in ages." He sounded broken, and lost, but I didn't have the words that would make things better. Was the dream the reason he'd seemed so happy this morning and had decided to come with me and Finn to the site and that he'd gotten quieter throughout the day?

"We might work up to that," I offered lamely.

He frowned up at me, and eased off the bench,

schooling his expression to one of a man who didn't care either way. "You forgot to add 'before you go' to that sentence." He left me alone in the empty shell of a kitchen, and I wondered how I'd let that happen, but thankfully I didn't have much time to think about anything, when my phone vibrated in my pocket. Nick had taken to sending me texts on a daily basis, consisting of observations about the day, or the kids, asking me how I was, always leaving the way open for me to reply with something equally innocuous that didn't take up too much brain space.

I struggled with what to say to my former best friend, when it had been me who'd shit all over us in the most spectacular fashion, and I steeled myself for the latest cute story. But it wasn't Nick, instead it was another email alert, and I didn't have to click on it to know who it was. Jim was the only one who had my temporary email address, and it seemed he hadn't given up representing me, and in his words, at no charge.

This was either news about the divorce, or something about how Graeme was trying to get hold of me demanding to see me and Finn. His messages were always the same about wanting to apologize, but I read between the lines. What my narcissistic ex really wanted was cameras to capture me and Finn visiting, and there was no way in hell I was going to expose Finn and me to renewed interest, nor to being anywhere near Graeme.

I always sent back a simple *no*.

Only this email was from Jim assuring me that since Graeme and I had agreed on all the significant issues related to ending the marriage, we'd most likely be able to complete an uncontested divorce.

I took the good news where I could.

Graeme had no grounds to disagree given his defense team had shot themselves in the foot. In an effort to garner pity from the jurors they'd announced that what happened had torn our marriage apart and that a broken home was the consequence. They'd tried playing on the sympathies of the jury and all that had happened is that everyone *knew* we were getting a divorce and there was no way out of it for Graeme.

So this email was simple, to the point, Graeme wasn't disputing custody, bankruptcy had come and gone, and there was no property or assets left. He didn't want me, or Finn, and if I ever considered him kindly I guess at least he was making things easy.

I pocketed the phone, feeling a small amount of weight lifting from me, and stepped outside to watch Finn and Micah throwing the ball to each other, scuffling at either end of their makeshift goals. I couldn't see Adam, but he could have gotten a cab and gone home, and I felt a shit ton of regret because the last thing I wanted to do was chase him away to a lonely house.

"We're doing barbecue, we'd love you to stay," Bernie said and startled me out of my musings. "Sorry, didn't mean to make you jump. The grill is on, it's six, and Finn is starving, apparently."

Finn was always starving according to him. "We'd love to stay. What can I do?"

"Nothing for now. Are you done for the day?"

"Just about." I needed to clear away, lock up, make things secure as per the health and safety rules, but yeah, I could finish today and call it a good one. "Did you see Adam at all?"

She shot me a knowing glance. "He's in charge of the grill."

I rushed through locking up, securing everything, then set out to follow the smell of the grill, and to find Adam.

And I was so pleased he hadn't left that the feeling blindsided me. I had to stop and take a few minutes to get my head straight.

I wanted him to go, I didn't want him to go. I wanted to make love again. I wanted to at least kiss him all over. I didn't want to hurt him. I wanted to stay here in San Diego with him. But I had to leave.

Wait. Why am I leaving? We're safe here. No one knows who we are. Surely something would have occurred by now if anyone knew where we were?

Only, when we were home, and Finn asleep, we made love and it was different from before. There was a desperation in Adam, and whatever I tried I couldn't get him to relax into the touch, and he whimpered in pain as he was coming. He'd tried everything to get me to press my fingers inside him, wriggling too much, demanding, but I wanted to be careful, and sure of what I was doing.

"I'm so fucking sorry," he muttered in my arms, then snuggled in to fall asleep. I hated that he felt he had to apologize for what he wanted, and that I was second guessing what I was doing and what I wanted.

Fuck my life.

Chapter Twenty-Two

Adam

WHEN I WOKE my first feelings were that I was warm and the alarm must not have sounded because I sensed that Cam was in bed with me. Then came the regret and guilt at being so demanding last night, followed by the messy connection of pain and sadness that overwhelmed me. Slow and steady wins the race—that was what the PT in the hospital had said to me, but I wasn't that kind of man. I was action, speed and heroics, so slow and steady was a death sentence to me. I'd pushed myself way too fast last night, and if I'd fucked up so that Cam refused to sleep with me again, I'd be destroyed.

How was it that I'd fallen so hard so fast? Was it just because he saw what I wanted and he didn't pity me. Was I so desperate that I—

"I can hear you thinking from here," he teased me, and I moved slowly to turn to face him.

"Sorry, for wrecking it all," I muttered, and waited for

him to lecture me about how I should know my limits. Instead, he chuckled and kissed me on the top of my head.

"Sorry for us getting so heated up and turned on that you lost control? Do you know how fucking sexy you were?"

Oh.

I hadn't been expecting that reaction, and the darkness lifted from my thoughts in an instant.

I reached for his hand and we laced fingers, lying next to each other and staring at the ceiling.

"I love you," I blurted the words out because they were so close to the surface, buzzing and poking at my thoughts, but he didn't say anything back, just rolled onto his side and rested his head next to my arm.

"Good morning to you too," he teased, and I get he was deflecting my announcement but I wasn't ready for him to do that.

"I mean it."

He bit his lip and wouldn't look me in the eye. "I'm not staying, Adam. I can't. You'll need to move on, so we need to be careful with what we're feeling." Regret dripped from every word as pain stabbed my heart. Then it hit me what he'd said.

"What are you feeling?" I pushed, and he muttered something incoherent before sitting up and scooting back so he was resting on the pillows.

"Right now, I'm regretting that Finn and I need to leave."

I scrambled to sit upright, going about as fast as I could manage. "Then what if you don't move on? What if you live here with me and nothing ever touches you or Finn, and this is the place you get to start again?"

He side-eyed me, and I saw confusion in his expression. "I don't know."

The last thing I wanted was to talk anymore about this now. I didn't feel hurt that he wouldn't say it back. My own self doubt as to why he'd even want to in the first place was enough to have me holding back. Still, I'd planted the seed in his thoughts, and it could sit there, and I might have even been able to prove that I was right about a new start. For now, I pulled the book from my nightstand and turned to the page I'd bookmarked, and then I pretended to read. He turned onto his stomach, and then checked the time. He liked to be up way before Finn, just so Finn never knew what we were doing, and I understood why he did that, but still, I wish he'd stay, because I was warm and cozy, and although he hadn't said he loved me, he had admitted he had thoughts about not leaving.

Or at least regrets that he still felt he had to.

"What is it that you're reading?"

I glanced over and got an eyeful of his gorgeous ass, as he lay on his front, his head resting on his hands. I leaned over to press a kiss on his shoulder blade. He was sleepy, and what I should've been doing is cuddling down into bed next to him, but I didn't want to give him any more thinking time and talking seemed like a good option.

"Pyrogeography."

"Like pyromania?" He blinked at me sleepily and I couldn't resist kissing any bare skin I could reach.

"Not like pyromania no. It's a mix of biology,

geophysical environment, alongside society and cultural influences on fire."

He wriggled to sit upright again, enthusiasm in his expression, the sheet catching on his thigh and stopping me from getting a good look at him, which was disappointing. I closed the book, after all I hadn't actually been reading it, but he stopped me and opened it back up at another page.

"I want to know what you're learning about." He cleared his throat. "Changes in ecosystems that often adversely affect the plants, animals, and humans that depend upon that habitat can be the result of fire suppression," he read. "Is this something you learned... before?"

"In my degree yes, it was an elective I took. You see, some wildlife depend on fire to regenerate, like there is a particular pine cone that only opens when it's in a fire, and some plants depend on the area being cleared so they can flourish. So the point is, with the forest fires we have, not all fire is bad, it's actually been part of our ecosystem to the point where some plants and animals thrive after a fire."

He frowned at the cover of the book. "So it's focusing on us messing things up, like global warming?"

I warmed to the subject as I talked about it. I'd ordered this book when I found out that Megan, the woman on the card Saul gave me, was one of the co-authors, and it intrigued me.

"Global warming is adding an entirely new slant on things, but this book talks about looking at fire historically, and we're talking way back before we stole the land from the people who were here before. They had a much better idea of how things should work, and we came in and bulldozed our way through habitats, building towns without a thought for fire. Ground fires will burn through soil that is rich in organic matter. Surface fires will burn through dead plant material that is lying on the ground. Crown fires will burn in the tops of shrubs and trees. In the book it explains a bit more about how ecosystems will experience a mix of all three and that keeps them going." God, that was a lame summary of what I was reading but those were the parts that made the most sense to me.

"You sound so enthusiastic about this, like Finn and his dinosaurs, or me with woodwork."

"I want to learn everything." I put the book back on the nightstand and wriggled to face him better. "Like, in the Northern Central Valley of Cali, there's evidence that fire has been more frequent in the past, but with fire suppression we've altered the landscape and then the fires now, whatever we do, they rush into towns, they destroy everything."

"Are you thinking about the teaching thing then?" he asked cautiously, after all he'd seen the encouragement and enthusiasm from my family to get me into using my degree to teach. I must admit working with Finn had given me an insight into where I might fit into a system of teaching—certainly not at college level, but with kids like Finn who were just learning how the world worked. It wasn't action and saving people, but maybe it was educating a new generation that would learn one day to live in harmony with fire. Somehow.

I was delusional.

"Not really, it's just that Saul knows this woman, Megan, one of the authors of the book actually, and she said she'd be happy to talk to me. Saul seemed to think she might have a role for me in her company, although what that would be I don't know."

"She didn't tell you what it was?" He looked puzzled, and I knew I had to admit that last stupid secret I was keeping.

"I haven't spoken to her yet, because what her company does is go out on sites and work with the land with controlled burns, and some days I can't even manage the grocery store let alone hike into the freaking wilderness."

"Then you tell her that upfront and you can see what she says."

"What if what she says is that she has nothing for me?"

He rested his head on his hands.

"You won't know until you meet her."

IT TOOK me the rest of the week to gather the courage to contact Megan. I hadn't mentioned the L-word again, but now I'd admitted it I felt a weight off my shoulders.

Cam could do what he wanted to with the information, and I would carry on keeping my declarations of love to myself until he either said it back and stayed, or didn't say it at all, and left. At least he'd kissed me good luck for the meeting with Megan, and even though I was so damn nervous about talking to her, the kiss helped.

I had this horrible dead feeling that she would take one

look at me and think that I wasn't capable of much, when I knew how far I'd come in the last year. I had to grab that cloak of invincibility and pull it firmly around me with not one hint of my worries showing.

She'd suggested a coffee shop to chat, and even though it was close by I didn't want to be going in there with a cane, so I'd taken a cab to the front door and was now sitting at a table waiting for someone to arrive who might be her.

She'd said to wait for a woman with purple hair, and that I would know the minute she walked in.

Her hair gave her away, but so did the sweatshirt with the flame logo on the front. She scanned the coffee shop, and I sketched a wave at the same moment she realized where I was, and she weaved in and out of the chairs to the table in the corner.

I began to stand. "Don't get up, I'm Megan, what are you drinking?"

She most likely asked me to stay sitting because she thought I couldn't, and that was the first of the negative brushes on my psyche, but again I pushed it aside.

"Coffee, I'll get it."

"It's on me."

She came back after a few minutes, pocketing a wallet and I noticed she didn't have a purse, or heels, or anything else I'd been expecting of the stunning woman on the dust jacket. Here she was, scruffy with a distinctive dark mark on her sweater, and a tear in her jeans.

"Sorry, just came off a burn, but I wanted to talk to you, and I knew I was going to be late if I changed." She smiled as she spoke, welcoming, the smile reaching her eyes.

"No problem. So, you know my brother."

She rested her elbows on the table. "The gorgeous veterinarian? Yes, I do, and he was the one who told me about the accident."

Well shit. We were going straight there?

"He did." I sounded flat, even to my own ears.

"I lost my first husband when he was only twenty-five, damned idiot went back into a house for a kid when it hadn't been cleared as safe by the bomb squad—he was a cop, I should have said that—turns out he ran out of the house, with the kid, and the blast caught him. The kid lived, he didn't. So I know all about heroes, and they're the best kind of people."

"Tell that to my chief."

She smiled again. "What's your degree in?"

If there was one thing Megan was, it was straight to the point.

"Fire science."

"Always wanted to be a firefighter, eh?"

"Pretty much."

"My degree is in ecology, but my post grad was fire studies, and this was way back in the early two thousands. When I set up FRM I had this wacky idea that working with the fire service, the electric companies, towns, all kinds of joined-up thinking, would be easy. Spoiler alert, it wasn't. The power companies had shareholders, the fire service had pride and limited resources, towns were strapped enough without adding extreme fire mitigation and allowing controlled burns..." She waved a hand in the air. "So I battled hard, won some, lost some, and when my grandson started school, then it hit me, I could advocate as much as possible for what I thought was right but—"

We were interrupted by the barista, carrying a tray of coffee plus two plates of sinfully rich-looking chocolate cake.

"This place is famous for its home-baked stuff, so if you don't like the cake, I'll eat both slices," Megan added a wolfish grin.

I slid the plate closer and pretended to hide it. "You might want to watch your own slice, in case I finish mine first."

She snorted a laugh, and fell on her cake as if she hadn't eaten in days.

Between mouthfuls she started to talk. "So, what was I saying?"

"Your grandson is in school," I suggested helpfully.

"Oh yes, but I should start from the beginning. First off my company is not part of anything that means homeowners can't get insurance. That is not what we are trying to do. We're saying that fire suppression in places like the Central Valley has altered the natural frequency of fires, and the landscape, and we work with land managers, landowners, and a ton of policy makers to inform ongoing efforts of natural restoration. In fact I have a team who deals specifically with laws, and policy, and all the high-level education, so that isn't what I would need from you."

"Okay." Wait? She actually wanted something from me? Even though she knew about the accident. "But you should know I take meds for pain, and have migraines, and it can be hard to walk and I lose hours, or sometimes a whole day." I blurted everything out before I could rethink everything.

"I'd already assumed as much," she murmured, and patted my hand. "That's all good to know."

"But I try damn hard with everything I do." She had to know that.

"You have a firefighter's instincts, of course you always do the best. So tell me what you know about pyrogeography."

I rambled about ecosystems, habitat vitality, and my understanding of the implications of fire suppression. It started out in fragments of learned information, but slowly over coffee and the slice of cake I relaxed and allowed more of my personality to emerge. "So the idea that fires are chaotic and unpredictable is the opposite of what pyrogeography endorses, that fire is part of ecological balance. Like in Yosemite National Park."

"They've had a very long fire use program," she said.

"Yeah, and when lightning fires occur in the park, they let them burn if they're not a threat to any humans. We need systems to start having fire back in them again."

I sat back at that final statement, realizing I'd said all I could really say.

She sipped her cooling coffee and examined me over the rim of her cup.

"Would you be interested in forming an education team for schools? We're talking grades one through eight? I have funding for a year, that's all I can offer you to start, and the money won't be amazing, but we have flexible working for the bad days, and you would be running your own schedule. Are you interested?"

I didn't have to think. Working with Finn, learning not to push myself so hard, understanding my strengths, all made that an easy question to answer. I had Cam and Finn to thank for this, along with the unwavering support of my friends and family. They trusted I could find a new way in life, and I wanted that so bad. I held out a hand, which she took.

"Hell, yes," I said.

She laughed then, and I felt an answering grin split my face. "You're hired."

Chapter Twenty-Three

Cam

"… and then she offered me a job, right there and then. I'd be working in schools, talking about fire safety but also about respecting nature, and it's just freaking awesome."

Adam kissed me again, which was what he'd been doing every few minutes since he'd arrived at Ringwood, post-interview. His enthusiasm was infectious, and all I wanted to do was kiss him back.

"So, I said yes, and she's emailing me a ton of information, and she's coming to the house Tuesday for us to start planning. I mean, I have so many ideas, and I wanted to ask you something. Is it okay to ask Finn to get involved with some feedback?"

"Sure."

He finally sat in the chair we'd positioned in the kitchen for him to chill on when he was visiting.

"So what are we doing today?"

"I'm nearly done with the final countertop, fifteen

minutes more, then you want to talk me into place with it when I connect it from underneath?"

"I can do that," he said, and I settled back to work, interrupted by the tone for a text. Only a few people had my number, and given that Finn was one of them, I checked every time. I'd had a few dropped calls from an anonymous caller, but given there was no message, and the number was unknown I expected they were just random misdials to a number similar to mine.

It was Nick. *When are you and Finn visiting for food? I'd love to talk? Bring Adam.*

"Are you okay?" Adam asked after a pause as I stared at my phone and the message.

"It's Nick," I explained, "he keeps inviting us over to his place."

"But you don't want to go?"

"I'm just being a coward."

"What actually happened between you and Nick? Feel free to ignore that question if you want."

I had a whole list of answers to that particular question, but unpicking everything was long-winded. "I fucked up. Nick's husband Danny died, and I met Graeme a few months after. Nick hated him from day one, only I was besotted with Graeme, and basically I ghosted Nick despite the fact that he was my best friend, and still grieving."

"That doesn't sound like you at all," Adam said.

I sighed heavily, the room closing around me, and put down the fine-grade sandpaper. "Let's get some air."

He followed me out into the yard and we ambled to the seating I'd been working on in my spare moments.

Micah and Finn were in the midst of painting one of the benches and there were handwritten signs all around warning of wet paint, but the other bench, under the shade of a large oak was naked of paint for now, so we took one end each, and Adam turned to face me expectantly.

"Nick called me the week after Graeme was arrested, when the news hit, and said that if I needed anything I knew where he was. All I could think was that I didn't need anyone's help with my husband, because even though I'd found him covered in blood I couldn't let myself think that he was guilty of what they said he was."

"You were protecting yourself and Finn," he said, and it was such an insightful comment I wondered why I hadn't told him all this before. *Because I'm ashamed of myself.*

"Graeme had this way about him—he was a true snake oil salesman—smooth, rich, persuasive, and he promised the best life for Finn, and for me, and I fell for it. Nick saw through him, but I didn't listen, and when Graeme was arrested I couldn't believe that everything I'd felt for him was based on lies. I should have listened to Nick, should have stayed here and been a better friend." I hung my head, resting my elbows on my knees. "It hit me the worst at Christmas, when the trial was at its peak, when I had a notification on my phone... god this is so stupid." I couldn't believe I was telling Adam this, because he'd look at me as if I was an idiot.

"Nothing is stupid," he reassured me, and shuffled along the bench awkwardly until he could press a hand to my shoulder in reassurance.

"There was a gif of a dancing elf, and it was a bulletin from the Single Dads forum."

"The one you set up with Nick that Ash goes to?"

"Yep. It was the end of a very old thread—something I was still watching, and it was this really cool news that an old contact of mine had asked his manny to marry him right in front of a mall Santa and he'd said yes. The forum had been the only private thing I'd had just for myself, but I could never keep up with the news because it hurt to see Nick's name whenever he was mentioned. Part of me was avoiding him online because I didn't know what to say about my situation as it began to change, and that was when I ghosted him, and it was easy because I was in New York, and his show had taken off, and he had his own life." I paused and considered where to go next.

"I watch his show. He's a good guy."

"Yeah. He is. At the start, when I first moved east, I'd told him everything about Graeme, but in hindsight I was just telling him the good stuff. I never mentioned the prolonged absences, or the loans taken out in my name, or the fact that Graeme's mood could turn on a dime. Nick didn't need to know that I regretted my choices, because he was dealing with the grief of losing his husband, and he was left to raise the kids on his own. How could I ever come back into Nick's life when mine was so ridiculously messed up and he'd been right about it?"

Adam smoothed a hand over my back. "Pride. Self-protection. The idiot gene. It could be all of those things."

"The idiot gene?" I side-eyed him, feeling unaccountably lighter just to have gotten that off my chest.

"Mom vows that all her kids have an idiot gene that she swears we inherited from Dad."

We exchanged smiles, because that was funny, and I knew his mom and dad and they were good people. "I definitely have the idiot gene."

"So how about you take up the invite to visit, tell Nick all of this, and start again."

"There's no point if Finn and I are leaving soon."

I wished I'd kept my mouth shut when his rhythmic rubbing of my back ceased for a moment, like a stutter in his support. I didn't mean to hurt Adam, but it appeared to be my default setting whenever I got close to anyone.

"I've still got time to persuade you to stay." He resumed the soft stroking and I felt a bit more weight leave me.

"I've been thinking of going to see him." I pulled out my cell. "He's invited us for a drink at his place. Said I should bring you, if you thought you wanted to. No pressure, but I could do with the friendly support." I shot him a quick look to judge his reaction.

"Thought I wanted to? Of course I do. Hell, I've seen his place on homes of the rich and blatantly freaking famous, it's gorgeous, right on the beach in Del Mar." He patted my back. "But of course, I'd mostly be there to support you. But, did you know he has an infinity pool with a hot tub?"

"You're so shallow," I teased, even if his joking made me feel even lighter.

"Hell, did I mention the hot tub?"

Chapter Twenty-Four

Cam

THERE WAS security at the gate to the community, a collection of beachfront mansions complete with two guards, and a list of who could go in.

They checked our IDs, but it appeared the heads-up that we would be there was enough to get the truck waved through with a smile. From then it was a turn left, as Nick had the first place in the row of six, and I parked up next to a beautiful pale blue Porsche with NK1 on the vanity plates. With cutting edge and apparently award-winning design, the house was a combination of white walls and glass, and when I caught sight of the ocean beyond, it was as if someone had taken a magical place and put it right down where it could be loved.

Adam let out a low whistle as he did a three-sixty, and Finn just stood with his mouth open. He'd been lured by the pool as much as Adam had, and both had all the gear they needed for today's swim-and-eat adventure. I didn't bring anything for me, because Nick and I needed to talk, and I wanted to get it over and done with so we could at least clear the air before Finn and I had to move on.

"This is some place," Adam murmured.

"Cam! Guys! You made it!" All three of us turned to face the wide front door and a grinning Nick standing in a flowery Hawaiian shirt and cut-offs. "Come in! Come in! Is anyone hungry?"

"Me," Finn said immediately as he climbed the steps.

Nick chuckled. "I bet you're always hungry, right?"

"Pretty much," Finn grinned, and it was the first real smile I'd seen that didn't involve the pool, Micah, or Cap the dog.

"Hang on." Nick moved to the bottom of the stairs. "Kids, we have guests!"

Various shouts echoed into the hallway as we took off our shoes and placed our bags inside the door. Nick was the father of three, his daughter Hannah through surrogacy, the boys Caleb and Mason adopted, with Mason, the youngest, being the same age as Finn. I heard the thundering of feet and then all three of them arrived to the hallway from different directions, and they stopped dead when they saw me.

"Uncle Cam is here," Nick announced, "with Finn and Adam."

Hannah glanced from me to her dad, and I could see the question in her teenagers-know-all expression. She remembered me for sure, and was old enough to know what I'd done to her dad was shit, and I could see her silently judging me. *I get where you're coming from, Hannah.* The boys on the other hand, either didn't understand the subtleties of me disappearing from their lives, or they just didn't care because they were very interested in Finn and somehow managed to encourage him from my side and into the kitchen as soon as Nick mentioned snacks.

"Hmm," Hannah glanced behind me at Nick. "Dad?"

Something passed between them, but of course all I could see was her expression which went from pissed, to disbelieving, to resigned. Then she spun away and stalked back upstairs.

Nick sighed. "Cam—"

"No," I interrupted and rounded on him, "don't apologize for Hannah, I deserve everything she throws at me."

Nick knocked his fist against my shoulder. "I wasn't going to apologize for her, because she's her own woman now." He wrinkled his nose at that and I wondered if that was a recent revelation. "I was going to say that things might be weird, but it will be okay." He shook hands with Adam, did this complicated fist bump bro thing, and then pulled me into a tight hug. "I'm so happy you're here."

"Me too," I admitted, even though what I needed to say to him created a ball of fear in my chest.

"Coffee? Beer?"

We followed Nick through the hall, Adam brushing his hand against mine, and for a second linking our fingers before letting me go. He was just reassuring me and I was grateful for it. We went down some steps to a huge kitchen, all granite, wood, and gleaming chrome sparkling in the afternoon sun. There was no sign of the boys at first, and then I spotted Finn sitting at a table in a sun room with

Mason, both of them watching Caleb on a video game projected onto a big screen, and Adam moved down to watch with them. I knew what he was doing—giving me time with Nick, but I wasn't ready to talk yet.

My eyes were drawn to the beautiful painting on the wall of Nick and his husband Danny plus the three kids, and a familiar grief hit me. Danny had been one of the good guys, and I'd grown close to him in the time I'd known him.

"I still miss him," Nick said from my side, and handed me a mug of coffee.

"Of course, you do. I do. Look, Nick—"

"Help yourself to food, boys."

I noticed it was only Finn who looked over at first, but then Mason scrambled over the sofa and led the charge toward the food, followed by Caleb and then Finn.

"Hollow legs on growing boys." Nick sent me a smile at the inside joke about having boys. "Whereas Hannah is vegetarian now, and super picky about what she eats. It's a worry, you know."

And so it went on, casual talk about life, and kids, and after we'd gotten through a ton of cold cuts, along with salad and bread, then had the requisite rest period, the kids went into the pool, and Adam joined them, although he headed for the whirlpool hot tub with a view of the ocean.

"Let me show you something." Nick snagged some sodas and left the kitchen, heading into the house, and I had no choice but to follow, although the feeling of foreboding was strong. This was the moment we were going to have a serious talk.

He led me up some stairs and we emerged into a

bedroom and then out onto a balcony where we could see the kids, and Adam, and the ocean beyond. Nick settled back in the chair and tipped his head to the sky. It was a beautiful day and a faint breeze carried the scent of the ocean up to this secluded space and I thought maybe I could sit up there forever. The difference between living in the sunshine next to the ocean and living in the middle of New York was marked. There was a different flow to life here, not any better, but certainly not worse, and small parts of it were twisting their way into my soul.

"Do you remember the night I called you after Graeme was arrested?"

"When?" Did he mean the single time I'd answered, or the other twenty times where I'd snubbed his calls out of shame?

"The first time, the one where I heard about what happened to Graeme, not the others that you ignored." He bumped a fist against my arm, and I winced even though his expression told me he was messing with me.

"Of course I do." I remembered sitting on my sofa. Finn had been asleep upstairs, untouched by the latest chaos that was the news of Graeme's arrest reaching national media outlets. Finn had been blissfully unaware that everyone at school would know for sure what had happened in full, instead of just passing around rumors that had already caused his peers to jeer at him so much that he'd come home in tears. Chaos, flashing blue lights outside the house, journalists, federal agents sitting in front of me and asking me a hundred questions I had no hope of answering. "The FBI were in my house, asking me if I had somewhere to go with my son, because they were going to strip the house, and when you phoned I didn't know what to say." It all came out in one run-on sentence, but it was all true.

"I meant it when I said I wanted to help," he murmured, and offered me the other soda, the surface was icy, beads of water collecting where I touched it, and the cold grounded me.

"You did help me, you gave me Adam's address."

We paused for a moment, and then he sighed. "I missed your face."

He held out a fist to bump and I didn't leave him hanging. "I missed you too."

"Still, I don't know how I fucked up, but I know I did somehow, so if I wasn't understanding enough, or too wrapped up in Danny, or... whatever. I'm sorry."

"What?" Is that what Nick thought? That it was somehow him who'd chased me away? He couldn't be more wrong. "You didn't fuck up, I did. I let Graeme tell me I had him and I didn't need you or the rest of the group, hell, that I didn't fit into your life anymore. Jesus, if anyone should be sorry, it's me. I turned my back on you when you most needed it, I ghosted you for no reason other than the fact Graeme convinced me that you were jealous and I believed him. I still don't know why even..."

"Jealous? I was jealous of him? What for?"

Christ. Here it came. Complete honesty. "He said you were in love with me."

The words hung there, and I know they sounded the death knell to our friendship, if it wasn't dead already. Then Nick snorted a laugh. And another.

"Did he know we tried kissing once? Did he really

think… oh my god…" Now Nick was laughing so hard he couldn't breathe, and I patted him on the back, and I couldn't help laughing alongside him. Everything seemed less awful, and although we had work to do, there was a glimmer of hope that we could be close again one day.

He might even visit me and Finn in Montana.

"I was the shittiest friend, you'd lost Danny and—"

"Don't. Let's forget it all. Okay?"

"Okay, as long as you know, and also, I might sound like a teenager but you're my best friend."

"Back at you."

More silence followed but it was a soft kind of space to think, and I was happy to sit there and stare at the expanse of sky over the ocean.

"I used to sit up here all the time with Danny," Nick murmured, and I didn't have to try hard to hear the sadness in his tone. "But I don't come up here much anymore."

"Too many bad memories?" I tipped my soda, the sweetness a full stop to the rest of my weird day.

"Not at all. Too many good ones."

"I get that."

"This was our place, when the kids were asleep we'd come out here and listen to the ocean and talk. We were here when he told me that…" He cleared his throat and sighed. "He poured me wine, a good one you know, as if he knew I'd need it, and then he told me about the shadow on his lung. He'd only gone for a routine checkup for the after effects of what they said was bronchitis, but instead they found the awful insidious darkness that killed him. I don't know how he did it, a whole week he kept it from me, and in that time everything was so normal. I didn't come up here for the longest time after I lost him."

Words failed me. For him to lose the man he loved more than life itself in such an awful way—I didn't know how anyone could bear that much pain. I didn't know what it would be like not to see Adam every day.

Fuck. Where had that thought come from. *I'm always going to be leaving.* One day soon I wouldn't see him unless he visited us at our fantasy safe space.

"Anyway, let's change the subject, I can't be doing all of that as well as having a big gay reunion with my best friend." He snorted another laugh. "Tell me about the work at Ringwood."

"It's going well." I felt a sudden urge to confide in him about Adam and how he'd impacted my life. There was love there for sure, affection, a need to be with him, and a terrible emptiness in my soul when I imagined the future without him. Finn loved him, he loved the house, Micah, he talked about going to school here.

Maybe I needed to rethink our lives? Maybe it would be safe here. I could start up that small company, build a reputation, make a life.

"Is that all I get? I want to know all about the cross threaded screws and the two by fours, and the widget gadget things or whatever," he deadpanned.

I snorted a laugh. "Well, we were fixing—"

"I was joking, I don't really need to know."

Adam climbed out of the hot tub, flexing his legs, and stretching, and I leaned forward to stare, a mix of seeing him so chilled, worrying about him, plus lusting after him in a way I'd never felt about anyone.

"How long have you been in love with Adam?"

"It's been a while…" Shit. I turned to Nick, aware I'd answered the question without any conscious thought.

"The way you look at him, it's different to how you looked at Graeme. That was all about security for Finn, about education, and all the things that Graeme was selling you. With Adam I see this light between you, a real happily ever after."

"I'm leaving," I said after a while, because it really was the only thing I could say.

"You don't have to."

"The press—"

"Will find you wherever you end up. You'll always be the partner of a man who nearly destroyed a bank, and stole millions from pension funds. It will be the same here as it would be if you went back to New York."

"Montana."

"Huh?"

"I was online last week and found this ad for a general maintenance person at this dude ranch in Montana. The role even comes with a horse."

"A horse." Nick's lips twitched.

"Apparently."

"You can't ride."

"I could learn." I *could* learn anything if I tried.

"You're actually afraid of horses, you remember that time—"

"Yes, don't go there."

Nick tried to stop a laugh. "And when you were twelve and we—"

"You know way too much about me."

"You know I could interview you, get your side of things, for the show…" he broached it so cautiously, but my back was up and temper replaced the calm.

"Jesus, Nick, is that why you invited me here? To get me to agree to media? You asshole. I don't know anything about the money, or what he did, I was fucking stupid but I wasn't complicit. Were you not listening…?" Now it was my turn to stop talking while he stared at me in silence, one eyebrow lifted. I knew I'd fucked up again because I *knew* Nick and he wasn't like the others, he wouldn't feed off the sensation for viewers. He wouldn't do that to Finn. But I was far from ready to give my side because I wanted it to go away. "Shit, Nick. I'm sorry."

After a pause, I extended a fist in the hope he'd see why I'd reacted so badly. He didn't hesitate to bump it.

"I get it," he murmured, and then we sat in peace for a while. We could have talked more, but what else could I say? I'd been the one to ghost him, ignoring his messages, not joining in on group posts in the forum, not even sending him a birthday card when we'd gotten so close. We'd created SDT together, one place for single dads everywhere, and it had become so much more than I thought it could be. It gave a safe space to all types of dads, bereaved, single, divorced, straight, gay, with adopted kids, or biological kids, I loved what we'd built, and then I'd left Nick when he'd been at the most vulnerable point of his entire life. Not only had he forgiven me for ghosting him years ago, but he'd called me when the shit hit the fan, and he'd organized a safe place for me and Finn to stay. He was my best friend, and I owed him everything.

He leaned over then and side-hugged me. "So let me tell you about this asshole teacher at Hannah's school, he's fucking with my head, and I need advice."

GETTING into the truck to leave Nick's place, I felt chilled. We had a lot of work to do to get back to normal—he didn't blame me, he blamed himself, and I was in this constant circle over coming to terms with my own behavior.

Adam belted himself in, looking as relaxed as I'd ever seen him, and in the back, Finn was staring out of the window. He'd slipped so easily into having fun with Nick's kids, and they'd exchanged cell phone numbers and promised to meet up. I had so much I wanted to tell Adam.

"You know we could put a hot tub in your back yard, build a structure over it to keep it shady, then you could use it every day if you wanted."

"Me first, you didn't answer my question."

"Huh?" I'd been so enthusiastic about telling him my idea that I hadn't even heard him ask me a question.

"Are you okay?"

"Oh. Yeah. Confused, relaxed, happy, sad, a million different things. Nick wanted to interview me, get my side of the story," I lowered his voice. "But what would that do to Finn?" My whisper levels needed work when Finn leaned on the back of my seat.

"I want to stay here with Adam," Finn interjected. "I want to talk to Uncle Nick and tell him that Graeme was bad and that we're not bad, and that people should leave us alone."

"It's not that easy, Finn."

He muttered and huffed and sat back in his seat. "It should be, because I have a friend, and I want to go to school and learn algebra the *right* way." I exchanged an incredulous look with Adam, and his lips twitched. "I love Adam, and Cap, and I really want my own dog, and I want people to leave us alone so me, you, and Adam can be a family for real, 'cause I know you love him as much as I do."

The impassioned speech hit me right in the gut.

"Finn—"

"What? I don't want to go to Montana, I don't even like horses, and Adam doesn't live in Montana, and neither does Micah, or Uncle Nick, or Mia, or anyone. Why do you get to make all the decisions, Dad?"

"I'm just trying to keep you safe." I stopped talking, because it struck me that in keeping Finn safe, or at least my idea of safe, I was taking away everything I wanted him to have.

"I know," Finn said, and then slumped back in his seat and put his headphones on. He was tired, closed his eyes, and I didn't have the heart to talk about anything right now. All I could focus on was the fact that he'd said he loved Adam.

Why was I finding it so hard? Was it because I was convinced we'd be separated soon. I don't think I'd let him inside like I should have—not even given him a chance to have something real.

But I'd *never* felt about anyone the same as I felt about him. The gates opened and I drove through, heading back to Adam's. *Home.* By the time we made it back I'd run through every scenario in my head, even going so far as imagining hordes of reporters in the front yard of Adam's house. As soon as I parked the big truck in the drive and killed the engine I turned to Adam.

"What if we stayed?" I went directly to the point.

"Stayed here? With me?"

"Yes."

He placed a hand on his chest, right over his heart. "Why?"

I held out a hand, and he laced his fingers with mine. "Because whatever I think about, it all comes down to one thing, Finn and I are in love with you."

He tightened his fingers and it was his turn to get confused. "Huh?"

"In love with you," I repeated. "Both of us."

"For real?" He sounded so surprised, but I'd connected on a level I'd never experienced before with red hair, freckles, and beautiful green eyes, not to mention his loving heart.

"I love you, Adam."

He gripped me. "Me too, I mean, I love you. Both of you. Please don't go, because we could do so much here as a family. Or you could take me with you, wherever you go?"

"I'm thinking maybe we could stay, if only we knew of a place to live…" I left that hanging and he pulled my hand up, kissing the back of it before releasing me.

"I want to kiss you."

"When we get inside."

"Not in front of me," Finn muttered, and opened the car door as he yawned. "And, Dad, tonight can you not set your phone alarm, because it wakes me up and I already know you both sleep in the same bed."

I didn't have anything to say to that, but Adam chuckled. "You're too clever for your own good, Finn Bellamy."

"I know." He puffed out his chest, and headed upstairs after a quick hug goodnight.

"I'll be up in a minute," I called after him.

"Don't worry, I'm asleep already. Night, Dad, and kiss Adam already."

Adam smirked at me, so I did the only thing I could right then and kissed him. We wasted time in the kitchen, stealing kisses, getting ready to settle in for the night when there was a knock on the door. Adam muttered something about friends who should stay away when he was getting his sex on, and I laughed. He half opened the door, when it was slammed inward, and a figure lurched into the house.

"Tell me where you put it!"

I went from tired to shocked to terrified in two-seconds flat.

Simon Frederickson. In Adam's house, a gun pointed right at Adam.

I instantly put myself between Adam and Frederickson, feeling Adam's hand on my back and hopefully shielding him enough to give him a chance to call 911.

"Mr. Frederickson. Simon, you don't want to do this," I said.

His eyes were wide, the same as that last day when we'd left court, but he looked gaunt and there was a madness in his eyes.

"Where's the money?"

"I don't know."

"I signed the fucking papers for him, I let Graeme Hastings take the money, so tell me where you've hidden it."

"Put the gun down, please. My son is upstairs—"

"You're fucking lucky you have your son. Mine won't even talk to me, he's ashamed of me, blames me for everything. Your husband stole my fucking life."

"Calm down—"

"I won't calm down." He waved the gun at me, his hold unsteady, and I imagined it going off accidentally.

"Dad?" Finn was right there on the stairs, only half awake.

"Go upstairs—"

"Stay where you are!" Frederickson and I shouted at the same time, and in the confusion, Finn scrambled back up the stairs. I would die before Simon shot Finn, and I threw out a question to get his attention.

"How did you find me?" I demanded, confronting him as if I had the upper hand, and he blinked at me for a moment, then sneered.

"People in low places found you using your social security number. You think we're all stupid or something? Did you really think I wouldn't find you and the money?"

"I called 911," Adam muttered behind me, and then in a move so slick it belied his pain, he pushed past me to and positioned himself between the gun and me, his hands out in front of him. "Sir, I'd like you to put the gun down." He kept his tone even, light, but with enough authority that I saw Simon's hold waver. It didn't last long, because he made a show of gripping the weapon hard, and raising the aim to point at Adam's face.

"Fuck you all," he snapped, and for a brief moment I could imagine shoving Adam to safety and jumping Simon, but the seconds it would take in my head could turn to Adam stumbling, to me falling, to the gun going off and all I could imagine was blood and death, and then Finn would be next. I searched desperately for a weapon— anything I could use, but there was nothing to hand.

"Sir, you've done nothing wrong yet," Adam lied then took a small step forward, leaning heavily on his cane and letting out a grunt of pain. "I can understand you're upset."

"You don't know a thing. Graeme Hastings stole millions, and you're standing there protecting the one man who knows where the money went."

"I don't know anything, I promise you. I lost everything the same as you."

Adam waved a hand behind him, telling me to stop talking, and took another small step forward, this time coughing with each agonizing movement. He listed to one side, pain in every line of him. "He's telling the truth, sir," he summarized. "Cameron Bellamy and his young son were victims as much as you."

Still no movement, not even a flicker of recognition in Simon's expression. I wasn't sure that Adam trying to use his skills at talking someone down was going to work. *I won't let him get hurt.* As the noise of a siren on an approaching cop car filled the hallway, I even began to move if only to yank Adam out of the way, but then Adam stumbled.

He'd taken another step forward, and Simon took his

eyes off me and couldn't help but track Adam's movements, it was enough for me to begin moving, calculating the chance of getting to Simon before the gun discharged.

In a flurry of motion, Adam began to fall, only he didn't fall, he swept his cane out, hit Simon's arm hard, and then took him to the floor as the gun flew across the hall.

"Get the gun!" Adam shouted, as he and Simon tussled for a hold. I scrabbled to grab it, hefting the weight of it and pointing it at the wall above Simon's head. Fuck if I was going to point it anywhere near Adam because I didn't know guns.

"Police! Drop your weapon!"

"I'm not the bad guy!" I shouted, because Simon and Adam were still tussling for control.

"Drop the weapon."

I couldn't. "Get him off Adam!" I yelled, and heard Finn sobbing on the stairs.

Someone yanked the gun from me, I don't know who, then the cops were there, helping Adam off Simon and cuffing Simon, reading him his rights, the blue of the patrol car throwing eerie shadows into the house.

"Wait!" I went to Simon. "I didn't know. I have nothing to give you. I wish to god I did."

"You must have known something." He began to cry— an utterly broken man.

"On the life of my son, I didn't know anything, and I don't know where any money could be. He lost it all."

The cop encouraged Simon to stand, helped him up

and out the door. At the last moment Simon turned back to me.

"On the life of your son you promise me." He was begging for me to end this for him, and compassion wormed its way into my fear.

"I promise you."

He began to cry harder, allowed himself to be taken away, and when the horror lessened I sought out Finn who was hiding halfway up the stairs, and held him tight. I focused on Adam, who was sitting on the floor, leaning against the wall, staring past the medic trying to help him.

"Ouch," he murmured up at me, and I went to my knees next to him with Finn in my arms, and I held them both tight.

"My heroes." I whispered for their ears only, even as my careful, safe world had disintegrated around me. How was I going to stop this? How could I really keep Finn safe? How could I stay and love Adam as I wanted to?

How was I going to make this a real family?

I dug in my pocket for my phone, and curled up with Finn in my arms, and Adam leaning on my side, I called Nick.

"We need to do the interview now. Right now."

"Of course, I'll be there in the morning and we can talk about scheduling—"

"Now, Nick. Please."

"What's wrong?"

"Someone tried to kill us."

Silence and then Nick cursed loudly. "I'm on my way."

This was how I was going to start again. With honesty and love, Finn safe and happy, and with Adam at my side.

This was the start of my forever, and I was going to tell everyone all about the real me, and I had to make it work. I couldn't hide if I wanted any kind of future for Finn and me.

I tucked Finn into bed, but he followed us back downstairs and curled up on the sofa next to Adam who had taken some heavy meds and was sleepy. Seeing the two of them at peace was a balm to my soul as I answered the last of the cop's questions, and fielded worries from Sean and Ash who'd come home from a family event to chaos. It was Sean who'd fixed what Adam needed from the locked box of meds, and he stayed until Nick arrived. He'd called to say he was bringing a camera guy with him, and they set up lights as best they could in the bright kitchen.

"Ready?" Nick asked. He looked polished, professional and in charge, and when I nodded, he counted himself in, then introduced me, and gave a brief backstory, then it was time for me to talk.

"Cameron, why don't you start at the beginning…"

Epilogue

Adam

One year later

CAM'S INTERVIEW had been a segment on Nick's news show, only five minutes, but it packed a punch and had gone viral with hashtags and social support. Carefully, and in a few words, Nick had unpicked the rumors that the defense team had created in order to paint Graeme as a victim, and Cam admitted that he'd been naïve. Whether Cam's admission that he should have known what was happening stuck, but the journalists on the front lawn, many on day one, had dwindled to nothing within three days, when all they got pictures of was the three of us going about our lives as if nothing was wrong.

And it wasn't.

There was *nothing* wrong in something *so* right, and almost a year later, divorce papers had arrived last week, and for the first time since I'd met Cam, he seemed to fully relax.

Micah was here this morning, after staying for an overnight pool event with a couple of kids from school. Finn was thriving, but he still had times when he needed his dad, a hug or a debate, or to be tucked into bed. Those moments were precious and perfect, and sometimes I was included, which made my already full heart even heavier with the love I had for the Bellamy men.

This afternoon we had a grand opening of sorts at Ringwood, and it was my first day of mobility after a small operation on my back to scrape away scar tissue to alleviate the pressure on my sciatic nerve. Cam's ability to stand up to his demons was inspiring, and I'd finally managed to stand up to mine, getting myself back into the hospital. It wasn't a fix, it was just another piece of the puzzle of my pain, but it was a positive step on my long path to recovery. Cam had been there when I'd gone under, and there when I'd woken up, along with my entire family milling around outside.

I was flat on my back in the house for a few weeks, moving slowly and working on as much of the fire history curriculum as I could, and a few days ago the PT announced that he wasn't needed to supervise my sessions and I could be released to my own care. I had a list of exercises, some that hurt, others that didn't, but the main thing was that when I walked, or slept, or breathed, the pain wasn't acute. It still didn't lead to energetic sex as I'd imagined it might, but last night's lovemaking had left me starry-eyed and so in love that it had followed me into today, and meant that Cam got a lot of kisses.

Much to Finn and Micah's disgust.

"Okay?" I asked Cam, as he straightened his tie. Summer in San Diego was at its most brutal, but he was determined to wear a tie with his new suit pants and light shirt, to look official. He'd moved from working at Ringwood, to another project off the back of it, and his company of one was going to grow from the ground up. Some jobs he got because of the interview, some through word of mouth, but either way he was doing well.

"What if this stirs everything up again?" he asked me in the mirror.

"We have to believe it's yesterday's news now."

He sighed again.

"Ready?" I asked.

"As I'll ever be," he muttered in disgust.

I straightened his tie, then kissed him. "Come on then."

Finn and Micah were already waiting by the truck—not the shiny red one Nick had *loaned* Cam, but a beat-up old truck Cam had bought with his own money. He'd spent a lot of his free time smartening it up, and tinkering with the engine, and it got him from A to B, which was all he wanted. He'd paid Nick back for the rent as well, even if Nick got pretty vocal about that, but in Cam's words, he wanted to start off right.

We made it to Ringwood early, and parked the truck, the boys running off to find Bernie for what they called celebration cookies, and that left me and my man standing inside the gate, ready to walk in to what I knew was a big surprise party. Of course, Cam didn't know that—he assumed it was Nick and a few other fundraisers, but what he didn't know wouldn't kill him.

"Always remember I love you," I reassured him, but he narrowed his eyes at me.

"Why do you phrase it like that?"

"Just in case."

"In case of what? What did you do?"

I wore my best innocent expression, the one he saw right through, and then kissed him before he could ask any more questions.

Kissing always worked.

Cam

"Surprise!" The large group of people called all at once as we rounded the corner. There was bunting everywhere, and it looked as if a party decoration store had vomited all over the new wing of the building. I just *knew* Adam had been up to something, but I thought it was a barbecue, or a few guys meeting up, not a full-blown event.

"So that was what the kiss was for," I muttered at Adam, who gave me that innocent smile of his I loved so much.

He knocked my elbow, and then got distracted when Cap began to dance around us, which left me to approach the group, including Nick, all his family, Leo, Sean, Eric, partners, kids, people from Station sixty-three, cops I recognized from barbecues, staff at Ringwood, and a ton of kids. Not to mention a couple of journalists who hovered at the side, plus local dignitaries. This was a *thing*.

Shrugging off my anxiety about all things public I did the rounds, shook hands, talked about the construction, and the tiny corners of peace that people found with cushions and books. Some of the kids were already making good use of it all.

Nick cornered me, a young girl on his shoulders, her eyes wide, and her lips curved in a smile. "This is Teegan, she's my new friend," he announced, and helped her clamber down. This wouldn't be a place for her, designed for kids older than her, but she climbed into the nest of cushions and laid back, staring at the ceiling where a crystal star hung and made prisms move on the wall as it spun. I crouched next to her.

"Hey, Teegan," I murmured, but she ignored me— didn't even look at me.

"She can't hear," Nick explained, "congenital hearing loss." I was sad for the toddler who wouldn't be able to hear the world around her, but smiled when she rolled onto her belly and kicked her chubby legs. "She's here with her foster parents, and I'm going through the process of adopting her."

Somehow I wasn't surprised, pulling him in for an awkward hug.

"Of course you are."

"It's what I want to do, something that Danny and I always talked about."

"I'm pleased for you."

"All being well, I mean there's a ton of paperwork, and meetings but I hope it goes right for us both."

He scooped her up out of the nest and she gave me a beautiful smile as she clung to Nick who stared down at her with such affection that I knew my best friend had already lost his heart to her.

"Here's where you're hiding," Adam announced, and

Nick gave me a wink as he left. "I want to show you something." I kissed him as soon as he said that, because I had all these responses I would normally give when he said those words, and he chuckled into the kiss. "Not here."

He tugged me into the empty kitchen, with its handmade cabinets and gleaming surfaces, and Finn hovering to one side, and then stopped and held out a hand.

"Finn, can you come here a minute?" Finn crossed over and then Adam held out a hand to me. "Can you help me?"

"Sure, with what?"

"I need to… hang on." He held out a hand, balancing himself against the counter and I realized there were pillows on the floor, and that he was lowering himself to kneel.

"Jeez, Adam, what are you doing?"

He didn't answer, just slowly coming to rest, and then he stared up at me as he rummaged in his pocket and pulled out a box.

"Cameron Bellamy, I love you. If Finn thinks it's okay, will you marry me?"

Finn glanced from me to Adam, to me again. "Sure. Can I go now, there's ice cream?"

"Yeah," I said. "Love you Finn-Bar-Boodle-Bod!"

"Daaaaad," he whined, but he was grinning, and then he hugged me hard, and then Adam tight around his neck. Without a word he left, and I remained with the question hanging between us. I crouched down so we were at the same height, and took the ring from the box, a simple gold band, feeling the weight of it on my palm. It meant everything to me—all those things I'd wanted from my relationship with Graeme, sharing, being dads together, making a family, maybe even adding to the family like Nick was doing with Teegan. Was I ready to start over again?

"I love you," Adam said. "As soon as we can, marry me, Cam. Make this even more real than it already is?"

And here in this beautiful place that had brought us together, with work that I'd created with so much love, it was easy for me to see a future that would last forever. So I closed my fist around the ring and then leaned in for a kiss.

"Yes."

It was the easiest thing I'd ever said.

THE END

Read Nick and Elliot's story in Listen, coming Summer 2021.

Newsletter

To keep up to date with news and releases, free stories and sales, sign up here:

Newsletter - rjscott.co.uk/rjnews

What's next in single Dads?

Listen, book 5

Coming September 2021

Nick and Elliot's story

Sign up for a release reminder

Jared (Boyfriend for Hire 4)

with Meredith Russell - coming 23 April

Top Shelf (Rebels 1)

with VL Locey - coming 25 June

Summer Drifter (Wyoming 2)

Coming July 2021

Sign up for release reminders

Never miss another release

To keep up to date with news and releases, free stories and sales, sign up here:

Newsletter - rjscott.co.uk/rjnews

FREE READS

You can also find free stories on my website

Also by RJ Scott

For an up to date list of all books please visit www.rjscott.co.uk

Montana (Cowboys, Ranchers, Mystery)

Crooked Tree Ranch | The Rancher's Son | A Cowboy's Home |
Snow In Montana | Second Chance Ranch | Montana Sky

Heroes

A Reason To Stay | Last Marine Standing | Deacon's Law

Single Dads

Single | Today | Promise | Always | Listen | Pride

Lancaster Falls (Romantic Suspense)

What Lies Beneath | Without a Trace | All That Remains

Texas (Cowboy, Rancher, Millionaire, Family)

The Heart of Texas | Texas Winter | Texas Heat | Texas Family |
Texas Christmas | Texas Fall | Texas Wedding | Texas Gift |
Home For Christmas

Legacy (spin-off from Texas series)

Kyle | Gabriel | Daniel

Harrisburg Railers (Hockey Romance)

Changing Lines | First Season | Deep Edge | Poke Check | Last
Defense | Goal Line | Neutral Zone | Hat Trick | Save The Date |
Baby Makes Three

Railers Volume 1 | Railers Volume 2 | Railers Volume 3

Owatonna U Hockey (Hockey Romance)

Ryker | Scott | Benoit | Christmas Lights | Valentine's Hearts

Arizona Raptors (Hockey Romance)

Coast To Coast | Across the Pond | Shadow and Light | Sugar
and Ice | School and Rock

Boston Rebels (Hockey Romance)

Top Shelf *(June 2021)*

Bodyguards Inc

Bodyguard to a Sex God | The Ex-Factor | Max and the Prince |
Undercover Lovers | Love's Design | Kissing Alex

Sanctuary (Bodyguards, Secret Foundation)

Guarding Morgan | The Only Easy Day | Face Value | Still Waters | Full Circle | The Journal of Sanctuary 1 | World's Collide | Accidental Hero | Ghost | By The Numbers

Sanctuary Box Set (including Books 1-5 in the Sanctuary Series

Ellery Mountain (Small Town, First Responders, Military)

The Fireman & the Cop | The Teacher & the Soldier| The Carpenter & the Actor | The Doctor & the Bad Boy | The Paramedic & the Writer | The Barman & the SEAL | The Agent & the Model | The Sinner & the Saint

Boyfriends for Hire (with Meredith Russell)

Darcy | Kaden | Gideon | Jared *(April 2021)*

In the Shadow of the Wolf (Paranormal)

Shattered Secrets | Broken Memories | Splintered Lies

End Street Detective Agency (Paranormal)

End Street Volume 1 (Cupid Curse / Wicked Wolf) | End Street Volume 2 (Dragon's Dilemma / Sinful Santa) | End Street Volume 3 (Purple Pearl / Guilty Ghost)

Kingdom (Paranormal)

Kingdom Volume 1 (Vampire Contract, Guilty Werewolf, Warlock's Secret) | Kingdom Volume 2 (Demon's Blood, Incubus Agenda, Third Kingdom)

Whisper Ridge, Wyoming (Cowboys)

Winter Cowboy | Summer Drifter *(Coming Summer 2021)*

Sapphire Cay (Tropical Island Romance)

Follow the Sun | Under the Sun | Chase The Sun | Christmas In The Sun | Capture The Sun | Forever In The Sun

Sapphire Cay Box Sets - Volume 1 | Volume 2

Salisbury

Heat | Ice

Standalone Christmas

Angel in a Book Shop | Christmas Prince | Jesse's Christmas | Love Happens Anyway | New York Christmas | The Christmas Throwaway | The Road to Frosty Hollow | Dallas Christmas | Cupcakes and Christmas

Standalone

Guarding Garrett | Alpha Delta | Seth & Casey | All The King's Men | The Gallows Tree | Spirit Bear | The Decisions We Make |

Back Home | Boy Banned | Deefur Dog | For a Rainy Afternoon | Moments | One Night | Retrograde | Secrets | Seth & Casey | Snow & Secrets | The Art of Words | The Bucket List | The Fire Trilogy | The New Wolf | The Soldier's Tale | The Summer House | Three

Free Reads

Available here on my website

Meet RJ Scott

RJ is the author of the over one hundred published novels and discovered romance in books at a very young age. She realized that if there wasn't romance on the page, she could create it in her head, and is a lifelong writer.

She lives and works out of her home in the beautiful English countryside, spends her spare time reading, watching films, and enjoying time with her family.

The last time she had a week's break from writing she didn't like it one little bit and has yet to meet a bottle of wine she couldn't defeat.

www.rjscott.co.uk | rj@rjscott.co.uk

NEWSLETTER - rjscott.co.uk/rjnews

facebook.com/author.rjscott

twitter.com/Rjscott_author

instagram.com/rjscott_author

amazon.com/author/rj-scott

bookbub.com/authors/rj-scott

goodreads.com/rjscott

pinterest.com/rjscottauthor